Shadows That Bind Us

Palisade Trilogy 1

Amber L. Werner

Contents

For my family.

NORTHERN DEPTHS
DOLN
NORWICH
MIDSPORT
GRANSEA
KINGDOM OF
DRACWOOD
MAGE KEEP
ABANDONED LANDS
EPRORA OCEAN
ORDDON OCEAN
GREENVALE
FLAMESMOAT
BOGSMOUTH
THE BOGLANDS
STONESHORE
RAIMIRE
SLINAS
MIDO ISLANDS
SALT CLIFF
SULAND WASTE
JORIA
SOUTHERN SEA

Prologue

Appearances can be deceiving. Delyth knew that better than most.

She stood atop a ridge, surveying an expanse of fertile land. Lush fields sprawled on rolling hills, laced with trickling streams and wildflowers. In the far distance, dancing waves kissed the sandy shore, the ocean sparkling in the midday sun. Most would agree it was a scene fit to adorn a finely crafted tapestry.

Delyth knew the truth. Hiding just below the surface, evil lay in wait.

"They're here, Sade Prim," said a voice behind her.

Delyth turned, tossing her long, gray braid over her shoulder. A dozen young men and women gathered nearby, clothed in pristine white robes that matched her own. They were so young. Such a pity what they were being asked to do. What she was asking them to do.

She drew a deep breath, focusing on each of them before speaking. "By now, you've all learned about our noble mission. Destiny has gifted you great power. We can teach you to harness that power to become a Palisade Mage. But before you can learn to control the elements, you must be willing to sacrifice some of that power for the protection of us all. For only those who are noble of heart may join our ranks."

She studied the young initiates again. Not one was fully still. They twitched and gazed around curiously, but they seemed at peace with their decision to be there. All except for one.

At the end of the line of initiates stood one girl, who looked on the verge of tears. While the others returned Delyth's gaze—some even smiling or blushing at the attention—this girl stared at the ground. She twisted her hands together, taking breath after shaky breath.

Delyth approached the girl and lifted her chin gently. "There's no shame in admitting you aren't ready to pay the price, child." She peered into blue eyes wet with tears.

She recognized her. Amora, the daughter of Remon, a skilled water mage. Delyth had met little Amora many times over the years, but this was the first time she'd spoken to her so closely. She was beautiful, even with her face reddened and puffy from tears, and no more than sixteen years old.

Perhaps she should take her aside for a private word? No. All of these initiates deserved to hear what she said next.

Delyth released Amora's chin and raised her voice, gazing at the entire line of initiates. "You've all been told what to expect, but don't forget—this choice is binding. The Palisade will be here next year, and the year after. I was a woman fully grown with a child of my own when I stood where you stand now. There's no harm in enjoying your youth before joining our ranks." She turned back to Amora.

This time the girl met her gaze, hands still at her sides. "Thank you for your kind words, Sade Prim." She rolled her shoulders back. "I'm ready." Her shaky voice grew steadier with each word. "I've been ready for this for a long time. I want to be a mage. I want my power to be awakened." She stood tall, her tears banished.

Delyth inspected the initiates once more. Her chest swelled with pride to see so many willing to join their ranks. They were brave. And ready. Ready as any of them ever were for what came next.

"Let's begin." Delyth stepped to the edge of the ridge. Taking a deep breath, she pulled at the surrounding air, drawing it closer, shaping it to her will. Air filled her lungs, comfortable and familiar, like slipping into her favorite robe at the end of a long day. The sky crackled with electricity. The hairs on her skin stood straight on end. She visualized what she wanted and exhaled. A massive wall appeared, stretching out from north to south as far as the eye could see.

A collective gasp rose from the initiates. The Palisade towered over them all, taller than the highest tree, blocking the view of the valley below. At first glance, it appeared to be made of metal that shined in the sun. Upon closer inspection, it became clear the structure was not wrought by a blacksmith, for it glittered strangely and pulsed, as if alive.

"Place your hands against the Palisade," Delyth instructed.

As one, the initiates complied.

Delyth gritted her teeth. No matter how many times she watched this ritual, it never got easier or less unsettling.

Each instant the initiates touched the wall, they aged. Delyth watched the man closest to her as the years sped by on his skin. Wrinkles and age spots that should take decades to form appeared in mere moments. His hairline receded, and a bald spot emerged; his black locks thinned and turned gray before her eyes.

This was the price they paid to keep the Palisade standing. And sooner or later, it wouldn't be enough.

"Sade Prim," her assistant for the ritual whispered at her side, a tense expression on his weathered face. "Shouldn't it be over by now?" His gaze darted over the initiates' faces.

Delyth patted his forearm, opening her mouth to speak just as the class let go of the Palisade and fell to their knees. She smiled at him instead and turned to address the initiates.

"Welcome back, my friends." Her smile widened, arms lifting skyward. "Let me be the first to congratulate you on taking the first step to becoming a Palisade Mage. Please, everyone return to Keep Hall. There's a celebration waiting for you."

The new mages murmured among themselves as they staggered to their feet. Delyth drew air into her lungs again to return the Palisade to its typical invisible state. It took a moment of concentration to complete the task, after which she gazed at the beautiful landscape laid out beyond the unseen wall.

No one had seen a trace of the creatures trapped beyond the Palisade for hundreds of years. No one even knew for sure what they looked like. The stories of the time were the stuff of myth and legend.

Some doubted they ever existed. They thought the mages fools to waste their time and power—their very lives—to keep watch over what appeared to be nothing more than an idyllic, untouched piece of land.

They were all wrong. They didn't know what she knew. But even before reading the journals of her predecessors, and her journey to the Northern Depths, she'd sensed the truth. She could feel it in her bones every time she looked at the Abandoned Lands. Something was out there still, waiting. Something evil.

Turning to return to the hall, she spotted one of the new mages still with her on the ridge. Amora rested on her knees, slowly tracing the new lines on her face, eyes closed in reflection. Her eyes shot open as Delyth drew closer, and her hands dropped in her lap.

"Don't worry, my dear." Delyth closed the distance between them. "You'll get used to it quickly." She patted Amora's back sympathetically. "The first time I looked in the mirror after my own ritual, I had a good long cry." She tugged the gray braid resting against her shoulder. "My hair used to be so glossy and thick. Now look at it." She sighed. "But no matter. Come tomorrow, you'll be so busy learning to use your magic you won't have a spare moment to stare at your reflection."

"I'm sure you're right," Amora said wistfully, a wry smile curving her lips. She grasped a vial necklace dangling on her chest, one common among mages. Eyes lighting up, she twisted the stopper free, spilling the contents into her cupped hand. Then she closed her eyes and pursed her lips, fingers straightening until her palm displayed a tiny pool of liquid. Slowly, an orb of water materialized in Amora's outstretched hand. It started out the size of a marble, slowly growing until it was the size of a large apple.

Delyth watched, her head tilting slightly. Her skin prickled with goosebumps as moisture whispered through the air.

Amora's eyes opened, widening with wonder. Then the water orb splattered to nothing, soaking her hand and sprinkling her robe with droplets. She laughed, shaking the remaining moisture free from her fingertips.

"I knew it would be water." Amora's eyes sparkled, her smile wide and infectious.

Delyth couldn't help grinning with her. "There will be time for practice tomorrow. Let's join the others." She pulled Amora to her feet. Together, they trekked down the ridge toward the hall where their brethren gathered.

They didn't have far to travel. Mage Keep, which served as both home and school for the Palisade Mages, rested beneath the ridge opposite the Abandoned Lands, south of the Palisade River's banks. The sprawling compound contained a jumble of different-sized buildings, none of which had ever been praised for their beauty or architecture.

Nevertheless, the sight of the keep warmed Delyth's heart. Though she'd traveled far in her youth and seen many areas much more beautiful, Mage Keep was the only place she'd ever consider home.

The keep appeared deserted as they approached, but that was no surprise. Everyone would be inside Keep Hall for the celebration.

Not quite everyone. A solitary figure strode in their direction. Delyth turned to Amora, sending her a small smile. "Head in without me. I have to speak to my daughter."

Amora nodded and picked up her pace, trading a glance with Ereni as they passed. Ereni hid her shock at Amora's transformation, but Delyth knew her daughter well.

"I didn't know Amora was joining the ritual today," Ereni said, once they were close enough to speak without being overheard. She raked a hand through her long brown hair, her blue eyes staring at Amora's retreating back.

Delyth pulled Ereni into a hug. At nineteen, she'd long outgrown the need for constant affection from her mother, but Delyth didn't let that stop her. Sometimes she needed to remember there were more things in life than ancient evil, magic, and responsibilities.

Delyth gave a final squeeze and released her daughter from the warm embrace. She grasped her shoulders, holding her at arm's length. Ereni was dressed plainly in a brown tunic and trousers. Still, it was like staring at a reflection of her former self. They shared such a close resemblance they could've been mistaken for sisters had they been the same age. As it was, she looked more like a grandmother to her daughter.

"I'm glad you're here, Ereni." Delyth dropped her hands but remained close, ignoring the confusion on her daughter's face. She spoke quietly. "I have something very important I need you to do. It's time. Pack your traveling bag and head to Flamesmoat. I have a letter that must be delivered, and you're the only one I trust to do it. Wait for a reply and return with it, personally." Delyth leaned in closer, voice whisper soft, though she remained smiling, as if relaying a pleasant anecdote. "If anyone should discover either letter, kill them."

Ereni's eyes widened slightly, but she showed no other sign of surprise at the request. "Of course, Sade Prim," she said with a smile.

Prior Boaz crept through the graveyard south of the church in the dead of night, leading a goat. The tiny lamp High Prior Sander carried brightened the shadows just enough to see a few paces ahead. Still, he stumbled more than once, his feet catching on rocks and roots littered in the crumbling cemetery.

They must be a strange sight—two old men in black hooded robes, clambering around in the dark. He clutched tightly to the rope, his heart swelling with pride to be chosen for such an important mission.

"We're almost there, son," High Prior Sander said. "You must memorize this route. When I'm gone, the responsibility will fall to you."

Boaz nodded, tugging the rope. The goat snorted, following closely. Boaz' brown eyes flicked over the battered gravestones. The names and dates carved on them had been worn smooth, lost to time.

Sander saw him looking. "Every so often some builder will come to you, offering to tear this place down. 'No one buries their dead anymore,' they'll say. 'Think of all the wasted space.'" His brow furrowed, and he stared at him intensely. "You must shut them down without question. This is a holy place. The holiest. Never forget."

Boaz gulped, shaking his head vehemently. "Of course, High Prior. I'll do exactly that."

"I'm not getting any younger, Boaz. After this year's Harvest Festival, I'm going to step down as High Prior. I want you to replace me."

His chest swelled even more. "I would be honored, sir."

"I'm glad to hear it, son." Sander stared ahead. "Now, let me introduce you to your most important responsibility." He shuffled forward and pulled a key from his waist pocket. He inserted it in a rusty lock on a small mausoleum. It opened with a *click*. "Since the first days of the church, every high prior has brought a goat to this spot on the same night each year."

Sander swung open the door, revealing—nothing. The tiny room was bare except for a large hole in the bottom. The slanted floor sank down into the earth.

Boaz tilted his head. "I didn't think we condoned sacrifice?"

"It's not a sacrifice exactly. More like a duty. The most essential of duties. Bring the animal," High Prior Sander commanded.

Boaz tugged the rope again, ushering the goat into the stone structure. The opening was barely wide enough, but Sander gave the beast a shove. Soon the small room engulfed the animal, and it clambered down the sloping path in the darkness.

"Where is he going?" Boaz asked.

"To his fate," Sander replied solemnly. He slammed the door, replaced the rusty lock, and spun to face him. "Every year, on this day. Don't forget."

He nodded, his stare glued on the tiny room. The goat's bleating reverberated behind the stone door, muffled but distinct. Suddenly the sound cut off mid-bleat, replaced by a sickening crunch.

He jerked back, inhaling sharply. A moment later, light flickered behind cracks in the stone door, and he fell to his knees, his heart hammering madly in his chest.

Sander squeezed his shoulder gently. "You see. Never let anyone shake your faith. We are doing god's work."

Boaz nodded again, his eyes full of tears.

"C'mon, son. We can still catch a bit of rest before the morning sermon."

He lurched up, following High Prior Sander back through the crumbling graveyard with tears rolling down his cheeks and a smile on his face.

Chapter 1

A hawk soared, gliding through an updraft before swooping down behind the tower looming on the edge of the Royal Grounds. Princess Kayda sighed, watching from her perch in her favorite oak tree. The summer breeze rustled the leaves, dry and hot but bearable in the shade. A well-worn book lay open in her lap, neglected today while her mind wandered.

The crunch of footsteps below broke her reverie. Her grandfather, King Quinton, and her half-brother, Prince Tarquin, strode nearby. They were dressed for hunting in russet-brown trousers and tunics, both carrying a bow and a quiver of arrows.

The family resemblance was staggering this morning, in their matching attire. Both were strikingly handsome. Tall and muscular with cornflower-blue eyes and dark-blond hair, although the king's hair was streaked through with gray. Behind them, a handful of house servants and courtiers trailed at a distance, where they could watch without overhearing the men's conversation.

She should climb down. Say hello. But then she'd have to talk to Tarquin. He might be blood, but she loathed the man.

Kayda suppressed a shudder, staying put among the thick foliage. Luckily, she'd chosen a fern-green dress today. Chances were good they would stroll past without noticing her. She did her best to stay motionless as the men drew closer, and their conversation rose to her ears.

"Ah, there's nothing better than the breeze in your hair and a good gallop about," King Quinton said, a genuine smile lighting his face. He was certainly in good spirits today.

Kayda grinned. She almost reconsidered staying hidden, so she could bask in his good mood. It was a rare sight to see him so happy and carefree.

"It would be much nicer if we need not be afoot. Let me buy a nice stallion for you, sire. It would be my pleasure." Tarquin's voice dripped with sincerity, but she knew it to be false.

Quinton's smile faded. "I'm afraid that won't be possible." His steps slowed, and his gaze shifted to that strange, far-off stare he wore so often.

Her blood boiled. Leave it to Tarquin to ruin someone's day. He knew better than to make that offer, yet he did it anyway.

"Oh, Grandfather, I can't believe I forgot. Of course, you can't." Tarquin's face was the picture of remorse as he wrapped an arm around the king's shoulders. "Please forgive me. It's just I have so much on my mind."

Kayda rolled her eyes. It was typical behavior for her brother. He had a way of saying the most cutting remark in one breath and begging for forgiveness with the next. What's worse was no one could see through the act, her grandfather included.

"It's all right, my boy," the king said, sounding distracted. "No harm done." He patted Tarquin's hand, staring off into the distance.

Tarquin withdrew his arm from the king's shoulders and moved to stand in front of him, halting a few paces away from her oak.

Kayda stifled a groan. Her nose picked the perfect time to need scratching. She wiggled her nose back and forth, keeping her hands glued to her lap, silently praying the men would continue walking.

"I wonder if you could help. You see, I've been approached by a group of merchants from Joria," Tarquin said.

Kayda's ears perked up. Her mother had been born in Joria.

"They've expressed interest in entering into a new trade deal with our great kingdom." Tarquin leaned in close. "An exclusive agreement," he added with a sly grin.

"An exclusive deal with the Jorians? Why, that's excellent news." The king's eyes regained their focus. His face lit with interest.

"I was hoping you would agree, sire. The deal would be mutually beneficial and would allow us to stop relying on those heathen Dolnmen to act as middlemen, of course." Tarquin's teeth gleamed in his self-satisfied smile.

"Ha, you're right on that account," Quinton said. "I would kill to see the look on Chief Aundrea's face when he hears the news." He laughed then, loud and long.

Kayda smiled in response until the motion set that traitorous itch traveling to her cheek. She closed her eyes briefly, praying the men would start moving again.

Her prayers were soon answered. The king patted her brother's shoulder and started walking. "Well, don't keep me in suspense. What are the details?"

Tarquin puffed out his chest, smiling widely.

Kayda's fingers curled in her lap. Her brother loved nothing more than being asked to talk.

"It was an impressive bit of bargaining I did," Tarquin matched steps with King Quinton. "You will be pleased to know I managed to convince the largest merchant group in Joria to agree to abandon Gransea port and to trade exclusively with us." He combed a hand through his hair, his eyes shining. "We'll save a fortune on goods that would normally have to run through Doln before reaching our ports."

"That's excellent news," Quinton said, "but what do they expect from us in return?"

"Just for us to build a new port on our eastern shores."

"Are you mad?" Quinton stopped in his tracks, his face flushing. "Absolutely not. We will not be building anything on our eastern shores."

The smug smile dropped from Tarquin's face.

Kayda stifled a smirk.

Tarquin quickly masked his disappointment, turning wide eyes toward the king. "Don't tell me you believe there's anything out there, sire. It's been hundreds of years since anything has been seen."

"Of course, I believe it." The king pressed his fingers to his brow, drawing in a deep breath. "Tarquin, our entire kingdom exists solely to protect the world from that cursed place. Has that drunkard father of yours taught you nothing?"

Tarquin flinched at the king's tone, pinching his lips together. "It's just a shame we can't use that land. Perhaps we could send an exploratory team beyond the Palisade and see what's out there? I'm sure the mages could be convinced to—"

"We will not be stepping foot inside the Abandoned Lands," Quinton said through gritted teeth. His voice was hard, brooking no argument. "That's my decision, and it's final."

"Of course, Grandfather." Tarquin adopted a nonchalant air, though she could tell by the set of his shoulders he was not as relaxed as he appeared.

The itch, forgotten while she listened to the argument below, returned to plague her. But they looked far enough away she could chance a scratch...

She slowly lifted her shoulder while moving her cheek to meet it, using the rough cloth of her sleeve to finally bring some relief. Eyes half closing, she spotted Tarquin's gaze lift in her direction.

Oh, no. Kayda gulped reflexively, remaining stock still. If only he would look away without noticing her. The moment seemed to stretch out infinitely until he finally looked away, taking a few steps forward toward the king.

In a single, fluid motion, Tarquin spun to face her, lifting his bow and nocking an arrow. Eyes bulging, Kayda had less than a heartbeat to scramble backward before the arrow hurtled through the sky. Weightlessness and the slap of leaves on her skin assaulted her as she lost her seat on the branch. Eyes closing in fear, she shrieked, clutching blindly for a grip to stop her fall and finding nothing but air.

But the hard wallop she expected never came. She cracked open an eye and found herself dangling from the tree upside down. The arrow pierced the hem of her dress before lodging in the tree branch, arresting her fall, leaving her hanging just above the ground.

"Why, Kayda, is that you, dear sister?" called Tarquin's voice from behind her, full of false surprise. "Whatever were you doing in that tree?"

With her heart racing and blood pooling in her ears, she couldn't think of a reply before her skirt ripped. She fell, thudding her head into the ground and landing in a heap on the grass. She groaned, rushing to fix her skirts and sit properly.

Her grandfather crouched beside her. "Little red, good gracious. Are you hurt?" The king's weary gaze traced her body as he clutched her shoulder to steady her.

She winced slightly and rubbed the back of her head. The panic and fear of the last few moments receded as she gazed at her grandfather. "I'm all right, I think."

"I can't believe I almost shot you." Tarquin chuckled, moving in front of her. "I saw that red hair of yours and thought I'd spotted a squirrel." He laughed again and crossed his arms, leaning against the tree, looking far too amused for someone who'd just barely escaped killing a sibling. "Don't you have better things to do with your time than hide in trees?" he added, raising an eyebrow.

Spotting her book to her left, Kayda snatched it off the ground. "I was only looking for a quiet place to read." Her voice was shaky, laced with a petulant tone she couldn't contain that made her grimace.

"Oh, please don't be mad," Tarquin pleaded, splaying a hand on his chest and crouching down beside the king. "You know I would never hurt you on purpose. I'm so sorry."

"Sure you are." Kayda pushed to her feet. Quinton and Tarquin followed suit. She glanced behind her and spotted the servants approaching.

Great. The story would be all anyone would talk about for days. She cursed inwardly. She considered saying more but settled for an icy glare. It wouldn't be seemly to argue. Besides, Tarquin would just make her look like the one at fault and he the victim.

Turning to her grandfather, she warmed instantly. He leaned toward her, his brow furrowed and lips pursed as he scrutinized her.

"I'm fine, sire, I swear. I'll head back. Enjoy the rest of your hunt." She forced a small smile and turned, crossing the field toward Kings Keep.

Kayda kept her head down as she passed the servants, not wanting to see them snickering. It wasn't everyday they witnessed a member of the royal family with half of their skirts dangling in their faces. Her cheeks burned, and though she tried to give the men's followers a wide berth, she could still hear their excited murmuring as she passed.

The nerve of Tarquin, shooting at her! She had no doubt he'd seen her sitting there and shot at her to teach her a lesson. There's no chance he'd mistaken her for a squirrel. He was an expert marksman. If he'd been aiming at her hair, he wouldn't have missed. No, he just wanted her to look like a fool.

Her shoulders drooped as she slinked away, picking up speed. He certainly never missed a chance to mock her appearance either. Her Jorian heritage meant she didn't have the dark blond hair and light skin the rest of the royals shared. Tarquin never forgot to remind her she was different. As if her having a Jorian mother made her lesser than him somehow.

She'd long ago realized Tarquin would take any opportunity to make her look bad. She lost count of all the chances she'd given him over the years. He always let her down. One might think a man nearly ten years her senior would've grown tired of teasing his little sister, but that was unfortunately not the case.

Like the day a few years back, when she begged him to remove a spider from her chambers. She shuddered at the memory. She'd trusted him that day when she confided her fear of the creepy insects. He'd acted so sweet and understanding, coming to her rescue. The next evening, she strolled into her chambers and found the entire room crawling with spiders. And of course, his laughing face was there to greet her as she raced screaming through the keep.

She'd called him out on it, but he had a way of spinning every situation like it was her fault. He would never do anything to hurt her. It was all for her own good, or just a joke. What a load of crap.

Kayda had lived in Kings Keep her whole life and knew the way by heart. Speeding through the immaculate gardens and manicured lawn, her mind reeled with outrage. She made her way inside through the back servants' entrance and headed swiftly toward her quarters.

She couldn't stop picturing the arrow coming straight for her. And the moment she lost her seat on the branch and plummeted through the air. She'd feared she was done for—that she'd break her neck, crack her skull, and force her grandfather to watch her bleed to death before his eyes.

All her life she'd dealt with Tarquin's bullying, but this was on a whole new level. He could've killed her.

As she opened the door to her room, his smug laughter replayed in her mind. She would give anything to wipe that stupid look off his face.

Her bedroom was her sanctuary. The one place in the crowded keep she could be guaranteed a little peace and quiet. Surrounded by light-blue walls and plush pastel bedding, she could relax and unwind. But not today. She still couldn't shake off the anger and humiliation burning inside her.

Feeling a chill sweep over her, she leaned down to check if any embers remained in her fireplace. A faint orange glow of flame appeared as the sound of her brother's awful gloating laughter rose again in her memory.

The flames leapt to life with a blast. She flew backward, landing hard on her behind. Her heart seized as the flames swallowed the fireplace, licking the edges and threatening to envelop the entire wall.

Gulping, she scooted backward away from the heat and bumped into something hard. Craning her neck up, she discovered her nurse, Izora, staring at the flames.

"What are you doing just sitting there, child?" Izora said, as calm as if gazing out an open window instead of at a raging inferno. "Fetch some water." She deftly grabbed the largest vase perched on the bedside table, tossed the flowers aside, and dumped the remaining contents on the flames.

Kayda sprang into action, thankful for her nurse's habit of bringing her a bouquet of flowers every morning. Within moments, the two women emptied half a dozen vases full of water on the flames, effectively extinguishing them. Surveying the wreckage of flowers, ash, and water, Kayda sucked in several gasping breaths and calmed her raging heart before turning a rueful smile toward her savior.

"Thanks, Izora. I don't know how that happened. The flames just appeared out of nowhere."

Izora shook her head, her short white curls bouncing with the motion. "I know what happened." She set a vase down on the side table and whirled to face her with a knowing grin, her eyes gleaming. "You did this. You conjured the flames. You have a talent for fire magic, Princess."

Kayda's breath caught. A fire mage... her? "No, that's not possible. The royal family has always possessed bonding magic, not elemental."

Was it even possible for someone to possess both types of talent? Shaking her head, she backed away from the steaming fireplace and sank down on the edge of her bed.

It couldn't have been her who'd done that, could it?

The bed shifted as Izora sat beside her. She smoothed the skirt of her flint-gray servant dress. "Believe it, child. The royal family may have always had bonding magic, and you may still have it, too. But you're forgetting one thing, my dear." She paused until Kayda turned from the fireplace. Izora stared straight at her, brown eyes warm, smiling tenderly. "Magic can be inherited from both parents."

Kayda gasped. "My mother was a mage?"

Izora had been her mother Solenne's companion before becoming her nurse when Solenne died from complications of childbirth. There was no one in the keep who'd known her better. But had she really been a mage? How could that be possible when Kayda had never heard a whisper of a rumor?

Izora's wrinkled hand landed atop Kayda's hand on the bedspread, her dark brown skin a few shades darker than her own. "I know you never got to know her. Your mother was an amazing woman. And yes, a powerful mage. She would've been very proud of you. I see so much of her in you."

Kayda teared up and wiped the moisture away with the back of her hand. Proud of her? What a joke. She had a father who ignored her and a brother who went to desperate lengths to embarrass her. Her grandfather always treated her with kindness, but with how busy he was ruling the kingdom and dealing with his own demons, she barely saw him.

A day would soon come when he would be gone, and she would be at the mercy of the new king and prince, who only cared if she married, mage or not. It was the blood that mattered most, after all. Since her brother and father showed no signs of bonding talent, it would be her duty to continue the royal bloodline. She was nothing more than a broodmare in her family's eyes. How could her mother be proud of that?

Izora must have sensed her internal distress. She squeezed her knee with surprising strength for her age. Kayda's gaze shot to her nurse's face, and she flinched from her intense glare.

"She would be proud. You'll be the first in your family—perhaps even the first in the entire world—to be a mage and have a bond-mate. You are going to do amazing things, Kayda. Amazing, incredible things."

A ghost of a smile crossed Kayda's face. She could always count on Izora to cheer her up. She returned the squeeze with a much gentler one of her own. "What now? We'll have to tell my family what happened first, I expect. Then send word to Mage Keep—"

Izora's laughter cut off Kayda's words. "Don't be ridiculous, dear. We won't be telling anyone."

"You can't mean that. Why can't we tell anyone?"

"You don't belong at Mage Keep. Your place is here. And besides, the longer you keep your talent hidden, the better. If you ever end up in trouble, you'll have a secret weapon at your disposal."

"But I'll need training. And there's no way we can keep this a secret."

Izora walked to the far wall, reaching out toward the lit candlesticks adorning the walls. "You'd be surprised what secrets people keep." She closed her eyes.

A chill ran up Kayda's spine. Then, to her astonishment, a ball of flame slowly formed on her nurse's outstretched hand.

Eyes opening, Izora smiled. "I'll clean up this mess. You need your rest tonight. Your training starts tomorrow."

Chapter 2

Crouching to inspect the empty trap in the underbrush, Conall caught a glimpse of ominous storm clouds peeking through the dense canopy above. His shoulders slumped. A storm was exactly what he needed to add to his day. He still had two more snares to check, and with his unwanted company in tow, there was no doubt in his mind he would end up drenched.

"Storms brewing." Brows furrowing, he stood, pointing to the break in the tree cover. "Maybe you ought to head home early. I can handle the rest on my own."

"Head home? From a little rain? I'm a man, not a mouse, boy," muttered his companion, Gael.

Gael was a large man, as broad as he was tall. His bulk suited him fine for the many chores they shared running their family farm, but was ill suited to tracking game.

Conall hadn't seen a single creature that day with Gael noisily trudging along, alerting all the wild game to their presence. It was strange he'd insisted on tagging along today, when he'd shown no interest in joining him in the past.

Then again, Gael had been acting strangely ever since Rhea, Conall's mother and Gael's wife, died a few weeks ago. Conall might not be overly fond of the man, but there was no denying Gael loved his mother deeply. He couldn't fault him for wanting some companionship during his grief. Even if he was scaring away all the game.

Steeling himself for more of the plodding pace and stilted conversation, he gestured to the left. "All right, the last set of traps are this way. Follow me."

Conall led the way through the forest, carefully avoiding the brambles and nettles that caused Gael to curse in frustration as they caught on his brown wool trousers.

He inhaled the salty tang of impending rain mixed with the familiar scent of wood and fresh vegetation. These woods were like a second home to Conall. He'd been hunting and trapping in them most of his life.

In the first few years, before the farm began to produce enough food to feed his family, his hunting and trapping had been essential to their survival. He had been only a child then, but hunger and desperation kept him coming back, practicing the few meager skills his father taught him.

He struggled at first, but with daily practice, it wasn't long before he became proficient enough with the bow to hunt small game. And through trial and error, he managed to find the best spots for his traps on their land.

Conall smiled, recalling the look on his mother's face the first time he'd brought home a kill. She'd been heavily pregnant with his sister Lark and heard the news his father died only days before. She'd moped around for days, barely getting out of bed, surviving on stale bread and watered-down broth that had nearly run out. When Conall placed that scrawny hare in her lap, her face lit up like it was a candy apple at the Harvest Festival.

Pain flashed inside his chest. His mother had been an amazing woman. Generous, loving, and so strong.

Those early years at the farm, after his father died, she managed to get it up and running with no help and two small children underfoot. She was always there with a smile and a helping hand for those who needed it, earning a reputation in nearby Greenvale as a great neighbor and friend.

Conall did his best to help, but he was only six when they moved. He hunted and did his fair share of work tending the vegetable garden, but the farm didn't make a profit until his mother married Gael.

Glancing back where Gael struggled uphill, Conall sighed. He had to admit, Gael saved their asses.

The money his mother received for their father's death at sea had run out before long, and she'd been more interested in following her late mother's footsteps as a healer than running a farm. She constantly made house calls, curing all the village folk of their aches and pains. She'd never been one to demand payment, always happy to help out of the kindness of her heart.

Gael had shown up around the time Conall turned fourteen. Within a year, he was married to his mother, doing the majority of work around the farm.

Conall hadn't liked him at first. Truthfully, it was hard to see how his mother found him attractive. He was a balding, coarse, hulk of a man.

His father had been so different. His mother claimed Conall had grown into the spitting image of his father. As the years passed, he struggled to picture his face clearly, but he remembered his father being tall and strong, with shaggy brown hair and hazel eyes that were always full of laughter, much like the image he saw when he looked into the mirror.

It was strange she could love two men who were so very different from each other. But Gael wormed his way into his mother's heart somehow. And despite his bristly attitude when working on the farm, he treated his mother like a queen and Lark like a princess, so Conall had grudgingly learned to live with the man.

As the trail became steeper, Gael's pace slowed even more. "You didn't tell me we had to climb a mountain today." He gripped tree branches and roots to steady himself with his right hand while keeping a tight grip on his bow with his left.

"There's a stream at the top of this hill, just ahead. It's a good spot for trapping." Conall kept the small smirk on his face hidden as he crested the ridge ahead of his stepfather. The old man should've stayed at home if he couldn't keep up.

The top of the ridge hadn't changed from his last visit. He stood on a flat area of grass with a small stream cutting through the middle. The stream began somewhere inside a rocky cliff that rose beyond their path and tumbled into a waterfall to the west, where a sheer drop gave way to the forest floor below.

Water splattered his nose. As he brushed the droplet away, he glimpsed gray fur in the forest to the east, along their much more gently sloped route home.

Finally, some luck. Fur that color likely belonged to a hare. The animal was mostly hidden behind a set of bushes, twitching, as if foraging in the underbrush. Inexplicably, a strange urge to leave the animal to its business came over him, but he shook off the feeling with a shrug.

Reaching into the quiver on his back, Conall's fingertips brushed the fletching of an arrow as Gael crested the ridge with a loud *thump*, and the mystery creature retreated with speed.

Nostrils flaring, Conall dropped his hand from his quiver and spun toward his first snare, which rested close to where the stream burst through the mountainside. He could see from where he stood it was empty.

"Conall, could you slow down for a moment?" Gael inquired, panting. "We need to talk."

Conall stopped, eyebrows raising. Gael was not the type for heart-to-heart conversations. At least now, his insistence on coming along today was starting to make sense.

"It's Lark." Gael frowned. "She's still got that fool idea in her head to go join the bloody mages."

Turning to inspect his trap again, Conall rolled his eyes. "Lark has been set on becoming a Palisade Mage for years. And she has the talent for it. Why stop her?"

"She's too young, for one."

"She'll be sixteen at harvest. They take initiates as young as thirteen, I hear." He knelt down to replace the bait in his trap. Gael and his mother had advised Lark against joining the mages in the past, but this was the first time either of them included him in the discussion.

Gael glowered at him.

"You know Lark. She's always been set on finding adventure. She could probably use it in her life now..." Conall trailed off as he finished setting the trap carefully back in place.

Lark had taken their mother's death hard. They'd been so close, spending practically every moment of the day together. It was as if part of her died with their mother. Grief cast a shadow on her heart, tormenting her. If becoming a mage could be the thing to bring joy back into her life, he wasn't going to stand in her way.

Raindrops fell in earnest, and the sky darkened to a sinister gray. He rose and picked his way toward the second trap, which sat closer to the waterfall and the cliff's edge. His brown tunic and trousers dampened and stuck to his skin.

Gael grabbed his shoulder, spinning him. "Those witches are not who you think they are, boy. They're liars and thieves."

He shrugged Gael's hand off. "What are you talking about, Gael? That's ridiculous. The mages are the most respected people in the kingdom."

Gael rubbed the back of his neck, staring off into the distance. "There's a reason your mother and I got on so well. Both of us had been in love before, you see. She had your father, and I had Seren. Seren was the love of my life." A wistful smile crossed his face, then he grew serious, meeting Conall's eyes. "No offense to your mother."

Conall nodded, and Gael took a deep breath before continuing.

"She had talent, too, you see. Decided she was going to become a mage. Protect the realm and all that nonsense." Gael shook his head vehemently. "What a load of crap that was."

"I don't understand..."

"They stole her youth."

"Her what?"

"I followed her to Mage Keep. I hid on the hillside while they performed her initiation ceremony. I saw that wall suck the life out of her before my eyes." Gael clenched his bow tightly with both hands.

Conall gulped, his mind brimming with questions. "When you say it sucked the life out of her, what do you mean?"

"Seren was eighteen when she walked up that hillside. After she touched the Palisade, she could've easily passed for fifty."

Conall's jaw dropped. He racked his brain for anytime in the past he'd seen a young mage. He'd spotted them countless times while at market or a Harvest Festival. His stomach clenched. He couldn't remember a single mage who wasn't gray-haired or wrinkled. "Surely, there must be a reason…"

"I found Seren after the ceremony. She told me they all give up a bit of power to keep the Palisade working. They do it to protect the realm from some ancient evil beyond the wall." Gael's stare turned flinty. "I saw beyond the wall. Stood there staring at it for half the day. There's nothing out there. Whatever they trapped, it's long dead. Those witches are forcing anyone with talent to waste their lives guarding a bunch of empty fields."

Conall let his words sink in. "Seren told you they forced her to do it?"

"Well, no." Gael's eyes lost focus. "She said it was her choice. Told me to go home. She had chosen her path, and it didn't include me."

Conall patted Gael's shoulder. No wonder he was so insistent Lark not join the mages. But Conall knew Lark. Forbidding her from going would only make her want to go more. She'd always been impulsive and hated being told what she couldn't do.

"Gael, you need to tell Lark what you just told me. She should be the one to decide," Conall said firmly.

"And what if she still wants to go? You would let your sister go, knowing the next time you see her she'll be as old as your mother?" Gael asked, voice cracking on the final word.

It would be strange, for sure, to see Lark aged prematurely. But what was the alternative? Keeping her a prisoner in her own home? And she would gain so much in return. The Palisade Mages were revered by everyone, welcome in every town. Plus, she would get what she always wanted—a life full of adventure and magic.

Conall met Gael's eyes and patted his shoulder once more. "I would. She deserves to know. And she deserves to choose for herself."

Gael stared back at him, his face blank.

Conall smiled, speaking gently. "Let me check this last snare, and we'll go back. We'll talk to her together."

He carefully made his way to the edge of the ridge, where the waterfall disappeared over the steep ledge. His trap nestled in a patch of mossy grass that often attracted birds. Conall sighed as he crouched down to add fresh bait. Another one empty.

"Jump." Conall startled.

How strange. He heard a voice in his head, clear as day. He ought to get some rest if his mind was playing tricks on him.

"Listen, little brother. He's aiming a killstick at you. Jump!" For a moment Conall knelt motionless, beyond confused.

Little brother? Killstick?

Then the full import of the message struck him, and he stood. He whirled around just as an arrow sailed through the sky, impaling his shoulder. Searing pain exploded, and his boots slid across the slippery moss. He staggered, trying desperately to ignore the pain and find his balance.

Dizziness struck him as gravity took over, but not before he caught a last glimpse of his stepfather glowering, bow drawn. His final thought before he slipped over the edge echoed in his ears, all the way down.

Gael, why?

Chapter 3

Stopping short, Lark peered nervously across the wide wooden bridge. Her stomach churned in time with the Riddle River below them. "You didn't tell me we'd have to go to Southmoat, Aunt Brenna."

Brenna was a plump, jolly woman, who wore her brownish-gray hair pulled back in a bun with strands escaping every which way. Both boots already planted on the wooden planks, she turned to address Lark, causing the hem of her simple brown dress to swing round her knees. She smiled.

"Don't tell me you're getting cold feet." Brenna motioned her forward. "The mages are at the docks, of course. I know the way; come on."

Lark frowned, standing on the cobblestone path in Northmoat. "Isn't it dangerous over there?"

Dozens of cramped buildings lined the street across the bridge. They were dingy and gray compared to the brightly colored shops and houses they'd passed in their walk through the Northmoat section of Flamesmoat.

Brenna positioned herself directly in front of Lark, blocking her view. "I've lived in Southmoat all my life. I won't let anything happen to you. Besides, it's only dangerous there at night, and we'll arrive where we're going long before nightfall." Brenna moved to her side, linking their arms together. "If we get a move on, that is."

Lark allowed her aunt to move her along, keeping pace with her along the creaking bridge. A cool river breeze swirled her brown skirt around her legs. She shifted the pack across her tan tunic that held a few snacks and a change of clothes.

Slowly, her apprehension subsided, replaced with excitement. This was it. The start of her first real adventure. She was going to become a mage.

A grin crept across her face. "I wonder why the mages don't keep their headquarters in Northmoat?"

"I imagine they want to be close to the port to welcome all the recruits coming from other parts of the world," Brenna said.

Lark's heart sped up. She hadn't considered that. She would meet people from all over the world. How thrilling!

They made it across the bridge and swung west toward the port section of town. Now that she stood on the streets of Southmoat, her stomach settled. Refuse lingered in the street gutters, and the wooden and brick structures were covered in faded, chipped paint. But although the buildings were more run down than the well-kept villas of Northmoat, they didn't seem so scary up close.

The streets bustled with activity. Children played while mothers strung wet washing on clothes lines between buildings. Men and women, young and old, stood talking animatedly with each other or moved through the streets toward some unknown destination.

Shaking her head, Lark giggled, attracting the attention of a young couple passing by, who smiled in her direction. "I don't know why I was so afraid to come here. It's just like back home in Greenvale. Although a bit more crowded."

She slowed and glanced inside the shop to her left. The smell of freshly baked bread drifted toward her, and her stomach growled.

"If I know my brother, I'm sure he's filled your head with stories of pickpockets, slavers, and thieves." Brenna chuckled, her pudgy face jiggling. "Truth told, Southmoat is not all bad. Why, your mother and father were from here, too, if I'm not mistaken."

Pain throbbed in Lark's chest. It should've been her mother taking her to meet the mages. If only she'd been able to save her...

Pushing the thought aside, she forced a smile. "You're right. They lived here before I was born. Then Father inherited the farm from some distant cousin, and they moved to Greenvale." Her smile brightened. "Do you think we have time to stop by Mother's old job? She's told me so many stories about the place."

"What place?" Brenna asked. "If it's on the way, we can stop for a moment."

"It was an inn called the Boggy Beaut. That's where my parents met. Mother was a barmaid, but on the night she met Father, she was filling in as the entertainment." She leaned in, voice hushed. "According to my mother, it was love at first sight. He was enthralled with her singing, and she with his charm."

Lark's smile faded as she noticed the pinched look on her aunt's face.

"I'm afraid that's nowhere near where we're headed." Brenna frowned sympathetically. "Another day, perhaps?"

Lark nodded, her heart sinking. "Of course. It was just a thought."

She sighed. It was probably better not to reminisce about her mother today. Today was about starting her future, not wallowing in the past.

As Brenna led the way through the crowded streets with the ease of a native, Lark was overwhelmed with gratitude. "Thank you again for taking me today, Aunt Brenna. I would've been lost without you. These streets are like a maze."

"Think nothing of it. You know I would do anything to help my brother." Brenna patted her arm gently. "And you, too, of course."

A pang of discomfort rose in her breast. Brenna was being so nice to her without realizing her help was something Gael would definitely not appreciate.

She lost count of all the times Gael advised her against joining the mages. She should've told Gael the truth in person, but she couldn't stand the thought of him trying to talk her out of leaving again.

With her mother gone, he was the closest thing she had left to a parent, and she couldn't bear disappointing him. When he returned from hunting with Conall that afternoon and found her goodbye letter on his pillow, he would not be happy.

She needed to tell Brenna the truth, at least. Brenna had been so kind these last few weeks, coming to help at the farm after her mother's death. She shouldn't have led Brenna to believe she'd be doing Gael a favor by guiding her through Flamesmoat. But when she'd woken up and found Gael and Conall headed out to hunt, and Brenna announced her plans to return to the city, she jumped at the chance to tag along.

The scent of saltwater grew stronger, and the first of many warehouses populating the dock section of Southmoat emerged in the distance. She needed to say something soon, or she would lose the chance.

"Aunt Bren." Lark's voice trembled. "I need to tell you something." She shuffled along, her eyes downcast. "Gael and Conall weren't exactly expecting me to leave today. I left them each a letter to explain, but you might not find they're happy I followed you the next time you head over for a visit." She snuck a peak at Brenna's face, and her eyes widened.

A grin stretched across her aunt's face. "Oh, I already knew that," she said with a chuckle.

"You did? And you helped me anyway?"

"Of course." Brenna smiled. "I do what I can to help my brother. Sometimes that means doing something he doesn't agree with. Any fool with half a brain could see you don't belong on that farm. He'll see it, too, eventually." She lifted her gaze to the darkening sky and frowned. "Let's pick up the pace. Looks like a storm is coming. It's not much farther."

It seemed the townsfolk had the same idea. The twisting streets became less crowded as everyone sought shelter from the storm.

Lark kept pace with Brenna easily. The older woman huffed with exertion but doggedly pressed on until she reached a large warehouse at the docks' edge.

Planted in the middle of a long line of buildings built of red brick common to the area, the warehouse appeared deserted from the outside. Lark didn't notice a number or any distinguishing feature to set it apart from the surrounding buildings, but Brenna marched purposefully to the back door and knocked without hesitation.

A few moments passed without reply. Just as Brenna lifted her fist to knock again, the door opened, revealing a middle-aged man with bloodshot eyes and a frown plastered to his face. He stuck his head out and looked left to right before focusing on Brenna and addressing her directly.

"Come in." He opened the door fully and disappeared inside.

Lark's heart sped up, fluttering as fast as a hummingbird's wings. Should she really be doing this? Leaving her family and everything she'd ever known?

A small part of her screamed to turn back. Head home. Forget this foolishness and return to the family she'd abandoned.

No. This was it. Her future was about to change. All she had to do was cross the threshold. Taking a deep breath, she strode forward and followed her aunt inside.

The warehouse was dimly lit. It took Lark a few moments to adjust to the darkness before she could make out most of her surroundings.

The building was enormous and almost completely filled with crates and boxes. Some were stacked neatly, others more haphazardly, lining the walls and forming row upon row of makeshift walls in the center.

As she continued to scan the building, the smile she'd been wearing faded away to nothing. This was not what she'd been expecting. Where were the mages? She shifted from foot to foot, waiting for someone to round one of the stacks and greet them.

Turning to take another peek at the man who'd invited them inside, she found him standing beside the closed door. He was of average height and build with brown hair and eyes, and he had one of those faces that was only remarkable in that nothing about it was particularly remarkable. He wore plain brown clothing, not the spotless white robes the Palisade Mages favored.

The hair stood on the back of her neck. He silently watched her, inspecting her body, the same way Gael looked at livestock. Why wasn't anyone talking? Brenna stood beside the man, watching him eye her up. Was this some test prospective mages needed to pass? Was he scanning her for talent?

"Are you a mage?" Lark blurted out, breaking the silence.

The man's eyes shot to her own, and he raised a brow. "Mage, me?" He exchanged a look with Brenna before returning his gaze to Lark and smiling, revealing a set of straight, yellow teeth. "No, I'm not a mage. I just work for them." He turned and gestured toward a door on the far right of the warehouse. "Come on; they'll want to meet you."

They followed closely behind the man, keeping their distance from the stacked boxes as best they could. A sour smell wafted around them, one that seemed vaguely familiar. What were they storing in here that smelled so unpleasant?

They stopped in front of the door. The man knocked twice and opened the door without waiting for a response, ushering Lark forward into the brightly lit doorway. "After you."

She smoothed her hands along her dark brown curls, wishing she had a mirror to check her appearance. Brenna grabbed her hand and gave it a gentle squeeze. "Go ahead, Lark. You look lovely."

Lark started through the doorway, breathing deeply through her nose. The smell assailed her again as she passed the man. This time, she recognized it. The stale scent of alcohol. It must have been coming from the man all along, not the boxes. She wrinkled her nose in distaste, squinting in the bright light after so long in the dimly lit warehouse.

Blazes, she must be making the most ridiculous face with her eyes scrunched up and her nose wrinkled. She fought to return her face to a neutral expression before the mages wondered what was wrong with her.

As her eyes adjusted, she found herself alone in a small room. It was empty except for a set of high, narrow windows lining the top of the far wall and a single cot that'd seen better days. She spun around as the door slammed shut behind her. The lock clicked shut.

"Let me out," she screamed, banging on the door. Her heart thundered, her stomach dropping as dread filled her.

This must be some mistake. Perhaps her aunt had teamed up with her stepfather to teach her a lesson about the dangers of Southmoat? Yes, that must be it. She would open the door, and they'd all have a good laugh. "C'mon, Aunt Bren, it's not funny. Let me out. Please!"

Her aunt didn't answer. The door stayed firmly closed no matter how much she pounded. The gravity of her situation sunk in. Tears welled in her eyes, and she clutched her neck, unable to scream or even make a sound.

She was so stupid. Something had felt off, but she'd ignored her feelings, trusting Brenna to lead her here safely. Never again.

She pressed her ear to the door. She could hear her aunt and the man talking on the other side.

"What did I tell you? Those hazel eyes, those bouncy, brown curls. I told you she'd be lovely. You'll score a fortune for her in Doln."

Doln? She stiffened. The man didn't work for the mages. He was a slaver, and he was going to sell her to a Dolnman!

"You didn't tell me she would be talented, Bren. I've half a mind to set her free here and now and forget the whole thing, lovely or not. Damn mages are more trouble than they're worth."

"Don't be so dramatic, Rasmus. You know talent doesn't matter a wit without training. You're not planning to stop by Mage Keep on the way to Doln, are you?" Brenna snorted.

How long had her aunt been planning this? She'd obviously met this Rasmus before. Lark had to at least try to gain some answers. And if she could hear them through the door, they could hear her.

"You can't leave me in here," she yelled, pounding on the door again. "Gael will come for me. You know he will." She stopped pounding, her chest aching as she remembered the letter she'd left on his pillow. "If not him, then Conall will come." A tiny smile lit her lips. "I promised to write him. I promised! When the letters don't show, he'll come looking for me."

Conall *would* come. Her brother would walk to Mage Keep himself if he didn't hear from her. Lark held her breath, waiting for some response from the other side of the doorway.

"Don't give me that look, Ras," Brenna said, her voice dripping with contempt. "She won't have anyone coming to her rescue. She doesn't know my brother at all."

"What are you talking about?" Rasmus asked, his words harsh and clipped.

"Oh, just that Gael would rather stay put where he is, on his precious farm. And with his wife and stepson dead, and his stepdaughter off to join the mages, he'll have exactly what he wants. It'll be so sad to lose his son to a tragic hunting accident this afternoon, won't it?"

Lark clasped a hand over her mouth, falling to her knees against the door. Her stomach filled with knots, her head reeled. She couldn't believe it. Gael wouldn't do that to Conall. It couldn't be true. They were family.

"Bren, you're colder than I thought. You really talked him into offing the boy for the inheritance?" Rasmus sounded impressed.

She was going to be sick.

"He worked his hands to the bone to turn a profit at that farm, only to be cut off by some boy when his bitch wife died. It ain't right." Her jolly aunt was like a different person, her voice laced with disdain. "Besides, you know I'd do anything for my little brother."

The world spun. How could she have been so blind? To think she had been worried about Gael being mad at Brenna for taking her to meet the mages. Her aunt must have been laughing at her the whole time while she confessed, knowing she was about to betray her.

She clutched her stomach, lurched away from the door, and collapsed on the worn cot. As the sound of talking quieted to a soft murmur, Lark laid silently and cried.

Chapter 4

Conall came to slowly, consciousness returning, bringing with it confusion and pain. He hurt everywhere and wanted nothing more than to sink back into blackness and escape.

No sooner had his mind awakened than he heard the voice return. The voice he now knew with certainty was not his own.

"Don't move, don't speak, don't move, don't speak," it said, repeating like a litany.

As if he could, he thought ruefully. *"Why?"* he asked the voice in his mind. *"Who are you? What's happening? Have I gone insane?"*

It was all too much. The voice. The pain. He wanted to cry out but heeded the voice, staying motionless and silent.

"We are the same, you and I. We shall meet soon enough. For now, be still. He watches."

He watches. Gael. He was still there?

He was so consumed with the voice and his aching body he'd forgotten what that snake had done. The pain in his shoulder was from him. It felt like the arrow was still lodged in his skin, the throbbing intensifying as he concentrated on the spot.

And the fall must have caused the rest of it. He wouldn't learn more with his eyes closed and lying still, but he could already tell he'd been struck in multiple places as he'd fallen down the ridge to the forest floor.

"You live, little brother. Your body will heal in time. So long as he thinks you dead, he will leave, and you will have time to heal. Just... don't... move."

"Yes, I won't."

Conall itched to open his eyes. To confront his stepfather. To show him his treachery had been wasted and he lived. But he knew that would be foolish. He'd likely only earn another arrow for his trouble.

He fought to ignore the pain. Warm rain fell on his face. The cold ground was hard against his back and legs. He listened to the soothing rain and the nearby trickling of the small waterfall. Had his body not been in agony, it would've been enough to lull him to sleep.

The water was loud in his ears, but not loud enough to drown out all the sounds around him. One particular sound he heard faintly, but nonetheless clear and unmistakable. A man crying.

Gael was crying for him? The realization almost made him laugh. He had no business feeling sorrow after what he'd done. They shared a home and family for years. Years. Worked alongside one another, celebrating birthdays and festival days together. And he'd shot him over a simple disagreement? It was crazy.

"My boy, my boy, what have I done?" Gael cried out between sobs, his voice filled with anguish. "Brenna... bloody blazes, I should've never listened to you."

Conall's confusion deepened. Brenna had something to do with this? Gael's sister had come to stay with them at the farm a few weeks ago, during the days leading up to his mother's funeral.

He racked his brain, trying to recall anything suspicious about her, but he'd been so filled with grief for his mother, so lost in his own memories of her, he'd not given the woman much thought.

Brenna had been a great help, taking over the everyday household chores of cleaning and cooking that his mother and sister always shared. Lark was happy to allow it, especially at first. She'd still been recovering from the sickness that infected both women and killed their mother. The familiar ache of grief rose in his chest, thinking of her.

Eventually, Lark recovered enough to return to her daily routine. Brenna seemed eager to return home to her life in Southmoat. But maybe not. Maybe her kindness was all an act. An excuse to creep close, to whisper plans of murder in her brother's ear. But why? What could she possibly want?

The farm. They wanted the farm.

Bile stung his throat. In retrospect, it was painfully obvious. Conall had been to Flamesmoat. He spent the first years of his life in the slums of Southmoat. No one in their right mind would be eager to return.

He should have known. He should have suspected. Now, his sister would be alone with those murderers. Trapped in that house with the only family she had left, not knowing they were responsible for her brother's death.

Not for long. Conall vowed to return to her. He'd pull his broken body along the forest floor if he had to, but he'd find a way to get back to Lark. He would save his sister.

The sounds of water and crying went on for ages. Conall's thoughts drifted back to the voice. It was silent now, but he had no doubt if he called out to it in his mind, he would receive a response. He didn't know who it was, or what exactly was happening, but he sensed instinctively he could trust it.

Twice it saved him. It said they would meet soon, and he found himself looking forward to it, if only for the opportunity to meet his savior and thank them properly.

He had a suspicion it would be more than a simple meeting. That it would change the course of his life. It was a curious thought, but one that brought him a measure of comfort. Despite the pain, or perhaps because of it, he fell asleep.

He awakened with a start. After listening carefully for a time and hearing no crying, he chanced opening his eyes to a tiny slit. The rain had stopped, and night was not far off. Unless Gael planned to spend the night fumbling through the darkened forest, he'd taken off hours ago.

Fully opening his eyes, he shifted on the cold ground, regretting the decision instantly as the pain that had become dull while he rested came into sharp focus. The agony stole his breath. Gritting his teeth, he lifted his head enough to look down at his body in the evening light.

He saw the damage the fall caused for the first time and shuddered. The arrow stuck out from his shoulder like a snapped twig; the fletching was broken and parts missing. He noticed his clothing was soaked, torn, and stained with blood in more places than he could count before the pounding in his head demanded he close his eyes.

He lay still, cursing his luck, gathering the strength to open his eyes. To find some way to move his battered body. He had to find shelter, build a fire, pull the arrow out. He'd not forgotten his vow. In fact, if it hadn't been for his burning desire to see his sister safe, he would've likely lay there and succumbed to the pain.

A twig snapped to the left. His eyes shot open. A large gray wolf sat on its haunches near his feet, studying him.

Conall should've been afraid. He should've been quaking with fear to find a predator so close, with him in no condition to defend himself. But gazing into the wolf's golden eyes, gratitude and tranquility washed over him. Something inside of him knew. The voice, his savior, was here.

"Little brother, you live." The wolf stood, pacing closer. A quick check told him he was male.

"Brother? You keep calling me that," Conall replied.

"What else would you have me call you?" The wolf tilted his head.

"My name's Conall. What's yours?"

"My name? I don't have a name." He yawned, lying down. *"Call me whatever you like."*

"All right, I'll think of something." Conall felt oddly comfortable talking with the wolf in his mind. It was so strange, like they'd known each other all their lives, although they'd only just met.

Magic. It was bonding magic. He was ready to admit what he'd only guessed at. What he'd only dreamed of. He was bonded to this wolf.

It made an odd sense to him. He always had a thing for dogs, for as long as he could remember. He loved them, and they loved him back.

As a child, he fantasized about owning a dog, but his family didn't have the means to take care of a pet. He befriended every stray in Southmoat, no matter how mean-tempered, sneaking little bits of scraps to them whenever he could. But it would be many years before he had a dog to call his own.

It was actually Gael who'd given him his first pup, Sunny. Shortly after proposing to his mother, he'd gifted Conall the sweetest, yellow mutt. From day one, he and Sunny shared a connection unlike any other in his experience. He raised her like a child and treated her more like a treasured friend than an animal. She was the best gift he'd ever received.

Looking back, that was the moment he'd started to accept Gael as part of the family. The realization stung, especially considering Sunny would treat Gael as her new master when he never returned from their hunt. One more reason he had to make it back. He had to survive.

"Do you think you can help me, brother?" The title would have to do until he thought of a name.

The wolf must've approved. His ears perked up, and his tail wagged. *"Always."*

"I have to get this arrow out. I'm going to break the bottom off, as best I can. Can you grab the sharp end with your teeth and pull it out from behind?"

"Arrow?" He rose and walked closer, examining Conall inquisitively.

Conall remembered the warning. *"Killstick. You called it a killstick."*

"Yes, I can try."

Conall sat up. Blackness clouded his vision. A fresh wave of pain slammed into him, and he struggled to concentrate on the task at hand. He better finish this quickly, while he still had the strength.

"Listen, I'm probably going to black out when you pull the arrow out. Do you see that tree?" He pointed to a massive star oak nearby. *"The ones that drop these?"* He used his knuckles to nudge an acorn resting next to his hand across the grass. *"If you can get some of the bark for me... like the skin, you know, of the tree... I can make a medicine when I wake up to stop infection."*

He'd listened to his mother and Lark enough to learn a few things. The fast-growing star oak trees, named for their star-shaped leaves, grew like weeds in Dracwood. Its scrawny branches made for poor climbing, but its bark might be the difference between life and death for him today.

"I can bring you the tree skin, little brother." His tail wagged again. *"Conall,"* he added.

Conall smiled. Maybe it was his imagination, but he felt like having the wolf here to help gave him a boost of fortitude. With him here it didn't seem so crazy to think this mad plan would work. That he might actually survive. He drew in a deep breath and got to work.

He'd lost his bow and quiver during the fall, but luckily, the pouches he wore strapped to his belt remained attached. Ignoring his body's protests, he reached into the pouch on his right-hand side and closed his eyes in relief when his fingers brushed against a smooth leather object inside.

It was a small blade he used to cut the twine for his snares and traps. He pulled it out, sliding his finger and thumb to remove the leather sheath covering the sharp edge. This ought to help.

Just that small movement had him panting. Sweat poured off his brow, plastering his brown locks to his forehead and stinging his eyes, despite the forest's coolness at dusk.

Should he start a fire? No. There was no time. He had to remove the arrow now. Before the wound started to fester and while he still had enough daylight to see what he was doing.

Now that he sat, the arrow dangled at an angle, swinging lightly with each heaving breath he took and sending little shockwaves of agony through his skin.

He just had to decide where to cut. The largest bend in the shaft close to his shoulder looked like it could work. He gritted his teeth, lifted the blade with his right hand, and began sawing.

On the first stroke, he screamed. The sound was so loud and jarring it sent the wolf scurrying back, tail between his legs. The second stroke brought forth a curse, uttered gutturally while his body shuddered. On the third stroke, the arrow broke, falling on his lap with a *plop*.

"Now, brother," he whimpered in his mind. Blackness already crowded the edges of his sight.

The wolf disappeared behind him. He heard him sniffing before the shooting pain in his shoulder told him the wolf had clasped onto the arrow with his powerful jaws.

"Pull!" he screamed.

His brother pulled. The last image he remembered after falling backward was the wolf standing over him with the broken, blood-soaked arrow clenched between his teeth.

Chapter 5

The storm had come and gone, the raindrops echoing strangely as they pelted the huge warehouse roof. Lark allowed herself to cry while the storm raged, but when the rain stopped, she let out one last heaving sob and dried her eyes on her sleeve. She forced the despair and humiliation deep down inside and sat up on the cot.

The warehouse was silent. The room she was trapped in dimmed as the sun worked its way closer to the western horizon. It truly was bare.

She pressed a hand to her temples. There was nothing in the room she could use to escape. She still had her pack, but the few pieces of clothing and half a loaf of bread would be less than useless as weapons.

In those last moments while the rain fell, she'd made up her mind. She *would* escape. She'd fixed that thought in her mind and was intent on seeing it through. There was no way she would end up as some Dolnman's slave.

No, she was going to find a way out of this mess. And after she was free, she would return to the farm and make them pay.

Her insides contorted with pain... Conall.

Brenna and Gael did not get to kill her brother, sell her to slavers, and steal their farm. No. They would *not* win. She was going to escape. She had to.

Determination fueling her, Lark stood and took another look around. After dropping her pack on the dirt floor, she climbed atop the cot. Despite her petite stature, by balancing on her toes, she could just peer through the bottom of the high, narrow windows.

Hope blossomed in her chest. Some kind stranger might be out there. She would call out to them, and they would come to her rescue—but of course, the street was deserted. Worse, it wasn't a street at all, but a tiny alley filled with even more crates and boxes, most looking decrepit and abandoned. Her heart sank. She wasn't likely to find help there.

After hopping down from the cot, she peered under it. Her eyes widened when she spotted something shoved to the back. Kneeling down, she reached under and slid out a large enamel pot. She opened the lid, then retched at the smell and closed the lid with a clatter.

That at least answered one question she had in the back of her mind, but it wouldn't be much help to escape. Although, it was rather heavy.

She sat back on her heels, an idea forming. Maybe she could land a lucky strike to Rasmus' head and slip out in the mayhem. She would need to distract him first with some ruse that would make him enter and turn his back. If she could just think of something...

A door slammed in the warehouse, and she almost jumped out of her skin. She shoved the chamber pot back under the cot but placed it within easy reach, just in case. After hopping up off the floor, she tip-toed to the door and pressed her ear against the wood.

"Well, well, well." She heard Rasmus' muffled voice. "What do we have here?"

"Pretty, ain't she?" said a second man, his voice deep and gravelly.

"Very, very, nice. Where did you find this gem?"

"The Joria Rose brothel. Seems her previous benefactor had enough of her." The new man laughed cruelly. "Don't want any other rich pigs around town sniffing at her, either. One of those 'don't play with my toys' types, I gather."

"Brothel, did you say?" Footsteps pounded across the room before Rasmus spoke again. "Pax, you know you aren't supposed to damage the merchandise."

"She was like that when I got her, I swear." Pax laughed again.

"Fine, fine. Stick her in the back room with the other one. Then come help me pack the wagon. We're leaving."

"Whatever you say, boss."

Footsteps headed in her direction. Lark scrambled back from the door and hopped onto the cot. She wrapped her arms around her knees and tucked her chin against her chest as the lock clicked and the door swung open.

One of the ugliest men she'd ever seen stepped into the room. He was completely bald, hulking in size and had a scar across his left eyelid that puckered the skin, leaving the eye looking like it was perpetually squinting. He gripped the forearm of a girl who looked not much older than she was.

Unlike the man, she was undeniably gorgeous, all soft lines and curves, her face so striking she would earn stares from any man with a pulse. She had dark brown skin and golden-brown eyes that were wide open in fear.

Pax let go of the girl's arm and dragged his hand through her short brown curls, gripping them tightly and forcing her head back. He stared into her eyes with a smirk and said, "I'll see you later, beautiful," before releasing his grip on her hair. Then, he shoved her inside and slammed the door shut. It locked with a *click*.

The girl smacked into the floor, catching herself on her hands and knees. Lark leapt up, intending to help her to her feet, but she backed away when the girl flinched at her touch and scrambled away, banging into the wall.

"I'm sorry. I didn't mean to frighten you." Lark perched on the cot and offered the girl a half smile. "I was only trying to help you off the ground."

The girl peered at her, silent and unsmiling. She was clothed in a tight-fitting, flimsy brown dress. The fabric blended into her skin so well she almost appeared nude. There was a bruise on her chin and a set of fresh scratches on her neck that looked red and angry.

"I got here right before the storm started. I had a look around, and there doesn't seem to be any way out of this room... Well, there is a chamber pot under the bed." Lark shook her head sheepishly, rubbing a hand on her neck, realizing she hadn't bothered to supply a name. "I'm Lark, by the way." She stared at the ground, wishing the girl would speak. "What's your name?"

"I'm Tiora," she said, after a moment of silence. Her voice was beautiful, too; a sweet alto.

Lark's gaze shot back to Tiora's face, and she found her staring out the window at the last rays of sunshine filtering through the glass. She looked forlorn, but her eyes held no tears.

"I would say 'pleasure to meet you,' but that doesn't seem right in these circumstances." Lark scooted sideways on the cot, patting the lumpy mattress' empty half. "You don't have to stay seated on the hard floor. It's not much better up here, but you're welcome to share the cot with me."

Tiora glanced at the bed before returning her gaze to the dimming view. "I'm fine here, thanks."

Lark's brow furrowed, but she didn't push the matter. She sighed. The chamber pot was out now. With two villains here, there was no way she could surprise them both. But she might get Tiora on her side. They had little chance of overpowering the men, but maybe the two of them working together could come up with a plan to outsmart them.

Before she could think of something to say to enlist the older girl's help, the sound of footsteps pounded in her ears. She sat stock still, gaping at the door.

Pax threw it open and sauntered into the room with an evil grin plastered to his ugly face. He was so large his muscles strained at the cloth of his brown tunic and trousers.

Lark couldn't stop the shudder that overtook her body when his eyes locked with her own.

"Blazes, how did I miss you earlier?" Pax licked his lips and prowled closer. "This is gonna be a fun trip. I'm gonna enjoy getting to know you two." He wagged his eyebrows suggestively, grinning even wider.

Lark's stomach clenched at the implication behind his words.

"Hands off that one, Pax. She needs to arrive unspoiled if we want the best price." Rasmus stepped inside and pulled the door closed behind him.

Lark's shoulders relaxed, until she glimpsed the items he carried, and her back knotted up again, worse than before.

Rasmus held rope and long strips of rough, black cloth. Handing half to Pax, he stumbled forward, and a whiff of liquor wafted off of him.

Lark angled her nose away in disgust. It only awarded her a brief moment of relief, for he came closer still; the smell grew much stronger.

"I'll take care of her." Rasmus glanced back over his shoulder. "Tie up the whore."

Lark's body rooted to the spot. She stared up at Rasmus as he unwrapped the rope between his hands. "You're not going to give me any trouble, are you, little bird?"

Lark's mind raced, her gaze flicking to the door. Could she make a run for it? Snatch the chamber pot and clobber Rasmus, race past Pax...

She considered it briefly, but the glint of silver at her captor's waist drove the thought from her mind. A man willing to trade in slaves would likely have no problem hurting or even killing a troublesome girl. Especially a slaver who'd been drinking.

She shook her head slowly, looking into the man's cloudy eyes. "Never mess with a man deep in his cups," her mother used to say. She would play the part of the obedient prisoner for now and bide her time until she could see a way out of this.

"Give me your hands." Rasmus' face displayed no sign of glee like Pax's but was just as frightening for all his stoic indifference.

She stuck her hands in front of her, and Rasmus went to work. The rope scratched her wrists, the loops dug into her skin. He wrapped the rope expertly, finishing it all with a knot and pulling it tight. She gulped, her stomach churning as he held up the strip of cloth he'd strung over his shoulder while he was busy with her hands.

"You're not going to blindfold me, are you?" she asked, her voice shaky.

He wobbled a bit as he slid the strip between his hands, then stretched it out. "Open your mouth."

Lark obeyed, shuddering as the rough cloth made contact with her tongue. Rasmus knotted the cloth tightly behind her head, then grabbed the rope around her wrists and tugged, pulling her to her feet.

She managed to catch a glimpse of Tiora tied in identical fashion, still staring impassively out the windows, before she was forced to follow Rasmus' lead.

He led her through the warehouse, weaving between the stacked boxes, and then through the back door. The street was much the same, except for a black horse and wagon that stood at the ready beyond the door. The wagon looked sturdy and the horse spritely and young. It pulled gently at its reins and nickered as they approached.

Rasmus tugged on her bound hands, leading her to the back of the cart. "Get in." He lifted the black tarp covering the back of the wagon enough so she could squeeze in.

She sat down on the edge and scooted backward but apparently not far enough.

"Further." Rasmus nudged her shins with his fist.

Lark scooted back as far as she could until her back pressed against something hard and unyielding. Tiora was made to squeeze in as well. The wagon was so crowded they were forced to sit crammed together like children vying for the best seat at the Harvest Festival parade.

Once Rasmus was satisfied they were arranged to his liking, he lifted the wooden, slatted tailboard and dropped the tarp. He sealed them in, shrouding them in darkness.

The cart swayed as the men boarded and Rasmus called out to the horse, "Ya." Then the cart surged forward, slamming her back against the hard object behind her.

Lark's chest rose and fell as she struggled for air. This was really happening. Her life was over. Everything she'd known and loved was lost to her. Even her pack lay back in that warehouse room, abandoned and forgotten.

She tugged at the gag, franticly trying to dislodge it now that the men weren't watching, but it was tied so tightly it wouldn't budge.

She tried desperately to calm her rushing heart, scanning the darkness for something to calm her panic. There was nothing. Only the taste of wet cloth clogging her mouth and the rough rope digging into her skin.

Suddenly, movement brushed her side. Tiora pressed her thigh against Lark's more firmly, and a moment later, a pair of bound hands landed on her knee. That small reminder that she wasn't alone helped immensely. Slowly, her breathing evened out, thanks to the kindness of the stranger beside her.

Time passed. Lark's eyes adjusted to the darkness. There were a few spots ahead of her where light leaked through the wagon slats. Leaning forward, she pressed her eye against the nearest spot and watched Southmoat as they drove through dusk. It was nearly evening, but there was still enough light for her to see.

Her stomach lurched. So that was the reason for her aunt's winding route earlier in the day. The wagon headed directly west, and the sights she saw were a far cry from the poor, but still respectable, neighborhood Brenna was so careful to showcase.

Beggars sprawled in the streets, a few covered in weeping sores or missing limbs. Dilapidated buildings crowded the dirty streets. Many appeared abandoned or like they might fall over in a stiff breeze. Children still ran in the streets, but they did not play. Instead, they fought one another or slinked in doorways, looking half-starved and desperate.

The wagon rolled on, the darkness outside deepening until all she could see was shadow broken by occasional glimpses of light shining from the seedy buildings. Finally, she leaned back, her shoulders and neck protesting after so long spent leaning forward.

What she wouldn't give for a hot bath. And a warm meal. Her chin trembled, and she closed her eyes. Would such simple pleasures ever be hers again?

The *clip-clop* of hooves on the hard-packed dirt slowed, and then halted, as the wagon rolled to a stop. Lark tensed, holding her breath.

"I'll just be a moment," Rasmus said. The wagon swayed with his shifting weight. "Have to stock up on libations. Stay with the wagon."

Lark peered through the slats but couldn't see much in the darkness. Just a rectangle of light and the sound of raucous merriment spilling out of a building as Rasmus slipped in. The moment dragged out with no sign of his return.

The wagon vibrated with the *tap-tap-tapping* of a booted foot. After an eternity of tapping, Pax cursed. The wagon jolted as he jumped down, followed by sounds of merriment once again breaking the night's silence.

Her heart skipped a beat. This might be their chance.

With all her strength, Lark shoved her fists into the tarp, looking for any weaknesses. A heartbeat later, Tiora joined in, and their fists pounded together in concert, like a crazed drummer in a frenzy. But it was no use. The tarp was tied on expertly, and their pounding had no effect.

Changing tactics, she kicked the wooden tailboard. Tiora joined in again, but being so cramped, it was soon obvious they wouldn't have the leverage needed to force open the lock. Shaking from exertion, Lark stopped kicking. Tears welled in her eyes.

Shuffling footsteps sounded from the opposite direction of the pub. Lark's breath caught. Had their attempt at escape attracted someone who might help?

A sound crinkled above her head, and a tiny corner of tarp peeled back, revealing the face of a stranger.

An old woman, wrinkled and gray-haired, peeked in at them, her brown eyes as big and round as the wheels of their wagon. "Oh dear, you poor things."

Lark tried to speak, to cry out help, but the gag only allowed her to mumble unintelligibly.

"There, there, little ones. Oh, I wish I could free you, but I haven't a knife for the rope—and the back—I haven't the key."

Staring at the woman with pleading eyes, Lark's heart filled with dread as she began to drop the tarp and leave.

The woman stared through the hole, remorse painting her face before disappearing. An instant later, she shoved her hand through and dropped something into the wagon. "I'll pray for you," she whispered, then she shuffled away.

Lark groped around in the darkness with her bound hands, searching for whatever the woman gifted them. After a moment, she found it, and a tear dripped from her lashes. The unmistakable softness of a fresh-cut flower flattened under her fingertips. She screamed her frustration into the gag, tears rolling down her face.

The pub door opened, and Lark pressed her eye to the slat. Pax exited, half dragging, half carrying out Rasmus, who had a bottle slung under his arm and another clenched in his fist.

Shoving the flower into her skirt pocket, she rubbed her face against her sleeves, brushing away the tears as the wagon rocked.

"Get up there, you lush," Pax said. He lifted the tarp's corner and eyed them both before hopping onto the cart and setting it in motion.

They traveled for ages. She'd long ago given up looking through the slats, for night had fully fallen. After they left the confines of Flamesmoat and entered the forested countryside, there was nothing to see, anyway. Just an endless expanse of woods and trees.

Her body was sore all over, muscles aching from being crammed in the back of the wagon for so long. When they stopped, relief washed over her, if only for the chance to climb out and stretch.

The wagon shifted, and a single *thud* landed on the ground before someone came round and unlocked the tailboard. Pax's face was revealed in the moonlit night. "Out," he said.

Lark moved to comply.

He looked at her stone-faced and shoved her back with his palm. "Not you." He pointed at Tiora. "You, out."

Tiora shrank back, but Pax grabbed her by her wrists and tugged, spilling her out onto the ground. He slammed the board back into place, locked it, and returned Lark to the darkness.

For a moment, she rejoiced. With Tiora gone, she had room to spread out, which she did at once, groaning as her muscles stretched.

Then came the sounds. Moaning. Skin slapping. Grunting and cursing.

Her blood boiled. Rasmus, no doubt blackout drunk, was not stopping it. She could do nothing to stop it.

Her stomach kinked up in knots with every disgusting groan. The momentary relief was long gone, replaced with disgust and guilt. She would gladly spend an eternity cramped together with Tiora to spare her this.

As she lay there listening, the cold night air chilling her skin, she made another promise to herself. One she was just as determined to keep. Before she escaped, she would see both of these men dead.

Chapter 6

Izora rapped on the door to Kayda's bedchamber early on the morning after Kayda summoned for the first time. The sun had barely crested the eastern horizon, but Kayda was already dressed in a cream and ivory-striped dress, ready for training.

Despite her nurse's instructions, she hadn't slept much. That night, her mind had brimmed with questions. And the morning had been no better. She was so full of excitement and apprehension about the day to come.

Izora breezed in without waiting for a reply. "Good morning, Princess." She placed a vase of flowers on her bedside table. "Up early, I see."

"Yes, I'm ready." Kayda jumped up from her bed, smoothed the bedspread, and nodded with satisfaction. "Are we training in here? Or shall we go to your quarters?" She was hoping for the latter. The musty scent of yesterday's events still lingered in the air.

"Neither." Turning on her heel, Izora led the way to the door, calling over her shoulder, "Follow me."

At this hour, the castle was quiet. Likely, there were servants awake in the kitchens and stables, but in the southeast wing, where the royal family slept in their private chambers, they were the only ones stirring.

Her rooms were the smallest in the wing, comprising a modest bedchamber, a closet-sized dressing room, and a cramped sitting room. They sat close to the corridor leading to the central hall, which Izora headed toward.

They called it the royal corridor. The entire path was hung, floor-to-ceiling, with portraits. Kings and queens of the past stared stoically out of the frames.

One day, her own portrait might be up there. Kayda suppressed a smirk. At least she would add a little variety to all the pale blondes and brunettes with her light brown freckled skin and auburn hair.

As they neared the corridor's end, they approached the largest painting. It was her favorite. Something about it always made her gaze linger on it as she passed.

It was a portrait of the first King of Dracwood, King Algernon the Great. According to legend, he'd been instrumental in blocking the Abandoned Lands, helping the mages along with his bonded animal, a dragon named Dru. Unlike most of the others, he was smiling, his tawny-brown eyes sparkling on the canvas. The painter must have been a genius of the time. The image seemed so alive.

Her favorite part of the piece was in the background. A casual viewer might even miss it, but Kayda's gaze always locked on the little detail. In the top left corner, camouflaged among trees, was the tip of a black-scaled tail.

She couldn't stare long today, so she settled for a passing smile and followed Izora out of the royal wing.

The central hall was the largest building in the castle and was rectangular, with four wings attached on each corner by a corridor. The royal corridor let out into the drawing room, a cheery canary-yellow room dominated by oversized settees and chaises, which connected to the main foyer and great hall.

Izora passed through the drawing room without pause and led Kayda through the great hall, which was brightly lit with daylight and deserted. Their footsteps reverberated through the cavernous hall. They scurried like mice, taking no time to admire the many colorful tapestries adorning the whitewashed brick walls.

Izora turned right at the back of the great hall and headed through the music room. Instruments of all shapes and sizes—the wood and metals polished to a gleaming shine—adorned the walls or sat waiting atop shelves and display racks. Today, the room was silent and still.

They passed through quickly, into the corridor leading to the northwest wing of the castle. This wing contained one of Kayda's favorite places in the whole keep, the library.

"You can't mean to teach me to summon fire in the library," Kayda whispered as they hurried down the corridor. "That would be disastrous."

She shuddered, picturing the wing going up in flames. Destroying all the tomes the library held would be a crime she could never forgive herself for.

"Don't fret for your books, child. We won't be training here." Izora smiled as she opened the door to the library.

They slipped in, and Kayda smiled, too, breathing deeply the familiar woody scent of the written word. Much like the royal corridor, the walls were loaded from floor to ceiling, only with shelves instead of pictures. Books sat neatly upon them in all sizes, shapes, and colors, covering a wide variety of topics. So many she could never read them all in her lifetime. She loved it here.

Kayda arched her brow. "Well, what are we doing here if we won't be training?" She crossed her arms. "Am I to study some books on magic before I'm allowed to practice?"

"No, don't be silly." Izora strode across the library toward a closet tucked away in a corner. On the way, she grabbed a large, three-armed candelabra off one of the shelves and lit it in the fireplace before motioning Kayda forward. "In through here."

Kayda followed, cramming herself inside behind her nurse, and then closing the door. The scent of lye soap permeated the room. She drew her elbows close, avoiding the stacked cleaning supplies while the dusty air tickled her nose.

"I don't see how you expect me to get much practice done in here. I can hardly move."

"Patience, my dear," Izora said. "Just a moment."

Kayda couldn't see what she was doing, but it was clear her nurse was doing something besides standing motionless in the closet. Before she could question her, the answer became obvious when the closet's back wall swung inward, revealing a stone stairwell leading into darkness.

Kayda squealed with delight. She'd thought she knew everything about the castle, but this was new.

She was about to follow her nurse into a hidden room... Forget reading about adventures; she was about to experience one for herself. Taking a deep breath, she lifted her skirts and followed Izora into the passage.

The steps were narrow, so they traveled single file. Kayda focused on the candles' bobbing light and held the rough brick wall to keep her balance. Her heart pounded with excitement.

It wasn't long before they made it to the bottom of the steps. In the candelabra's dim light, she could see the beginnings of an underground chamber of some sort. "What is this place?" Kayda squinted into the darkness.

The light dimmed even more. Kayda looked back at her nurse as a chill filled the air.

Izora cupped a hand near one of the candles, eyes closed. When she opened her eyes, the candle's flame split into four distinct balls. The flames separated, then floated to the corners of the room, pausing just below the ceiling and hanging suspended as if from invisible dangling sconces.

"Wow," Kayda exclaimed, impressed with the display of Izora's talent as much as the underground chamber's size. It was massive, comparable in size to the great hall. The walls were made of brick and stone, but the floor appeared to be hard-packed dirt.

There were several doorways hewn into the stone walls. Most of them were open to reveal passages leading off into more darkness, but one on the far wall had a wooden door that blocked her view of what lay beyond.

Kayda itched to explore it all. Especially that door. What would she find if she walked through that doorway? Forgotten treasures? Ancient relics of the people who once inhabited this keep? A voice inside of her hummed with wonder and curiosity and called out to open that door and discover what hid behind it.

"I never knew this was down here. How did you find this place?" She turned and found Izora watching her.

"Oh, I have my ways. These rooms were once used as storage. At some point, they stopped using them. From the looks of it, they're prone to flooding." She nodded toward the discoloration shading the bottom of the brick walls. "This room should serve us fine for our training."

"All right, but what about the rest of this place?" Kayda stood on tip-toe, peering into the darkness beyond the closest opening. "Have you been down all the halls and passages?"

"I've been through some. It's all the same—just more empty rooms like this one and locked doors."

"Oh." Her shoulders slumped. It wasn't the mystery she'd been hoping for, but she wouldn't let a few empty rooms dampen her enthusiasm. She was about to learn how to summon fire. "So, how do we start?"

"Before we begin practicing, there are a few rules you need to learn." Izora planted herself in front of her, meeting her eyes, her face serious. "Never try to summon without your source element nearby. Luckily, the fires in this old castle are always lit, but that won't always be the case everywhere you go."

Izora removed something from her skirt pocket and placed it into Kayda's hand. It was an oblong metal box about the size of a deck of cards. Kayda smoothed her fingers across the top, admiring the intricate etching of a flame engraved upon it.

"It's a tinderbox. It has flint and steel inside," Izora explained. "I'll teach you how to use it."

"Thank you." Kayda lifted the lid and peeked inside. "But I don't understand. Why can't you just summon flames from nothing?"

"You can, dear. But that doesn't mean you should. Using a source that's already there—you'll find it's as easy as breathing. Summoning a flame from nothing—that's much harder to do, and it has a cost."

"A cost?" She snapped the tinderbox lid shut and placed it in her skirt pocket.

"Yes. Sometimes it might take your energy. Mages have been known to black out when they lose their source and still try to summon."

"That doesn't sound so bad. I mean, you would recover quickly, at least."

"Well, that's just for simple things. Like the little trick I did earlier to light the room." Izora nodded toward the closest fire orb, still suspended from the ceiling. "But if you try to accomplish something bigger without a source—well, the price is a bit steeper."

"What would happen then?"

"You pay with your life."

"It... kills you?"

"In extreme cases, it can. More likely, it will age you. Years of your life, gone in the blink of an eye." Izora sighed. "It's a steep price indeed."

Kayda gulped, eyes widening. Years of her life... The thought of having to pay that price was frightening, but it wasn't enough to stop her from wanting to learn all she could. "All right, so always use a source. What else?"

"You have to remain close to your source if you want the magic to last." Izora held up the candelabra at eye level, the flames dancing merrily. "If I snuff out this candle right now, the flames I summoned will disappear, too. I could use my talent to keep them lit for a short while, but without the source, the magic will only have my own energy to use for fuel."

"And then the costs... Yes, I see." Her brow furrowed. "Hmm, it's too bad I don't have air talent. I bet they don't have to worry about any of this."

Izora chuckled. "Some of us do have it a bit easier than others, I'm afraid. But that's life. You have to work with whatever talents you're given." She backed up a few paces and placed the candelabra on the dirt floor. "Remember those two rules, and you'll be fine. Are you ready for your first lesson?"

Kayda nodded eagerly. "Yes. What should I do?"

Izora sidestepped a few paces, watching Kayda intently. "Approach the candle. That flame will be your source. You don't have to touch it, but you should be close enough to feel the flame's heat."

Kayda complied. The candle warmed her skin. It didn't feel any different today after learning about her talent then it had all the multitude of other times in her life she warmed her hands around a flame. There had to be more.

"This is the part that will take practice. You have to visualize what you want the flames to do. Concentrate. See the flame take shape in your mind."

Kayda bit her lip, flinching away from the flame. It couldn't be that simple, could it?

Izora must have seen the confusion on her face. "It's not as easy as it sounds. At least, not at first. You'll have to learn to empty your mind of all else in order to concentrate and visualize properly. But once you've mastered the basics, you'll find you can shape the flames into whatever you desire."

Kayda's jaw dropped. "Anything I desire... Wait, then why didn't you make the flames disappear from my fireplace yesterday?"

Izora chuckled. "I could have, but I didn't want to scare you before we had a chance to talk. But there's a reason I brought a vase full of water to your room every day. I've been waiting for this day for a long time." She rested a hand on her shoulder, giving her a squeeze. "I know you can do this, Kayda."

She still hadn't wrapped her head around this incredible gift she'd been given. Her whole life, she'd been expecting a completely different talent. Now she could control flames, too.

It was a lot to get used to, but she was up for the challenge. Setting her shoulders back, she reached forward, and the flame's heat kissed her skin once more.

"Try to clear your mind. Start with something small, a ball of flame floating in your hands. Visualize it clearly, the heat... the shape..." Izora instructed, backing away a few paces.

Kayda closed her eyes and tried to empty her mind. She started to picture a ball of flame resting in her palms, but a question interrupted her concentration.

"Wait, if you have to clear your mind, then how did I summon the flames in my room?" She turned to her nurse, raising a brow. "My mind wasn't clear at all."

"Sometimes, when a mage first discovers their talent, it's an instinctual response to extreme emotions. More often than not, it's a response to danger, a life-or-death situation." Izora raised an eyebrow of her own. "If the rumor floating around the keep is to be believed, then you had quite the scare yesterday."

Kayda shivered. The arrow streaking toward her flashed through her memory. She recalled the terror of that moment, and the anger she felt later as she stirred the coals in her fireplace. That must have been the trigger.

A smile crossed her lips. Just this once, she could be thankful for her brother's bullying. If he hadn't shot at her yesterday, she wouldn't be down here learning to summon.

Izora cleared her throat, interrupting Kayda's musing. "Try again, please."

Kayda nodded. She focused on the flame topping the middle candle. She pictured the color of it. The heat. The way it danced in the air. Closing her eyes and lifting her right hand, she tried to picture the flame moving, forming a small sphere floating above her palm. She emptied her mind and thought of nothing else but the flame. The warmth, the power.

A chill swept through her, like an icy breeze stroked every inch of her skin. Lifting her lashes, she squealed with glee when she saw a fireball the size of an apple resting exactly where she pictured it above her outstretched palm. She turned to share her excitement with Izora, only to witness the fireball vanish when her concentration broke.

"Blazes." Kayda frowned. "I had it for a moment, at least."

Izora squeezed her arm. "No, no. That was excellent, Kayda." She tilted her head, a smile stretching across her face. "You're a natural, just like your mother."

Kayda's chest swelled with pride. She was going to be a mage, like her mother. She beamed.

Izora dropped her hand from Kayda's arm and took several steps back. "Again."

Chapter 7

Conall awoke dazed, with a luxurious warmth pressing against his face. A musky scent wafted off his pillow. His nose twitched. The pillow twitched back. He startled, rolling away in surprise, jostling his battered body and awakening fully.

"Blazes." He groaned and clamped his eyes shut, breathing deeply through the pain. His skin was scratched and bruised all over, like he'd been through a thresher. His shoulder burned where the arrow had been, and his body screamed in a dozen places.

The sound of water was missing.

Opening his eyes, he took stock of his surroundings. Shadows blanketed the walls of a shallow cave. It was small, just wide enough to fit a man and wolf inside, with a little room to spare. The cave roof loomed high above, ensuring he could stand without smacking his head on the ceiling, but he would have to crawl to get out. The only light came from the mouth of the cave, by which he could tell a new day had dawned outside.

"How did we get here, brother?" Conall eyed his silent companion, who yawned lazily before replying.

"I pulled you in when you would not awaken. It's not far from where you fell."

"Thank you." He smiled. That was a good call. Sleeping on the wet ground next to a waterfall would've been a bad idea in his condition. The wolf had saved him again. Time and again, he proved himself a true friend.

Hmm, maybe he could call him Buddy? No... that wasn't quite right.

"Did you get the bark?"

"Yes." He rose from his stomach and stretched out his hind legs before walking back a few paces to the cave wall, picking up the bark with his jaw, then depositing it in Conall's outstretched hand.

Conall inspected the bark and sighed. He grabbed his waterskin from his belt loop and swigged a few long swallows before casting his gaze about for a large rock he could use to grind the bark into a paste.

There. *"Please, can you bring me that rock?"* He pointed to it and grimaced as he raised himself into a seated position.

The wolf rolled it with his snout until it landed next to his thigh. Conall got to work, using the stone floor and the rock to grind the bark, adding water one splash at a time until he made an ugly concoction that would hopefully be enough to stave off infection. He'd watched his mother and Lark enough times to know what to do, although he doubted they'd ever worked with such primitive tools.

He smiled crookedly at the soggy mess. They both would've laughed at his attempt and made him start again had he been home with them. For today, it would have to do.

Grimacing again, he unbuttoned the top few buttons of his tunic and peeled back the bloodstained cloth covering his shoulder. The wound looked as bad as it felt—red and black and swollen, weeping fresh blood from where his shirt had been glued.

He suppressed the urge to heave and scooped big globs of the oak paste onto the wound. Though he couldn't see the exit wound, he heaped paste onto his back, gritting his teeth with agony.

He pulled a bit of folded rag out of one of his belt pouches. He always kept some with him when trapping, for cleaning his hands and knife after handling a fresh kill. His empty traps had been a stroke of luck, after all. The fabric was old and worn but blessedly clean.

Holding one end with his teeth, he tossed half the fabric over his shoulder, then smoothed the rest over the front of the wound. That would have to do for now. He rolled his sleeve back in place, ignoring the searing pain as he jostled his wound, and lay down on the cave floor, totally spent.

He must've slept. When he opened his eyes, the cave shadows had lengthened. Was it afternoon outside, or dusk? Feeling a pressing need to know and to relieve his aching bladder, Conall decided to venture out and explore.

The wolf was no longer in the cave. Perhaps he had similar thoughts.

Rolling up to sitting, he groaned. That hadn't yet gotten any easier. His body protesting, he leaned forward on his knees, and being careful not to put much weight on his left arm, he crawled through the mouth of the cave into the forest.

From the sun's position, it appeared to be late in the afternoon as he knelt, squinting. The cave let out into a small clearing surrounded by trees. The waterfall peeked out behind trees to the left, a few dozen paces away. He smacked his dry lips together. He ought to head there, to fill his waterskin before dark.

He tried to stand. That was a mistake. His right ankle screamed in pain as he placed his weight on it. Falling back to his knees, tears pooling at the corners of his eyes, he crawled between the trees, searching—there.

He grabbed a large stick just the right size for a crutch. Once again, he stood. With the stick under his right armpit, he hobbled toward the waterfall, pausing behind a tree to take care of his other pressing business.

It appeared so close when viewed from the clearing, but his injuries and hobbling pace made it feel like twice the distance. When he made it to the trickling stream, he collapsed next to it in relief, bathed in sweat, wishing he'd remained resting in the cave. He quickly emptied his waterskin with a few gulps and refilled and emptied it twice more before his thirst was quenched.

Scanning the cliff wall, he spotted the path his body had taken on its way down. Below the top of the ledge lay freshly turned earth, dislodged roots, and torn plants that told the story. A story of betrayal.

Even now, so many hours later, darkened stains marred the spot where he'd lain bleeding, shot, and pretending to be dead. A shiver swept down his spine. He should be dead, but he wasn't. He was alive, and he would set things right. He must.

His stomach rumbled, reminding him he hadn't eaten since yesterday's breakfast. He reached for his belt pouches, planning to nibble on the dried meat he'd brought with him, but at that moment, the wolf appeared. His tail wagged, a freshly killed hare dangling from his jaws.

"Little bro—Conall, you're awake. Good, good. I brought meat." He dropped the hare at Conall's feet, tongue hanging, looking particularly pleased with himself.

Hunter? No... still not right. The name had to be perfect.

"You can still call me little brother, if you like. I don't mind it," Conall said.

"Good." His tail wagged again, a bit faster. *"It is a habit of all wolves to call each other brother, sister, and the like. Sometimes, I forget you are not a wolf. I went searching for a pack of my own, and I found you, so to me, we are brothers."* He nudged the hare with his snout. *"Eat up, little brother. You need to regain your strength."*

"All right, all right, but not before I cook it." He picked up the hare and grabbed his blade.

"Cook?"

"Gather some dry sticks, and I'll show you."

Conall skinned the hare quickly. He grimaced with pain every time his shoulder jostled, but luckily, years of practice left him so deft at the task he could do it in his sleep.

The wolf spent the time waiting gathering sticks as requested. Then he watched Conall spear the hare's carcass with a stick, licking his chops as Conall stabbed the end of the long branch into the ground.

Conall rinsed his hands in the stream and stacked the wood for a fire. He pulled out a worn metal tin, dented and scratched in a dozen places. He popped it open, grabbed what he needed, and within moments, the scent of smoke filled the air as the fire caught.

"Brother. Fire. Fire!" The wolf backed away from the smoke, pacing, tail between his legs, reminding Conall of his dog Sunny during a thunderstorm.

"It's safe. It's how we cook. The fire won't spread, I promise."

His words seemed to comfort the wolf, but he was still wary. He stayed far back from the fire, until he caught the scent of roasting meat, then he began licking his chops again and creeping closer.

"C'mon, brother. It's almost done." Conall beckoned the wolf forward.

The wolf appeared at his side as he was ready to pull the meat from the spit. Conall used his knife to split the hare in half and placed the wolf's portion in front of him.

He sniffed the steaming meat before licking it cautiously. *"It's warm,"* he said before taking a bite, then proceeding to devour it with relish. *"I like it,"* he proclaimed between bites.

Conall laughed. He ate his own portion more slowly but with just as much pleasure. There was nothing else quite like a simple meal over a campfire with good company. He inhaled, lifting his nose, the scent of wood fire and foliage calming some part deep inside him.

Could that be the answer? Woody... Forest? No, still not it.

He rubbed the back of his neck, polishing off the last of his meat. It would come to him. Perhaps after a night's sleep. Drowsily, he made his way with his brother back to the cave, eager for rest and a chance to heal.

He awoke in the night, bathed in sweat, awash with pain and screaming at some half-forgotten nightmare.

The wolf was at his side in an instant, curling up next to his good arm, staring at him with golden eyes in the dark. *"It's all right, Conall, I'm here."*

He clutched a fistful of fur, comforted instantly, but still scared witless, knowing the infection he'd hoped to avoid was the cause of his state. He hoped with all his might he would overcome this. That his battered body still had enough fight left in it to see him through this fever and alive on the other side.

He spent the night drifting in and out of consciousness, plagued by unrelenting visions. Lark was trapped in the farmhouse while it burned. He stood outside watching but could not move to save her, no matter how he tried. His heart raged as he listened to the torturous cries, the pleas for help. It drove him half mad with agony.

Suddenly, he was in front of a wall that gleamed and pulsated with a life of its own. Lark was there, too, and he watched the life being sucked out of her. He screamed, glued to the spot, unable to move. His throat ached like he'd swallowed broken glass before she heard him, only to turn her ancient face his way, looking drugged.

A smile split her face, ear to ear. She held on tight to the wall, forcing him to watch while the ravages of time wore on her. Her skin decayed, ending with only bone. Her skull still stared back at him, smiling... always smiling.

He saw his own face, glowering at him with shame. Or... it was his father. His own face so similar, those hazel eyes gazing into his own with regret. He'd sacrificed his life on that ship to ensure his family's survival, and what did he get in return? A weakling, a victim. Couldn't protect his own.

No—those were not his father's thoughts. They were his own fevered imaginings.

There were monsters. Great behemoths in the waste, trying to drag him under. Sand filling his throat, hot and choking.

Reptiles slithered in the water, waiting for the moment he let down his guard to plunge him into the salty depths.

Phantoms stalked him through an unending expanse of snow. The cold and fear froze deep in his bones.

His whole body, covered in vermin. The squirming, squealing bodies full of sharp teeth. They would eat him alive.

Darkness blanketed the sky. A black creature, so huge and fearsome, soared through the clouds. Swooping down, it rained fire on the ground, surrounding him with flame. Panic turned his blood to ice.

Run. He had to run.

He awoke with a start, heart still pounding. But his nightmares receded, the way such things do, until they were only a feeling. A niggling discomfort he couldn't fully banish.

Dragging the back of his hand across his forehead, he huffed out a sigh. The fever had passed. His body was weak and his throat drier than it had ever been. He grabbed his waterskin and emptied it, not minding the way it sloshed out from the edges and dribbled down his sweat-soaked neck.

Something twitched to his right. The wolf—his brother—lounged beside him, head resting on his front paws, watching him. Gratitude washed over Conall. He gently stroked the wolf's fur, and soon, fell into a dreamless sleep.

Days passed. The wolf hunted by night while Conall slept, and they feasted each morning. Before long, Conall's body began to knit itself back together. The pain receded slowly. He feared his shoulder would never be the same, yet that, too, began healing.

Throughout it all, the wolf stayed with him. Following him out wherever he went, glued to his side. Then one day, it came to him.

"Shadow. I think I shall call you Shadow, brother." Turning to gaze into his companion's golden eyes, he waited for a response.

"Shadow... Yes, I like it. I'm Shadow." Raising his head to the sky, he let out a single, heartfelt howl.

Conall placed his hand on Shadow's back. Looking at the mouth of the cave, he smiled, feeling bittersweet. *"I hope you're ready for a journey. Tomorrow, we're leaving. I have to save my sister."*

"We will, little brother. Together."

Chapter 8

The days passed by in a flurry of activity for Kayda. Every morning she rose with the sun and crept through the sleeping keep with Izora to practice her magic in the forgotten depths of the castle.

Steadily, her skills improved until she could call the flames at ease. Izora tested her concentration at every turn, distracting her in a million ways. At long last, she became adept at keeping the flame burning, no matter what her nurse did to divert her attention. A bud of pride bloomed in her chest, but she knew she'd only just begun. She was eager to continue her training, relishing learning to control her talent with a fervor she'd not yet known in her life.

Early one morning, Izora did not come to meet her at their usual hour. Refusing to sit and wait, Kayda pulled on a simple turquoise dress and set out to discover the reason for her absence. Stealthily, she made her way through the castle, searching all the common areas on her way, but finding them empty and silent.

Had Izora gone on ahead without her?

She made her way to the tunnels through the library. After the first day, her nurse had shown her the secret that revealed the entrance to their training room. A simple lever hid in a decorative pattern inlaid in the closet wall, which served as clever camouflage.

But when she opened the hidden door, she found the room still swathed in darkness and closed the door hastily after calling down, "Izora...?" and hearing no reply.

Perhaps she'd overslept?

She headed to Izora's quarters in the keep's northwest wing. She made her way quickly through the library and music room. Then she skirted the back of the great hall, avoiding a servant with his head and shoulders in the main fireplace, likely stirring the coals, preparing to rouse the fire to life for the day.

She opened the door into the staff corridor that bordered the greenhouse and slid inside the candlelit hallway. The cramped, windowless passage enabled the staff to reach the northwest corridor from the keep's back entrance without being seen by the royal family or any visitors who came to enjoy the lush vegetation and exotic flowers in the greenhouse.

She paused. A sound from the greenhouse caught her attention.

Who could that be at this hour?

Her curiosity piqued, Kayda tiptoed to the adjoining wall, placing her ear on the cold plaster. It was obvious this wall had not quite been made up to the keep's high standards. But the thin walls afforded her the ability to hear a bit of what was said.

Tarquin. Kayda recognized her brother's arrogant, self-absorbed tone, though she couldn't make out all the words. She listened carefully but only picked out perhaps two words out of every ten Tarquin uttered.

"Old man... mages... port... regret..." It made no sense to her but raised her hackles nonetheless. What was he doing up this early?

A voice answered him, so quietly, or from such a distance, she couldn't make out a single word, only an incomprehensible whisper. The tone differed from Tarquin's, but in such a register, she couldn't be certain whether the speaker was a man or woman.

Who could he be meeting at this hour? She had half a mind to sneak outside and peek at the pair through the greenhouse windows, but the conversation ended. Silence returned to the keep, broken by the sound of a door opening and closing in the distance a moment later.

Sighing deeply, she removed her ear from the wall and tried to push the mystery aside. She could not forget her purpose. She had to find Izora.

As she approached the door to the northwest wing, she tried to remain calm. It was not like Izora to forget to tend to her. She was always there, the most constant presence in her life. Izora had even been known to drag herself out of bed while suffering from colds and injuries to check on her young charge. Kayda couldn't help but worry something was very wrong with her nurse.

The door slammed behind her, and Kayda grimaced. Well, if Izora overslept today, she was probably awake after that. But at least she'd made it to the staff rooms. Within a few steps, she was at Izora's door and knocking gently upon it.

"Come in," came Izora's voice from within.

Breathing a sigh of relief, Kayda set a stern look on her face, opened the door, and stepped inside. Upon seeing her nurse sitting on her single bed in her small, neat room, the stern look dropped from her face as if it had never been there.

Izora sat there in her flint-gray dress, clutching a letter, looking lost and miserable. "Oh, Kayda. I thought you were someone else. What are you doing here?" Izora straightened her shoulders, pasting a smile on her face.

"When you didn't come for our lessons, I worried something had happened... Has something happened? Are you all right?" Kayda eyed the letter warily, her brow furrowing.

"Yes, dear, I'm well. Just a bit of bad news from an old friend. Nothing you need concern yourself with."

Izora rose from the bed and strode toward Kayda. She rubbed her shoulder and glanced at her with a sad half smile. "Thank you for worrying about me, Princess, but as you can see, I'm quite all right. I'm afraid we'll have to skip our lessons today." She maneuvered them both so Kayda was poised to leave the small room. "Why don't you take the day off, do something fun? Read a book. Take a walk. We'll get back to it bright and early tomorrow."

Kayda withdrew, feeling even more confused than before. What was in that letter? Who was it from? If she knew anything about her nurse, she would let her know when she saw fit and not a moment sooner. Her shoulders sank as she made her way back through the staff corridor and through the door to the great hall.

"Got ya!" a familiar voice accosted her.

Kayda nearly jumped out of her skin.

"What a surprise to find you here, sister," Tarquin said, seeming not to care that his words echoed off the vast room's walls in the early morning stillness. He was dressed in a flashy blue silk tunic and spotless tan trousers today, topped with his haughtiest glare. "It's not enough for you to spy on my hunt with Grandfather, you have to spy on my trysts, too?"

"I wasn't spying on you." Kayda's cheeks burned, and she shot him a sour glare.

"That's a load of horseshit." His jaw jutted out at an angle as he leaned in, pointing at the door she'd just exited. "I heard you slamming doors in the servant's corridor while I was engaged with my paramour in the greenhouse." He smirked. "I mean, it really isn't seemly to lust after your own brother. Perhaps we should find you a husband quickly, before you do something rash."

Kayda saw red. Of all the disgusting, egotistical things he could have said, that was the foulest.

"I was checking on Izora. If you must know, she's not feeling well. The world doesn't revolve around you." She stepped around him, heading for her quarters. "And I couldn't care less what you do, or who you do it with."

The fact that he stuck around to confront her—would've likely confronted anyone who came out of that corridor next—made Kayda even more suspicious. He shouted so loudly about his supposed paramour she suspected the whispering party with him in that room was anything but. What was he hiding? She *knew* he was up to something.

He caught her arm before she could get far and spun her to face him. "Don't leave like that, sister. You know I didn't mean to offend. We'll go our separate ways as friends, no—as loving family—ought to." He smiled, flashing that fake vacuous grin he wore so often.

Raising an eyebrow, she pulled her arm free from his grasp. "Sure, let's." She turned and exited the great hall.

What was that? Tarquin being Tarquin, or an attempt to displace her suspicion?

She returned to her quarters and sank down onto the oversized chaise that took up most of her cramped sitting room.

Try as she might, she couldn't set the incident out of her mind. Those few scattered words replayed in her ears. She couldn't help wondering if this secret meeting had some connection to the trade deal Tarquin had discussed with her grandfather. The four words she overheard certainly seemed to suggest a connection.

Tarquin had no love for the mages. It likely stemmed from the seers' announcement the family talent had skipped him. But he was always eager to be useful despite his lack of bonding talent. He trained with the castle guard habitually and jumped at every opportunity to be seen at public events with the king.

Could he still be planning to move forward with his plans to build a port on the land the mages protected? Behind her grandfather's back, no less?

Oh, it was no use. She could sit around guessing his motives all day, but without knowing more of what was said in that room, she couldn't be sure. All she had was a feeling. An aching wrongness she felt to her core.

It was time to pay her grandfather a visit. She would share what she learned with the king. Perhaps he knew something that could help set her mind at ease. At the very least, she would gain some company and a fresh perspective.

It was not far from her suite of rooms to the king's. She knocked, bouncing on her toes as she waited for an answer.

Quinton's personal servant, Evander, slid open the door, but only halfway. His bushy white eyebrows knitted together as he stared down at her. She was tall for a girl of fifteen, but Evander always made her feel like a child.

He swiveled his neck in both directions, checking that she was alone, no doubt. "I'm afraid the king is feeling poorly today. Can you come back later?"

"Who is it, Evander?" the king's voice called from within.

Evander frowned, turning to speak over his shoulder. "It's your granddaughter, Your Majesty. She can come this afternoon, when you're feeling more yourself."

"Nonsense, man. Send her in. If anyone should see me like this, it ought to be her."

Evander frowned again, the lines on his forehead so deep they could swallow a coin. He obeyed, opening the door wide and stepping aside.

Kayda entered, swallowing reflexively and stopping just inside the doorway.

Evander pulled the door closed without a sound and disappeared into the king's dressing chamber.

These rooms were the best in the keep. No expense had been spared to make King Quinton comfortable. The large sitting room was upholstered in the finest Jorian silk. Knick knacks and curiosities from all over the world were displayed on shelves decorating the walls.

Normally, she loved to spend time here and came whenever offered an invitation. But something was off this morning that had Kayda's palms sweating.

The room was a wreck. Clothes were strewn everywhere. All the carefully collected artwork and collectibles lay scattered or broken. Some had obviously been thrown into the walls and even the fireplace, if the multicolored ash and broken shards of pottery inside were any indication.

In the middle of all this disarray, wearing only a crimson robe and his underclothes, was her grandfather, sprawled unceremoniously on a large settee, holding his head in his hands.

He glanced up as she drew closer, a lopsided smile spread across his face. "Sorry for the mess. It just gets a little too... crowded in here sometimes." He shoved some clothes and the battered remains of a map off the sage-green settee cushions and then gestured for her to join him.

She approached warily and perched on the cushion's edge. She'd heard the rumors—the same rumors everyone had. Until today, she hadn't truly believed them. In spite of all his quirks, her grandfather had always been good to her. Good to everyone, all throughout the entire kingdom.

It couldn't be true... that his use of bonding magic had driven him mad. She gulped, taking another long look at the mess scattered around her. It was the same magic she was expected to inherit.

"Have I told you about the time I flew?" Quinton blurted out, a wild grin flashing across his face. "Oh, it was amazing. Right over the Riddle River. Ha!"

Kayda quirked a brow, clenching her dress in her hands.

The King didn't seem to notice her discomfort. He rambled on, a faraway look in his eye. "It was all good fun until the damn harbormaster caught me. Blazing big-mouth, had to go tattle to my father."

"The harbormaster caught you flying..." Kayda said, the word trailing off into silence.

"Quiet!" King Quinton exclaimed out of nowhere. He closed his eyes and applied pressure to his temple with his fist.

"Maybe I should come back later," she said after a moment, moving to stand.

"No." His arm shot out sideways, blocking her from standing. His abrupt tone set her heart jolting.

"I've kept you sheltered from my condition your whole life, but you should see." Quinton opened his eyes. They were strangely murky and stared at some point above her shoulder. "You should look and see what your future might hold." His voice cracked on the final word, and his eyes met hers.

His arm fell, coming to rest between them. Some of the cloudiness in his eyes retreated. "I'm sorry. What was I saying?"

Kayda shook her head and forced a smile. "Nothing important, Grandfather." She patted his hand gently, deciding not to burden him with her suspicions. "I just came to invite you to breakfast, that's all."

He stared at the wall again, his voice distracted. "No, not today, dear. I've some... things that require my attention, I'm afraid."

"I understand. I'll leave you to it then." She squeezed his hand, then stood.

"Little red, fetch Evander for me before you leave, please."

She nodded once, then picked her way across the mess to the dressing room. Same as the sitting room, it appeared as if it'd been caught in the midst of a storm. She found Evander standing tall in his servant's uniform, setting things to rights.

He continued his work, smoothing the wrinkles from one of the king's tunics. "He gets this way, sometimes. Ever since his second bondmate passed." He stared at her directly, compassion filling his eyes. "You'll do well to learn from this, Princess. The king is not wrong in that." He placed a wrinkled hand on her arm. "Don't bond more than once, if you can help it."

Evander's brows knitted together, his words earnest. "Their voices will never leave you. Can you imagine having your dearest friends living only inside your own mind? Being the only one who can hear them? The constant reminder of them—you never get the chance to heal your grief. It must be maddening." His hand dropped from her arm, falling to his side.

A shiver raced down her spine. Her only thought was to escape. "I... have to go now," she replied lamely. "He's asked for you." She turned on her heel, left the king's rooms, and leaned against the door, shaking in the hall.

Was that what her future would be like? Locked away in her rooms, tortured by voices in her mind?

A portrait of King Quinton hung across the hall. He smiled at her, young and carefree. His arms draped around his beautiful queen and his beloved brother, both now deceased. All three of them looked so merry. The man in that wreck of a room was a shadow of his former self. So afraid of what might happen were he to bond with another that he hadn't set foot in a stable in over a decade.

She'd spent most of her life eagerly waiting to discover her bonding talent. It was what made her family special. The royal trait might skip a generation but always bestowed someone in the royal family the gift to speak to an animal companion.

For her grandfather, it was horses. He told her stories about his love for the beasts. Even as a boy, he'd been drawn to them.

Before, when he would tell those stories, she ached inside, like something was missing. Despite being introduced to all manner of creatures during the course of her life, she'd never experienced the instant connection he described.

She had longed for it so badly. For the first time in her life, she felt grateful instead.

Before long, she calmed enough to head back to her rooms. Her thoughts returned to Tarquin and his suspicious meeting. She began second guessing her decision to not tell her grandfather, but seeing him like that... it would've been selfish to add more worry to his day.

She paused outside her father's rooms. Maybe he could help? She wouldn't know if she didn't try. She planted her feet in front of the door and knocked.

"Bloody blazes," a slurred voice shouted from within. The next instant a crash sounded as something thudded into the door, vibrating the wood. "Leave me alone."

She let out a heavy sigh and escaped down the hall. She couldn't say she was surprised. It was a sad fact that all he cared about was having enough to drink.

Perhaps Izora? No. She was clearly dealing with some disaster of her own, if that letter was any indication.

Kayda would have to shoulder this burden alone, but that didn't mean she was giving up. She would learn the meaning of those scattered words, one way or another.

Chapter 9

The days melded together for Lark. They traveled by day, with Lark and Tiora crushed together, sweltering under the tarp in the heat. Every night they stopped to rest and parked the wagon somewhere off the road in the forest. Rasmus would sneak off to the nearest tavern or drown himself with the bottles of liquor he stashed in the front of the wagon. And every night, without fail, Pax took Tiora. Lark sat there shivering and seething, locked in the back of the wagon, night after night, wishing she were anywhere but there.

After the first night, Rasmus removed their bonds and gags, but not without threatening to replace them should either of them try to escape. Though Lark spent many hours scheming about how to do just that, an opportunity had yet to present itself where she could put the idea into action.

At least without the gag, she could talk to Tiora. It took Lark a few tense days to convince the older girl to open up, but eventually, they started sharing stories with one another. They whiled away the dull days of travel with conversation that began with unemotional descriptions of their respective homelands, but quickly became more personal, until Lark felt a closeness to Tiora she'd previously only shared with her mother and brother.

One afternoon, Lark fanned herself in the back of the wagon while the sun beat down unmercifully on the tarp above them. "Tell me again about Joria."

Sunshine slipped through cracks in the wooden slats, brightening the wagon just enough for Lark to note Tiora's wistful smile. "We lived south of Joria on the eastern banks of the Peat River. It was hot, just like this, all year round."

Lark groaned. "I don't think I could stand it."

Tiora giggled. "Well, it wasn't all bad. We spent the hottest part of the day resting in the shade. Or better yet, swimming in the river."

"Swimming would be amazing right now." She pictured the cool river water rushing over her skin, sighing. "It sounds so nice. Why did you leave?"

"My mother—she got sick. She was a dyer, contracted with traders in the city. When she couldn't meet her quota... someone had to do something."

"I don't understand. What about your father?"

Tiora scowled. "He was long gone. Only stuck around long enough to give my mother me and my sisters. Then he disappeared to parts unknown."

"So, it was up to you to take care of your family."

"Exactly. I would do anything for my mother and sisters. There was only one way I could get the money we needed. I made sure it was more than enough to pay for a healer for my mother." Tiora's fingers tangled in the hem of her brown dress. "I walked to the city and sold myself to a Jorian slaver." She grimaced, her eyes downcast. "You must think I'm so stupid."

"No, no." She grabbed Tiora's hand, her heart breaking for her. "I understand. My mother got sick, too." Lark's voice was thick with pain. "I would've done anything to save her. It's one of the biggest regrets of my life that I couldn't." Tears welled in her eyes.

Tiora squeezed her hand. "I'm so sorry, Lark."

"I miss her like crazy." She sniffled. "I couldn't save her."

"You can't blame yourself. People get sick every day. Even if you were trained as a healer, it's not your fault."

Lark scrubbed her cheeks, fighting for composure. Tiora was sweet to say that, but deep down, she knew it was her fault. Nothing was going to change that.

"It must have been exciting to be a healer. Did you ever birth babies?" Tiora asked.

Lark smiled. Those, at least, were happy memories. "Yes. Many times."

"Wow, what was that like?"

"Incredible. There's nothing like seeing a mother hold her child for the first time." Her smile fell, brows knitting together. "It could be awful sometimes, too. When the babies or mother didn't make it."

"That must be hard to watch."

"You can't even imagine." She let go of Tiora's hand and hugged her knees to her chest. "Once there was a baby. A boy. My mother handed him to me after his mother birthed him while she tended to the mother. It'd been a long, hard delivery, and the baby, he wasn't crying."

"Oh, no." Tiora frowned, listening raptly.

"I tried everything. Slapped his bum, rubbed his back, cleared his mouth and nose. Nothing worked."

Tiora's hand rose to cover her lips, eyes wide. "Was he dead?"

"My mother thought so. But I wasn't ready to let him go. I grabbed some of my mother's salve and started rubbing it on his chest." She shook her head slightly. "I'm not even sure why I thought it would work. It's supposed to treat skin irritation. But I rubbed and rubbed and rubbed some more."

"And it worked?"

She laughed. "No... But then I placed my hand on that little babe's chest." Lark closed her eyes, recalling the moment so clearly it was almost as if she was back there with the babe nestled in her arms. "I closed my eyes and wished. I wished with everything I had in me he would just breathe." She opened her eyes, smiling slowly.

"And did he?"

"I felt something then. A tingling vibration, like the ground was quaking beneath me and shaking my whole body. Some power moved through my hand into the boy's chest. Then he let out the biggest, most beautiful cry."

"It was a miracle." Tiora smiled, eyes bright.

"No—it was magic."

Tiora's smiled dropped.

"My mother told me that day, my grandmother, she'd been talented, too. That salve had a few ingredients, all of them from the earth."

Tiora's mouth fell open. "You're an earth mage? Why didn't you tell me before?" She punctuated the question with a punch to Lark's knee.

"Hey, no need to get violent." Lark rubbed her knee. "And I'm not a mage. At least, not yet."

Tiora's eyes darted back and forth. Lark could practically see the wheels spinning in her mind.

"But you summoned. If you summoned once, you could do it again." Tiora grabbed her hand, squeezing tightly, those golden-brown eyes staring into her own with such intensity. "You can do it, Lark. You can free us."

Lark looked down, breaking eye contact. "I can't... I've only been able to summon that once. I don't know how it happened in the first place, or how to do it again."

The wagon stopped. Tiora dropped Lark's hand and shuddered.

Lark tensed, waiting for the rocking of the wagon and the thudding of the men's footsteps. She'd been so caught up in their conversation that she hadn't noticed the light in the wagon slowly diminishing.

The tarp lifted a few moments later. Fresh air rushed in to greet her. She sighed as a breeze swept through, cooling off her sweat-soaked skin. She caught sight of Pax watching her, that scarred eye winking at her lasciviously, and she snapped her mouth shut, wrapping her arms around her chest.

The villain laughed, reached behind his back, and tossed something at Tiora. She flinched but caught the waterskin, then opened it and hastily drained a portion before passing it to Lark. She drank, too, the lukewarm water a blessing after the afternoon spent sweltering under the tarp.

Rasmus appeared, retrieving the key he wore dangling from a length of cord wrapped around his neck. He opened the backboard and motioned for Lark to hop down. "I'll take this one first. Get a fire started," he said to Pax.

Lark jumped down, her muscles protesting from so many hours spent cramped in the back of the wagon. She took a moment to stretch and heard Pax call out to Tiora behind her, "Make yourself useful and gather some sticks, whore."

Fire spread through her veins, but she said nothing and followed Rasmus across the clearing.

She searched for a sign of anything to tell their location, but it was no use. They were in a clearing, much the same as any other she'd ever been in. Trees loomed on all sides, and there was no sign of a road, stream, or anything else she recognized. The sweet melody of a sparrow broke the forest's stillness. From a distance, she could hear running water, though she couldn't see its source.

Rasmus stopped behind a star oak tree, trampling a patch of dandelions. "Be quick about it." He shuffled a few steps to the left but kept his stare trained on her, his face impassive.

Though he watched with little interest, Lark's cheeks burned all the same as she crouched behind the tree and relieved her aching bladder.

They returned to the clearing. Lark was made to collect sticks while Tiora took her turn with Rasmus. The hair on her spine raised as Pax watched Lark's every move. His eyes on her felt much different from Rasmus', and she was thankful to see the pair return, so she no longer had to be alone with the hulking man.

Soon, the fire roared, and the scent of meat roasting made her stomach rumble. Rasmus made them sit back in the wagon but left the tarp pulled back and the backboard down, which was a luxury after so long spent crouched beneath it. He handed each of them a stick with a piece of meat dangling off it; the aroma made her salivate. She'd just begun to tuck in when a voice called out beyond the clearing.

"Hello, my friends."

Lark jolted, almost dropping her dinner, as she searched the forest for the voice's source.

A man stepped out of the trees to their left, beaming and waving both hands. He was middle-aged, with dark brown skin and long, dark brown hair plaited in a multitude of small, neat braids that were decorated with beads in every color of the rainbow. His tunic was multicolored, too; the bright silk covered his lanky frame and glittered in the firelight.

"I saw your fire from the road and smelled the delicious aroma of roasting meat. Would you care for some company tonight at your campsite? My group of travelers and I are stopping for the night. We'd love to trade some entertainment for a full belly and the pleasure of meeting some new friends." He spoke with his hands and projected his voice in a strong, pleasant tone that marked him as a natural showman.

Excitement stirred in her breast as the man bowed with a flourish.

"I am Dausius of the Wandering Bards. It's a pleasure to make the acquaintance of such fine folk as yourselves."

Rasmus and Pax watched the man curiously, both with a hand on their sword hilts. They exchanged a look, then Rasmus spoke. "I think a bit of entertainment would be a welcome diversion. I'm Rasmus, and this is Pax." He nodded in his direction. "You can go fetch the rest of your group and share our fire tonight."

Dausius' smile never wavered as his gaze slid over Lark and Tiora, seeming to note the fact they'd not been introduced but not pressing the matter. He bowed again and disappeared back into the forest, presumably to go fetch the rest of his group.

A traveling show! Lark's pulse quickened. Maybe she could use this turn of events to her advantage. Visions of her and Tiora escaping while the slavers were distracted played in her mind. She did her best to hide her excitement, chewing her meat silently while she waited for the return of Dausius and his group.

They didn't have to wait long. Dausius returned moments later, leading a white and brown spotted horse and wagon.

The wagon was similar in size to the one they sat in, but his brought a smile to her face. Bright paint and intricate patterns decorated the sides in all the colors of the rainbow. The bed was uncovered, and perched in the center, among a number of trunks and boxes, sat a large hawk upon a wooden tree branch.

Lark's breath caught as she stared at the majestic creature. She'd never seen a bird of prey from such a close distance before. Its strength and power, even at rest, was a magnificent thing to behold.

Three people trailed the wagon. Each of them dressed identically to Dausius—minus the beaded hair. The rainbow silk threads of their multicolored tunics gleamed in the evening light.

The first two, a short-haired boy and girl with a single, long braid, appeared so similar she was sure they were related. The pair appeared to be in their late teens, with olive skin, brown hair, and brown eyes.

A young man, wearing a large, brimmed hat that obscured much of his face, lagged a few paces behind. He was much paler than the rest but taller and more muscular, too. He wore a thick leather glove on his right hand and had a finely made lute strapped to his back.

Dausius stopped and parked the horse and wagon in the clearing. Then he raised his voice and swiveled toward the men seated at the fire. "Please, allow me to introduce my companions and fellow performers." He spread his arms wide, smiling broadly, adopting a theatrical voice. "Hailing from the exotic jungles of Raimire, I present to you, Mazen and Meital."

The brown-haired pair stepped forward, both offering a shallow bow and a mischievous grin.

Dausius continued, "They learned their deadly knife skills fighting for their lives against jungle cats and venomous snakes, but the only danger these twins face now are each other."

They reached behind their backs in unison, each of them revealing a set of four small daggers that glittered dangerously in the setting sun's light. Without a word, they casually juggled them, tossing them in ever-widening circles and flawlessly swapping them.

Lark gasped with delight. Glancing sideways, she saw Tiora's gaze dancing as she traced the blades' flight through the clearing.

The pair ended the display by throwing each knife into the grass, all eight lined up neatly in a row.

Lark and Tiora clapped, earning a wink from Mazen. Tiora giggled until Pax glared in their direction, cutting her laughter short.

Dausius broke the tension, stepping forward with an exaggerated bow. "Thank you, thank you., You are too kind. Please, save some applause for the last members of our group."

The tall man stepped forward, lifting his gloved arm and whistling. The hawk flew to him and landed on his outstretched arm.

"Behold, the beautiful and fierce hawk Whisper and his handler, Aren," Dausius said.

Aren reached into a pouch on his belt with his free hand. Whisper's eyes locked onto the movement, and he looked like a coiled spring, ready to fly at any moment. Aren tossed some small morsel into the air. Whisper flew at lightning speed, snatching it mid-flight in his beak, and then landing back on his wagon perch.

Lark and Tiora clapped once more, as Dausius spoke again. "Thank you, Aren and Whisper. Please take a bow."

The hawk tilted its head forward repeatedly, and Tiora laughed again, but Lark's attention was caught entirely by Aren.

Before bowing, he removed his hat, revealing a face that rivaled Tiora's for its beauty. He had light blond hair cut short and ice-blue eyes that sent a shiver down her spine when they locked on her own. Her hands stilled their clapping as she returned his stare, and she found herself leaning forward without consciously deciding to.

He looked away first, straightening from his bow and replacing his hat.

Lark blinked, shaking off her strange reaction.

"Bravo." Rasmus clutched one of his bottles in his fist and took a long swallow. "Come, join us 'round the fire and have a bite to eat."

"You're most kind, good sir." Dausius swaggered in the fire's direction, the beads in his hair clacking as he signaled his performers to follow. Meital and Aren headed over directly, but Mazen detoured in their direction, a playful smile on his face.

Lark's brow wrinkled when she realized his intentions.

Tiora was still admiring Whisper and didn't notice the boy's gaze zero in on her as he approached.

"Will you lovely ladies be joining us?" Mazen asked, glancing at her and returning his gaze to Tiora.

Tiora jolted at his voice, her mouth dropping open as she met his stare.

Dausius spun to view the scene and shot daggers with his eyes at Mazen.

"No, they will not," Pax announced, his voice hard and cold. He stood with his fists pressed on his hips, a feral grin flashing across his face.

Tiora's shoulders slumped, and an echoing disappointment spread inside Lark's chest.

"Toss me the key, Ras." Pax thrust out a hand.

Rasmus shrugged and pitched the keys at him.

Pax caught them and strode to the wagon, shooting a glare at Mazen, who retreated with his hands in the air, a pleasant expression plastered to his face.

"It's bedtime for the lovely ladies." Pax stalked closer, grinning maliciously.

Tiora's eyes shone with unshed tears. She made herself small on the wagon floor, preparing for the tarp and backboard to lock them in.

Lark let out a heavy sigh, took a final look at the traveling show, and did the same.

It wasn't long before Pax shrouded the wagon in darkness. The setting sun and shadowy tree cover permitted little light to shine through the cracks of the wooden slats.

Lark fumed, clenching her fists together so hard her nails dug into her palms. Her hopes to sneak away during the performances were dashed, and as she noted the sounds outside, she realized Pax was preparing to hitch the horse back up to the wagon. The bastard wasn't even going to allow them the simple pleasure of listening to the performers.

The wagon jerked forward. Quiet sniffling broke the silence inside the wagon bed.

Tiora never cried. Not even after that monster returned her to the wagon each morning. It looked like missing out on the show was the final straw for her. Lark wrapped an arm around her, pulling her close. Tiora's tears wet the linen of her tunic as she shuddered.

The wagon stopped, and Pax jumped down, slapping a hand on the side. "Pleasant dreams, ladies." His laughter faded as he strolled back to the fire.

Lark held Tiora while she cried and silently prayed for that to be the final time they saw Pax that evening. She fell asleep with the sound of a lute whispering in her ears.

She startled awake at the sound of the backboard opening. It was Pax, coming for Tiora. Lark's arms were still wrapped around her friend, and seeing that vile man's profile lit in the moonlight, she clutched her closer, even as her friend moved to go with him.

"No," she whispered.

Then Tiora's hands closed on her own, prying her fingers free of her arms. "It's all right, Lark. I can do this."

Lark shook her head, tears filling her eyes, but she released Tiora and let her climb down from the wagon. She covered her ears when the sounds began but couldn't block them out entirely. The familiar grunts and groans seemed more forceful tonight and were joined by a new, more frightening sound. Cries of pain.

Anger burned in her chest, and shame. How could she sit here night after night listening? It was killing her to do nothing, but she had to be smart and bide her time. She rubbed her wrists, remembering the rope biting into her skin. All hope would be lost if she got herself wrapped in bondage again.

Pax returned Tiora to the wagon as the first rays of dawn brightened the sky. Lark scooted back, her stomach clenching.

Tiora's cheek was swollen, and from the way she winced as she sat on the hard wooden slats, she suspected that wasn't the only injury she'd sustained that night. Despite the pleading look Tiora sent her, Lark couldn't help glaring at Pax as he slammed the backboard shut with a laugh, obviously not caring about the damage he inflicted on her friend.

"Tiora, what did he do to you?" Lark whispered. The sound of Pax's footsteps trailed off into the distance. "I'll kill him, that bastard!"

Tiora reached out her hand, managing a sly smile despite her swelling face. "I hope so." She deposited a fistful of fresh soil on her palm.

The cool dirt slid across Lark's fingers, its earthy scent filling her nostrils. She nodded. "I'll try." She owed it to Tiora, to herself, to do something. She stuffed the dirt in her pocket to wait for her chance.

Tiora winced again, and a pang of sympathy struck Lark. "Can I do anything? Do you want me to check your injuries?" she asked, wishing she had her mother's book and the right herbs so she could tend to her properly.

"No, I'll be all right." She sighed deeply. "I just wish we could've watched the show last night. It's been so long since I've heard any music."

Lark's face lit up. "Well, we'll fix that." She closed her eyes briefly, and when she opened them, she began to sing. It was a cheerful song, one her mother had sung to her as a child.

Tiora listened with her eyes closed and a small smile on her face. When the song was over, she lifted her sleepy lids and whispered, "That was beautiful. Your mother named you well." She closed her eyes again before she noted the blush warming Lark's face.

It wasn't long before the sounds of the camp rising and the performers making ready to leave echoed throughout the clearing. By the time Rasmus came around to give them each a chance to empty their bladders, the other wagon was gone.

Lark's stomach quivered as their own wagon rolled along the bumpy forest trail. Pax had stayed too far away for her to try anything with the dirt that morning. They had another long, sweaty day of travel to finish before she would have another opportunity.

Tiora spent the day resting, and Lark refused to wake her after the night she'd been forced to endure. She rested, too, or tried at least, but often her mind wouldn't allow it, replaying all she'd overheard that night, keeping her anger smoldering.

Finally, the wagon stopped for the night.

"Pax, I'm going to ride into that town we passed a few miles back. You can handle feeding the girls tonight on your own." Rasmus jumped down from the front wagon seat.

"Whatever you say, boss," Pax replied.

The horse whinnied, and soon the sound of galloping echoed in her ears. It quickly faded away.

Lark wet her lips, rubbing her sweaty hands against her skirt. She'd expected to feel fear in this moment; instead, giddy anticipation tingled up her spine as the backboard swung open and Pax sneered in at them.

"Please, take me, I have to go now," Lark blurted out before he said anything, making a show of pressing her thighs closed and bouncing her knees up and down.

She expected him to say something cruel, even make her wait just because he could, but he surprised her.

"Fine." He moved aside so she could hop down. "Then back in with you, and me and the whore will have some fun," he added, leering at Tiora as he shut the backboard again, leaving them alone in a clearing practically identical to the last.

Lark dug in her pocket while his back was turned, scooping the pile of loose soil into her palm. This was it. She was going to kill him.

As soon as he whirled around, she pretended to trip, catching herself with her palms on his chest. She started to wish, like she had with the babe, but before she had the chance to set the thought in her mind, Pax shoved her away. The handful of soil sprinkled down his shirt and landed on the grass at his feet, and Lark's heart dropped to her stomach.

"Watch it, you clumsy bitch," he spat, not noticing the dirt dusting his clothing.

Lark cursed inwardly, her mind spinning as she tried to think of some excuse to place her hand on his chest. She grimaced, realizing what she would have to do and prayed there was more dirt in her pocket.

As he led the way behind a nearby tree, she searched her skirt pocket as circumspectly as she could. At first her fingers only brushed cloth, and her heart thundered madly. Then she dug further and found something flat and crinkly, crushed in the far corner. The flower! She said a silent thank you to the old woman who'd gifted it to her on their trip out of Southmoat so many days ago. Tucking the dried flower into the center of her palm, she put her plan into action.

"I was lying, just now." She slowed, eyes half lidded and a sly smile on her lips. "The truth is, I've been feeling a little left out."

Pax stared at her, raising a brow, that scarred eyelid looking even more grotesque with the action.

Lark swallowed her disgust and closed the distance between them. "It's not fair I have to stay locked away in that wagon while the whore gets to have all the fun." She followed the statement with a pout and pressed her chest forward, drawing his gaze downward.

This had to work. She held her breath, hoping it had been enough to bait him.

Time stretched out, neither of them moving. His eyes searched hers, then zeroed in on her upturned lips. Had he seen through her seduction? Sweat beaded on her forehead. She was sure he was a heartbeat away from laughing in her face and pushing her to the ground. But then he struck.

Shooting out a hand, he gripped the brown curls at the nape of her neck and jerked her head back. His mouth landed on hers, hot and oppressive, and she shuddered as his tongue invaded her mouth. Her body screamed at her to spit out the vile thing, to pull away. Instead, she pressed closer and wedged the flower between them, flattening it directly over his heart.

She remembered the sounds. The awful, disgusting sounds clogging her ears every night. The bruises that evil monster left on her friend. She closed her eyes and wished. She wished with every fiber of her body for his heart to stop beating.

She felt it then. Her whole body thrummed with energy, the same as before. The vibration coalesced in her palm, her skin tingling. Then it jolted through her hand and entered his chest.

For one excruciating moment, panic filled her. It hadn't been enough. He was still at it, tongue still moving, choking the air from her mouth. His fist still clenched around her curls.

Then he pulled back and clutched his chest, eyes bulging. His vile tongue still dangled from his mouth, a string of spit hanging.

Lark backed up slowly, a smile spreading on her lips.

He saw her smile, and his eyes filled with fear and panic. He reached for the hilt of his sword, but it was too late. With a sickening *thump*, he collapsed, slumping face-first in the grass.

Lark stared at his back, covering her lips as she fought to overcome the intense disbelief raging inside her. Then she drew her sleeve across her lips, wiping off his foul taste. She crouched down, fished the cord and key out of his tunic, and hurried to free Tiora from the wagon.

Tiora gaped at her as she let down the backboard. She hopped down, heading straight for where Pax's booted feet sprawled on the ground still twitching, the front half of him hidden behind a large oak tree. Lark let her go and watched silently as Tiora screamed with rage, and the *thud* of her boots kicking that monster sounded over and over again.

Finally, Tiora stopped and rounded the tree, her brown dress covered with flecks of red. "You did it." Her face lit with joy. "Lark, you did it!" She ran to her, pulling her into an embrace and bursting into tears.

Lark's muscles relaxed, and she sagged against Tiora. They stood there, clutching each other and crying. Lark was so overwhelmed with relief, she didn't register the sound of a horse's footfalls approaching.

"Ho, Pax, just forgot my coinpur—" Rasmus' voice trailed off as he took stock of the scene.

The girls sprang apart, backing away slowly from the horse. Lark's heart hammered with the rat-a-tat-tat rhythm of a woodpecker.

No. No, no, no! He shouldn't be back. They were free.

There was no way she could repeat the same trick with Rasmus. He would tie them both up again, keep them trapped in the wagon, bound and gagged, until they reached Doln.

His brow furrowed as he spotted Pax's body lying still and half hidden behind the tree. He dropped the reins, gripping his sword hilt. His mouth opened, and Lark gulped, preparing herself for the order that would come next.

Instead, his body shook as a wet *thunk* interrupted the clearing's stillness. His eyes bulged, his mouth widened, and blood poured out. A scarlet flood coated his chest in an instant. He slumped forward, a blade lodged in the back of his neck.

Lark's mouth dropped open at the crunch of footsteps.

Meital stalked forward from the forest, shoved Rasmus' body from the horse, and retrieved her dagger. Then she whistled sharply, and Lark flinched, her wide eyes searching the forest as more footsteps sounded.

Dausius strode into the clearing, Mazen and Aren following closely. "I'm sorry, we've not been properly introduced, my ladies." He smiled. "Which one of you is the singer we heard early this morning?"

Lark stared, tongue tied, still trying to process the events of the last few moments.

Tiora spoke up. "I'm Tiora, and this is Lark. She's the one you heard singing."

Dausius' smile widened. Leaning toward them, he offered his hand. "Tiora, Lark, it's a pleasure to meet you. Have you ever considered joining a traveling show?"

Chapter 10

"*What do you think?*" It was early morning on the day they'd chosen to return to the farm. Conall stood staring at the sheer wall of rock and dirt he'd tumbled down so many days ago. "*If I can make it up there, it will cut out a full day of walking, maybe two.*"

"*What about your shoulder?*" Shadow sat beside him, his golden eyes shining like wheat caught in a sunbeam. "*You'll need two arms for that climb.*"

Conall shrugged his shoulders and winced at the answering twinge where the arrow had been wedged. He grimaced, taking a last look up at the wall, and spun to face south. Had he been in better shape, he could've made that climb, but Shadow was right. He couldn't chance it. Another fall could set him back weeks in recovery time if it didn't kill him outright.

"*All right then, we'll take the scenic route.*"

"*Wise choice, little brother.*" Shadow's tail wagged.

The day was bright and cool. The forest sang with activity from insects, birds, and all manner of creatures.

Conall inhaled deeply, gazing at the waterfall and cave that had been his home during his recovery. It was an adventure he wouldn't soon forget—living off the land with a wolf as his only companion—but he was ready to head back to civilization. It was time to say farewell to the forest and set things right at home.

They set out heading south. This part of the forest was new to Conall. He'd always stopped at the top of the ridge, never choosing to venture down the cliffside.

Shadow, at least, was at home in these woods. He trotted happily by Conall's side, leading the way whenever the trail split.

"How is it you know these woods so well, brother? Did you learn the paths by heart while you hunted for us?" Conall asked, watching as he expertly wove between trees and branches on the trail.

"No, I've been here many times." Shadow's tail stilled its wagging, and he slowed his pace. *"This land is part of my pack's territory."*

"Your pack... I thought you said you left your pack?" Perhaps now he might learn more about his bondmate. Shadow had been vague so far about his past.

"I did. And I found you, little brother." His tail wagged again, and his ears perked up as he stared off into the brush to their right.

Conall lifted a brow. *"I didn't realize you were so close to me all along."* It was strange to think they might have crossed paths before this.

"The pack's territory is very large. We weren't always so close. This is near the edge." Shadow stilled, his eyes and ears the only thing moving as he tracked something.

Conall stilled as well but saw nothing. *"Huh, I guess that's why we haven't seen any of your brothers and sisters so far."*

"They're not my brothers... not any longer." Shadow darted into the nearest bush, spooking a hare, and then tearing off into the distance, fast on its trail.

Conall sighed. Every time he brought up Shadow's pack, he found an excuse to dodge the subject. He had to find a way to let his friend know he could talk to him about anything. It was obvious there was something in his past he was reluctant to think about too closely.

Conall headed after Shadow, his steps lingering as he waited for his bondmate's return. He still had problems with his own family to consider. He clenched his fists, kicking the dirt trail.

There was the question of what to do about Gael. The part of him that still burned with anger wanted to creep into the barn at night, grab his second-best bow and quiver, sneak into the farmhouse, and shoot an arrow right through that murderer's heart while he slept. It would be a fitting end for a man who would shoot his own stepson and leave him for dead.

Conall sighed again. As much as he wanted revenge, he could never go through with that plan. The smarter play would be to head for town, tell the townsfolk and magistrate his tale—with the broken arrow and still healing wound for proof—and bring the town's wrath down on that villain.

Conall smiled. He wouldn't have the pleasure of pulling the trigger himself, but he would watch Gael hang. He would get the farm back the right way. It was his by rights, inherited from his father, and he had every right to march inside and tell him to leave...

But there was no way he was going to just let Gael leave. He wanted justice, and he would get it.

The one decision he was wrestling with was what to do about Lark. She was still there on the farm with Gael. Every moment she spent in his presence was another moment he might harm her.

He thought back to their argument in the forest. Gael acted so concerned for her, so eager to keep her from becoming a mage, but after what he'd done to him, Conall couldn't be sure he wouldn't do something just as thoughtless to Lark. What if she put her foot down and insisted on leaving? Would he shoot her, too?

His stomach churned. Could he head straight to town to tell his tale when he couldn't be sure what Gael was doing to Lark on the farm? He could go to her first, but then he might show his hand to Gael. If Gael realized he was still alive, he would have the chance to flee, escaping justice for attempted murder.

A movement in the brush ahead, and a flash of gray fur signaled Shadow's return. He trotted up beside him, the hare clutched in his jaws.

Conall grinned. *"I suppose now is as good a time as any to stop for breakfast."*

Shadow dropped the hare, sitting on his haunches and licking his chops.

As much as he wanted to race back to the farm, he couldn't push his body too hard. Though his ankle had healed, his shoulder still pained him. And though he didn't want to admit it, he still had a way to go before his energy was back where it'd been before the fall.

After breakfast, they walked again. Conall took breaks every so often, careful not to overtax his body, but they made good time through the forest despite the stops. Shadow was an expert guide, never taking them down a path that required much exertion. By the time they stopped for the night, they'd covered a fair distance and drew close to where they would turn toward the farm.

Conall constructed a simple shelter out of sticks and leaves and started a fire before night fell. He gazed at his bondmate, feeling immensely grateful for his presence. Without Shadow, the loneliness that washed over him while he sat in these woods, away from his family and friends, would be overwhelming.

Still, it was a beautiful night for camping, and despite the circumstances, he found himself smiling as the last rays of daylight faded in the sky. It felt good to be doing something. His journey home had begun, and he would soon set things right on the farm. His shoulder and feet ached, but his heart was at peace as he fell asleep that night, curled up next to his brother under the stars.

They woke the next morning to find a fog had rolled in while they slept. When they set out for the day, it had not yet dissipated entirely, forcing Conall to step carefully in the haze.

Shadow seemed on edge, ears and eyes constantly roaming, searching the forest. *"Brother, could you do me a favor? This fog has me all turned around. Do you think your shoulder can handle a climb today?"*

Conall lifted his shoulders a few times. His left was still sore, but if he kept most of his weight off it, he suspected he could manage a climb. *"What did you have in mind?"*

"That tree there." Shadow approached a large pine. *"It looks plenty tall. Can you get to the top and tell me if you see a stream off to the right? I don't want us headed in the wrong direction."*

Scrutinizing the tree, Conall nodded in agreement. *"Good eye. That looks like an easy climb."* The tree branches were spaced evenly and close to each other. *"Shouldn't take long at all."*

He made it about a quarter of the way up without having to put much weight on his left shoulder, then he paused for a breath and smiled. He glanced down, spotting Shadow pacing back and forth. *"Don't worry, my shoulder is holding up."*

He climbed up halfway and glimpsed water off in the distance to the right, where Shadow expected it to be. He shifted, preparing to climb down and tell his bondmate the good news, but he stopped in his tracks as the haze parted and revealed three large wolves stalking toward Shadow.

"Brother, watch out," he cried.

"I see them, little brother. Stay where you are." Shadow headed toward them, hackles raised, growling, and looking ready to fight.

What was he doing, going after them all on his own? There was no way Shadow could win this fight—three against one.

All three wolves were large, with gray hair and strong, lithe forms. As they caught sight of Shadow's aggression, they snarled and growled in kind, circling in on him as a team.

He had to get down there. He had to help his brother. But what could he do? His bow was lost, and his arrows lay broken and discarded beside the waterfall. The only weapon he had was the tiny crafting blade he used for his snares. That would be practically useless in a fight with wolves.

Conall's breath caught in his throat as he realized Shadow sent him up that tree to get him out of the way.

Down below, the biggest wolf stalked forward, his left ear missing a sizable chunk of skin and fur at the tip. He was ferocious. His jaws snapped, lips curled back, his stare locked onto Shadow's neck.

Shadow stood strong, looking fierce and fearless despite the odds stacked against him.

Conall's stomach dropped to his feet. The other two had disappeared, probably using the trees and fog to hide their movements, preparing to jump at Shadow from behind.

He had to do something. Tearing his gaze from the tense standoff below, Conall searched the forest in vain, desperate to find a weapon or some way of causing a distraction. The snarling intensified as he spotted a dead branch of a star oak, caught up in the pine above him.

That could work! He just had to reach it.

He climbed, then gritted his teeth as he stretched his left arm to its limits to grab it. He pulled. At first, the stubborn branch refused to move. Then he pulled harder, ignoring the shooting pain in his shoulder until it finally dislodged.

Yes! He stashed the branch in the crook of his arm, balancing carefully as he dug in his belt pouch and retrieved his tinder box.

He chanced a glance below and grimaced. The lead wolf dashed toward Shadow, his jaws snapping. Shadow deftly avoided him, spinning on his hind legs and closing his jaws on the attacker's haunches, drawing blood.

There was movement in the bushes behind Shadow. *"Look out behind you,"* he called, just as the second and third wolf sprang out of the fog-shrouded forest. Shadow let the leader go, barely managing to leap away before the other wolves pounced.

Conall gulped. His fingers felt fat and sluggish as he raced to light the dried leaves on fire.

This had to work, and fast. Shadow couldn't last down there much longer.

The three wolves backed up, snarling and snapping. They were poised to attack in tandem.

A chill swept over him as he fumbled with the flint, striking against the steel, praying a spark would catch. It had to.

An ember caught, bursting into flame faster than he thought possible. He gasped, holding the makeshift torch tightly and raced down the tree as fast as he could. He dropped to the ground, landing directly behind Shadow.

"Get out. Get away, you bastards," he screamed, his own voice gruff and foreign in his ears after so many days of silent communication.

The wolves jerked back and stared at the fire.

Conall strode in front of Shadow swiping the stick in an arc. "Get out of here, you filthy mutts!"

Conall's heart pounded wildly. He was certain the wolves would attack at any instant, but his fears were negated a moment later when two of the wolves took off, tearing through the woods in the direction they'd come. The wolf with the torn ear sent a final snarl in Shadow's direction before he joined his companions, fleeing the flames.

Conall stumbled back a step, his legs wobbly. He turned to Shadow, lowering the flaming branch but keeping hold of it, in case the wolves still watched from the trees. *"Are you okay?"* He searched his bond-mate, not picking out any obvious injuries.

Shadow stood at attention, staring off into the forest where the wolves disappeared. *"I'm fine, thanks to you, little brother."* His shoulders relaxed, and he circled the area, peering closely into the forest. *"I do not think they will return, but let's be on our way just to be safe."*

"Who were those wolves?" Conall dropped his torch and stomped out the remaining flames before they began picking their way through the forest. *"I thought you said this was your pack's territory?"*

"That was my pack." Shadow's head dropped. *"Or what's left of it. I told you when we first met, we're the same."* His head lifted, those golden eyes staring at him. *"My father died. The new alpha didn't want me around anymore. Leave or die. Those were his orders."*

Conall's heart twisted. No wonder they were bonded. Both of them had been betrayed. *"The one with the torn ear... was that him?"*

"Yes." The fur on his back quivered as he snorted. *"You're not the only one who has someone out to kill him. I'm glad you were there with me, Conall."*

He smiled, tussling the fur on Shadow's head. *"Always, brother."*

"Can I ask you something?" Shadow tilted sideways, leaning into Conall's hand as he scratched him behind the ear. *"What did you say when you were swinging around that branch?"*

"What do you mean?" Conall stopped scratching, glancing at his friend curiously. *"You didn't understand me?"*

"No. Did you understand what I said to the alpha?"

"That was talking? I just heard you two growling and snapping at each other." Conall rubbed his shoulder, massaging the ache that reignited during his climb. For some reason, he'd assumed they would understand each other when they spoke, but it was good to know their communication's limits. *"I called them filthy mutts."*

Shadow snorted again and wagged his tail. Conall grinned, sensing his friend's amusement.

Then Shadow stopped, body tense and nose raised, scenting the air. Conall tensed as well, stopping next to him. They'd turned toward the farm, and the woods had finally begun to look familiar. He noticed nothing out of sorts.

"What is it? Why have you stopped?"

"Smoke... I smell smoke. A lot of it. Something ahead is burning." Shadow's gaze darted all over as he sniffed. *"Something big."*

The farm—Lark. Even though he couldn't see the flames, something inside of him knew. It was his home burning. He gazed at his brother, eyes speaking volumes, and without either of them saying or thinking a single word, they took off running.

Chapter 11

"Are you sure about this?" Dausius asked. His hands were still for once, resting on his hips as his brown eyes searched her face.

Lark pressed her lips together and nodded. "I'm sure. This is the perfect time. With everyone in Greenvale watching the show, I'll have no trouble getting in and out without being noticed."

Her nerves thrummed with anticipation. They stood in the forest outside the town's limits. She'd waited days for the show to reach her hometown. And as luck would have it, they arrived at the perfect time.

Everyone had already gathered in town to head for Flamesmoat in the morning for the annual Harvest Festival. Gael never missed it, so she could be sure to have the privacy she needed to retrieve her belongings. She was ready to go back to the farm. She had to know for sure if what Brenna had said in that awful dock warehouse was true.

Dausius pursed his lips and crossed his arms. "I just wish you weren't going alone."

Footsteps crunched behind her. "She won't be." Tiora strode out from behind a tree, wearing a multicolored tunic and trousers borrowed from Meital, a knapsack strung on her back. "I'm going with her."

Lark smiled and linked her hand with Tiora's. "Don't worry, Daus. We'll be in and out, I promise. Then we'll meet back here after."

Dausius shrugged his shoulders dramatically, letting out a loud sigh. Then his long arms pulled both of them into a tight hug. Tiora stiffened beside Lark, but after a moment she relaxed and wrapped her arm around Dausius, returning the hug.

Lark laughed, reveling in the embrace. They'd only been with this strange crew for a few days, but they'd already begun to feel like a family.

"Stay safe, girls," Dausius said at last. He ended the embrace and waved as he joined the others on the trail to Greenvale.

Lark turned to Tiora as Dausius disappeared into the trees. "You don't have to do this, you know. Gael will be in town watching the show and preparing to trek to Flamesmoat in the morning, just like everyone else. I won't be in any danger."

"Danger or not, you shouldn't have to do this alone, Lark. You were there for me while that vile man—" Tiora's voice caught, and her chin quivered, but she drew a deep breath and continued, "You were there for me, and I'm here for you."

Lark nodded, blinking quickly to stop the moisture filling her eyes. "All right then, let's do this."

Leading the way with a confidence born of familiarity, she started down the well-worn trail that led to the outskirts of Greenvale and her family's farm. The trail was devoid of people, but the solitude didn't help calm her nerves. Her senses were strained, searching for signs of any stragglers on their way to the show, ready to vanish into the trees should anyone appear. The last thing she needed was for someone to recognize her and tell Gael she was headed to the farm.

It was late afternoon when they started down the trail, but when they made it to the turnoff to the farm, the sun was setting. The sight of her home, surrounded by the pink, purple, and orange clouds of sunset, stole her breath.

Not so long ago, she'd thought she'd never have the chance to return. Now, instead of racing inside and reuniting with her loved ones, she crept through the woods like a thief in the night. She set her jaw, straightened her shoulders, and headed for the barn.

Tiora had been silent as they hiked through the forest, but as they began their trek across the wide, green grazing field surrounding the barn, she spoke. "Lark, there's another reason I wanted to come with you today." Her eyes were downcast, her voice barely above a whisper. "I know you trained as a healer." She gulped, her stride slowing. "I... there was this awful-tasting tea they made us drink at the brothel." She cleared her throat. "Do you think—"

Lark squeezed Tiora's arm. "I know it well. When we get inside, I'll brew a pot. My mother ought to have stored all the herbs we need." Her heart ached as relief flashed across Tiora's face, and she wished she could kill that bastard Pax all over again.

They crossed the field and stood poised to open the barn door. Lark closed her eyes, whispered a silent prayer, then pushed.

Growling resonated from the building's shadowy depths. "Sunny?" she called, stepping into the large barn. The musty scent of animals assaulted her nose.

Her brother's mutt darted forward, her tail wagging like a flag caught in a storm wind.

"Sunny, I missed you, girl." She laughed and crouched down, stroking her soft golden fur.

Tiora giggled as Sunny sniffed her hand and licked her fingers.

"I have to check something in here before we head inside the house." Lark led the way inside the barn, passing the goats and cattle, all tucked into their pens for the night and indifferent to their presence. "My brother always comes in here when he gets home. It's where he stores all his bows and trapping gear." Lark reached a ladder and grabbed a worn, wooden rung, staring at the top of the loft where a high window lit the space with the last of the day's sunlight. "I have to see if the letter I left for him is still there."

She climbed in a few quick steps and held her breath as she took her first look around. Her heart filled with glee. The letter—it wasn't where she'd placed it, atop the trunk where her brother stored his trapping supplies. Did that mean... was Conall alive?

But as she stepped off the ladder, she spotted the white parchment lying beside the trunk, and her heart fell. She lifted it with shaking fingers. It was still sealed. Even worse, two of the hooks her brother used to display his bow and arrows on the wall lay empty. She sank to the loft floor and clutched the letter to her chest, letting out a gasping sob.

She'd hung onto hope for so long that Brenna had been lying. That her brother was still alive. She'd prayed Gael would not have the heart to go through with the evil plan his sister whispered in his ear. Now she had to face the facts. Conall was gone. There was no way he would've missed her letter. Even if it had fallen to the loft floor immediately, it was still right there in plain sight. Her brother was dead.

Tiora climbed up after her and hugged her as she cried. "It's all right, Lark. I'm here."

Lark clutched her friend, grateful not to be alone. She let herself feel the grief of her brother's death for the first time and wept with abandon.

Her brother and her mother were both gone. She couldn't do anything to bring them back, but she could do something to make things right. She remembered her vow. There was no way she was going to let Gael and Brenna win.

Lark wiped her tears and pulled free from Tiora's arms. "C'mon, we better go in the house."

The light in the barn had dimmed even more as she cried. She ruffled Sunny's fur as she stepped back onto the barn's packed dirt floor. "I'll be back for you, girl. I promise. But for now, you'll have to stay in the barn." She offered the old mutt one more gentle pat on her head, then shut the barn door and turned toward the farmhouse.

Passing her mother's herb garden, Lark shook her head. Weeds strangled the once neat little rows. As they approached the house, she shivered. The darkened interior no longer buzzed with life and laughter but stood empty. She opened the back door and wrinkled her nose. It even smelled off. No longer full of the scents of food baking or fresh herbs hanging to dry, it reeked of sour ale and rotting vegetables.

She froze in the doorway, her gaze the only thing moving. Dirty dishes and empty bottles crowded the kitchen counter and packed the washbasin. A single place was set at the table, the used cutlery and dish still waiting to be cleared away. Pain stabbed her chest. This was not her home any longer.

Lark opened the door and ushered Tiora inside. "This is it. Sorry about the mess." She winced as the stench of stale alcohol sparked a flashback of Rasmus. "...and the smell." She picked her way past empty bottles, treading carefully across the soiled floor that likely hadn't been swept since the day she'd left. "I'll put the kettle on. Have a seat." She stirred the hearth in the center of the room, bringing the fire back to life.

Tiora's chair skidded across the floor. "It's a lovely home if you ignore the mess. It must've been nice growing up here."

A wistful smile tugged at Lark's cheeks. "It was. It was wonderful." Her smile dropped, and she left the hearth. She stood on her tiptoes and opened a nearby cabinet bordering the ceiling. "That's over now. After today, I'll be glad when I never have to set foot in this house again."

She pulled out an old book and rubbed her hand across the smooth leather cover. Her mother's book. She leafed through it, sighing as she noted her mother's familiar handwriting filling the pages. She stopped on one of the first pages and bustled about the kitchen, visiting several shelves and cabinets until she'd assembled a variety of different-sized jars and containers on the table.

The kettle whistled, and she returned to the hearth to grab the steaming pot. "I'll have that tea ready for you in no time. Let it steep while it cools, then you can drink it while I collect the rest of my things." She set to work, adding a pinch of this and a dash of that to her favorite ceramic mug. She set it in front of Tiora and squeezed her shoulder gently.

"Thank you." Tiora gazed into the cup with obvious trepidation. "I wish I didn't need this, but I can't..." Her eyes teared up, and she sniffled. "I just can't."

Lark bent down, staring into Tiora's watery brown eyes. "You don't have to. And you don't need to explain why to me or anyone else." She saw the pain written all over her friend's face, and her blood boiled with rage. "I'll be back in a moment. I just have to grab a few things from my room."

It wasn't fair her friend had to deal with these consequences. Both of them had been forced to change their lives so drastically, through no fault of their own.

All her life she'd followed the rules and listened to her elders. She'd helped her mother heal countless people, often without asking for a single thing in return. Look where that had gotten her. She was sick of other people thinking they could walk all over her and take advantage of her kindness. And she'd learned the hard way not all of her elders deserved respect.

Lark charged into her room and collected the pouch of herbs she'd come for. Grabbing a knapsack from her closet, she packed the fragrant bundle inside, along with a change of clothes. She grabbed a few more things that looked like they might fit Tiora and clutched them in her arms.

Her eyes welled with tears as she surveyed the room. Memories of her childhood flashed in her mind. Her mother brushing her hair and reading her bedtime stories. Conall playing dolls with her on the floor, humoring her, despite being six years older and likely bored to tears. But that was all in the past now. She took a steadying breath and a final look around, then shut the door.

She found herself drawn to Conall's door. She slipped inside, the metal hinge squeaking as it swung open to reveal the room—cold and desolate.

Lark exhaled a shaky breath. A part of her had been hoping he would be there, curled up in his bed, ready to jump up and yell at her for leaving without a proper goodbye. Now that would never happen. Gael and Brenna had seen to it that he would never greet her again. She gritted her teeth, shut the door, and spun on her heel.

Tiora set down the empty mug as Lark reentered the kitchen. "Did you find everything you needed?"

"Just about." Lark dropped the bag on the table and handed the clothes to Tiora. "I thought you might like these." Then she grabbed the spell book, stashed it inside the bag, and pulled the cord closed.

She slung the bag around her shoulders. "That's everything. Let's get out of here."

Tiora rose from the table, stuffing the clothes in her knapsack. Brow furrowing, she inclined her head toward the table, still littered with jars and containers. "Do you need help putting these back where they belong?"

"No. Leave them." Lark lifted the lid off the closest container, giving the contents a sniff before casually dumping the aromatic herbs in a heap on the wooden floor near the door. She grabbed the next pot, sliding it aside without opening it and picking up a large jar behind it. She walked a circuit of the room, scattering handfuls of brown herbs all along the floor, atop cabinets and walls.

"I thought you wanted to be in and out with no one the wiser?" Tiora asked from the open doorway, frowning. "What's the mess for?"

"My mother taught me a lot about herbs." Lark glanced up from her task, setting the empty jar on the table and selecting another. "Gael wanted this farm so badly he killed my brother for it." She lifted the pot's lid and tossed the contents down the hall leading to the bedrooms and family room. "I'd rather watch it burn than let that monster stay here."

Carrying the empty vessel to the hearth, she used a set of metal tongs to place a smoldering coal inside. She strolled over to join her friend in the doorway. Tiora backed away slowly, staring at the jar glowing ominously in the moonlight outside.

Lark spun to face the kitchen, letting the jar warm her hands as she took a last look at the house that had once been her home. She expected to feel reluctant, even sorrowful, but all she felt was a burning conviction that this was the right decision. That murderer did not deserve this place. This home that was once so full of love and warmth did not belong to him.

Lark stared down into the glowing jar and upended it. She dumped the coal into the pile of herbs near the door and backed away as the dry leaves burst into flames.

Shoving the door closed with her boot, she turned her back on the house, grabbed Tiora's elbow, and hurried toward the barn. "C'mon, we better let the animals out to graze. The flames probably won't spread to the barn, but you never know when the wind might change direction."

They set the cattle and goats free. Sunny helped, weaving around the stragglers and nipping at their heels to encourage their exit.

As they abandoned the empty barn, she gazed at the house. The kitchen was already engulfed in flames, and the fire spread quickly into the center of the house. A loud *thud* caught her attention, coming from the back bedroom.

Her breath stilled. That was her mother's room. Gael's room.

Tiora stumbled back, her hands shaking. "Lark, did you hear that?"

Lark's heart thudded madly as she remembered the empty bottles littering the kitchen floor. Could he have been asleep in the bedroom the whole time they were inside?

"Bloody blazes," a voice from within exclaimed.

Rage burned in her veins. She knew that voice.

Gael coughed loudly between curses. Another *thud* sounded, closer to the front door. It was him, staggering drunkenly through the burning house, making his way toward fresh air and the freedom of the night. The freedom her brother would never again enjoy.

Lark sank to the ground, digging her fingers into the soil. Her gaze never left the house as she concentrated on the spot where she'd heard the sound. She wasn't going to let him leave.

With everything inside her, she wished for that bastard to be buried inside the house he wanted so badly. Closing her eyes, she pictured the ground opening up and swallowing the house. A tremor struck her, pulsating through her bones and rattling her teeth. The power flew into the earth through her fingers. Then a great bellowing *crunch* made her eyes fly open.

Blazes. The unburnt side of the house now rested halfway into the ground.

She gasped, pulling her hands from the ground and covering her mouth. As she knelt in the dirt with Tiora and Sunny standing motionless beside her, what was left above ground of the front door—just the very top—jolted wildly as Gael attempted to shove it open. Smoke, and the sound of his hacking coughing, were the only things that escaped.

Finally, the door stilled. Lark stood and turned her back on the farm. Tiora stared at her hands, still covered with the wet, brown soil.

Brushing her fingers along her tunic, Lark rubbed the dirt from her skin. "Let's go. We're done here." Without looking back, she set off for the forest trail.

Chapter 12

Kayda hurried along the cobblestone path. Red silk swirled around her legs, the crimson color dulling in the thick fog that had arrived in Flamesmoat overnight. "I can't believe we're late. Grandfather will not be pleased," she said to Izora as they approached the centuries-old brick cathedral. The bell tower rang, signaling the start of the Harvest Service.

"Oh, I'm sure he'll just be happy you came at all this time," Izora replied with a chuckle.

Kayda clasped her hands together and rubbed her knuckles.

If she'd only gone to the renewal ceremony this spring, she wouldn't be so late today. She thought she'd allotted enough time for dressing after her morning training session, but she hadn't counted on the growth spurt she'd been through this year requiring alterations to be made to her ceremonial frock. They had to summon a trio of seamstresses to the castle, who added several inches of silk to the bottom edge and the bust of the gorgeous, cumbersome gown.

Now she would have to scurry past everyone already assembled to take her place at the front of the pews. She shuddered, picturing all those eyes upon her, whispering under their breath.

The path split. Izora grabbed her hands, unclasping them and giving them both a gentle squeeze before placing her hands at her sides. "You look lovely, Princess. I'll see you later, at the feast." She sent a gentle smile her way and set off down the path to the front entrance.

Kayda swallowed her apprehension, approaching the side door to the church. Thankfully, that entrance was reserved solely for the royals. She wouldn't have a dozen sets of eyes on her as she navigated the stairs with the thick layers of fog-dampened silk bunching about her legs and threatening to trip her.

Her eyes widened. A pair of men stood closely atop the steps, speaking in hushed voices. With the bell tower still chiming, she had no chance of overhearing what they said. How strange to find them cloistered here outside of the service, when everyone was meant to be inside.

She didn't recognize the man facing her, but she noted his features—dark eyes and hair, light skin and a full beard—before he spotted her staring. He said a final word to his companion and hustled down the steps, onto the path she'd just exited. She paused, watching the black-cloaked stranger's back retreating in the fog before she turned to address the second man as he spun to greet her.

"Hello, Tarquin."

Her brother was dressed in a suit of matching red silk. He looked down at her from atop the stairs, his brows scrunching together before he plastered a wide smile across his face. "I see I'm not the only one making a dramatic entrance." He moved sideways, making room on the top step. Then he offered his elbow, quirking a brow mischievously. "Shall we?"

She stared up at him, eyeing his proffered arm like a snake in the grass until the smirk dropped from his face.

"I can tell you're nervous." His expression warmed. "You don't have to walk in alone. C'mon, I promise, no tricks."

She swallowed, considering. Just when she thought he could not be any more awful, her brother did something sweet. She should hold her head up high and march in on her own. But the part of her that remembered the handful of good times they'd shared as children insisted she give him the benefit of the doubt.

Well... they were both late. Kayda linked her arm with Tarquin's. He opened the door, and they entered as the church bells concluded their chiming. As all eyes flicked to them, she let out a shaky breath, grateful she had her brother to share the spotlight. With him there to lead her, his grin spread from ear to ear, she could set her gaze to the ground and ignore the dozens of eyes inspecting her.

They strode down the polished, tiled aisle, their footsteps echoing in her ears despite the muffled chatter of the assembly. They reached the front pew as High Prior Sander emerged from the curtained alcove at the front of the building.

Everyone stood to honor the prior's entrance. The king, wearing a crimson silk suit identical to her brother's, smiled at her and Tarquin as they slipped in next to him in the front pew. He showed no sign of displeasure at their tardiness. Her father, Prince Gideon, was absent, as usual.

As Kayda's stomach settled, her attention was drawn to the High Prior.

High Prior Sander was a somber man who rarely sported a smile on his wrinkled face, and today was no exception. He adjusted his black robe that was lined with red silk stripes down the side—the color a perfect match for the bright crimson the royals wore, but the fabric was not nearly so fine. He marched out front and center and mounted the podium steps that raised him high enough so all those in the back of the spacious building could view his speech.

"Please be seated." High Prior Sander's deep voice boomed through the room.

Kayda smoothed her gown and admired the decor as she waited for the room to quiet and the sermon to begin. The Church of the Dragon was palatial and imposing. Brightly colored tapestries adorned the walls, along with majestic stained-glass windows with intricate etchings—muted today in the foggy morning—that rivaled those in the great hall of Kings Keep.

The centerpiece hung suspended from the ceiling above the prior's head; the massive skull of a long dead dragon, so huge it made High Prior Sander—one of the tallest and stoutest men she had ever met—seem puny in comparison. She shivered as she marveled at its size and imagined the ferocity of the extinct creatures who had such large, sharp teeth.

"Thank you all for coming to join us in prayer this morning. Today, we ask the Lord Dragon to bless our harvest..." High Prior Sander's voice was strong and soothing. It wasn't long before Kayda's mind wandered, tuning out the message she knew by heart after attending these services her entire life.

Her gaze slid sideways. She smiled at her grandfather. He was clear-eyed today, staring intently at the prior as he delivered his sermon. He'd always been so devout, his bonding talent proof enough for him to take every word as truth. It was the church who upheld their right to rule, stating in their holy text that those of the bloodline of the first King of Dracwood would inherit the gift of bonding and prove essential in the future when the Lord Dragon tested the world again.

Tarquin sat on the other side of the king, fingers tapping repeatedly on his knee. His stare was fixed not on the priest, but out the stained-glass window behind him. Kayda returned her gaze to the prior, keeping her face impassive. For her grandfather, and the assembled public, she would at least give the impression of listening, even though the droning sermon was not inspiring her rapt attention.

Her half-brother ignoring the sermon was no surprise. Though Tarquin pretended to be as devout as their grandfather when they were in public, she suspected his belief in church teachings was not the driving force behind his actions. He certainly behaved like he didn't believe there was any higher power out there, ready to reward or condemn him for his actions in the afterlife. No, Tarquin lived every day doing exactly as he pleased, with no thought to any rules of behavior the church espoused.

As for herself, she wanted to believe. She tried her hardest to live by the church's teachings. She sought to embrace their highest values of honesty, kindness, and charity in her daily life. For the rest—if she were honest with herself—she had her doubts.

Her gaze was drawn again to the skull, suspended above them like a menacing chandelier. She didn't doubt dragons had once existed, but she found it harder to believe they would return to save them all from some future danger. Add to that the idea that her children, or even herself, would have some role to play in that conflict, and her skin moistened with sweat under all those layers of silk.

"Please, join me in asking the Lord Dragon to bless the royal house of the Kingdom of Dracwood." High Prior Sander's voice interrupted her musing.

She took a deep breath and stood with her family, turning to gaze upon the parishioners. Her heart raced as all those adoring eyes fell upon her standing in her crimson dress, the color a visual reminder of the blood the royals carried.

The common people held so much love for her family. They expected so much from them. Kayda couldn't help but feel uneasy with their eyes upon her and unworthy of their devotion. She bowed her head and lowered her lashes as the prior prayed, grateful to escape the public's scrutiny.

"Holy Father Dragon, spread your protective wings over our king and his heirs, so they may serve your children and all who believe. Bring to them, on this day of harvest, all the great fruits of our world, so they may reap the benefits of your everlasting love in this time of plenty. Finally, please bless them with your wisdom and bestow them with your strength to weather the storm to come."

A moment of silence stretched out. Then the prior raised his voice again. "King Quinton, please do us the honor of lighting the holy oil. As our Father Dragon's flame burned bright, so too, shall the fire that burns in our hearts."

Her grandfather strode forward. Kayda lifted her head and spun forward again, watching the king clasp hands with the prior and smile fondly at his old friend. "Thank you so much for your prayers, High Prior Sander."

He plucked a taper from a candelabra on the wall and used it to light the wick of the laumarle oil lamp that the prior settled on the podium for all to see. The rare oil sent a bright white light flickering into the air. Despite costing a fortune, the oil would be left to burn all day long, warming the hearts of all who visited the church.

The king turned to address the parishioners, "Thank you all for your great faith in the Lord Dragon and our kingdom. Everyone is welcome to join us at the feast to celebrate the coming harvest."

Cheers erupted throughout the room, and voices rang out calling, "Bless you," and "Long live King Quinton."

Kayda smiled. The love the people felt for her grandfather washed over her like a warm wave. He sauntered forward, grinning and waving at the common people. He gracefully made his way to her side, offering his elbow to escort her to the feast. She accepted and made her way down the church aisle, Tarquin following closely behind them.

They exited the church from the front, where another group of people waited outside to watch the royal family's procession through the outskirts of Flamesmoat and the great field surrounding the city. The fog had lifted, chased away by the bright morning sun.

They were met by a large group of the castle guard, around thirty or forty armed men. Their silver, ceremonial armor glittered as they circled them, providing a buffer between the royals and the common people as they strode down the streets of Northmoat.

Kayda kept her eyes trained forward and a tight grip on her grandfather's arm as they strolled through the city. The shops and houses on the route were decorated with bright flowers and shimmering ribbons. Townspeople ringed the streets, and children perched on their parents' shoulders, grinning as they passed.

The king seemed to enjoy himself, waving at all the people lining the streets.

Kayda's stomach wobbled. She loved seeing her grandfather in such good spirits but couldn't help feeling uncomfortable being on display.

They drew closer to the edge of the city, their steps sinking as they traversed through the shallow gully ringing the city. Centuries ago, it was erected to protect the people within, filled with flame, giving the city its name. But it had been out of use for so long it was overgrown with grass and barely discernible from the surrounding fields, allowing them to pass through easily.

Throngs of people amassed outside, waiting for their arrival at the feast site. Tumblers and jugglers wove through the crowds, delighting children with their antics. A bouquet of delicious smells wafted in their direction, making her mouth water. People sat upon blankets of all shapes and sizes, drinking, eating, and laughing with family and friends.

Kayda sighed as she spied the nearby tables. Most were already full of people, many she recognized from the castle, but the grandest table of them all sat empty, except for the great heaping plates of food piled high upon it. Her grandfather spotted it and ambled in that direction.

A scuffle of some sort broke out to the right. Several guards peeled off from their procession, headed toward it.

Kayda tore her gaze from the waiting feast, craning her neck. The guards and townspeople closed in on the source of the disturbance so quickly she couldn't see anything.

"Don't worry, my dear." King Quinton patted her hand, which rested in the crook of his elbow. "The guards will take care of it."

She turned to her grandfather, abandoning her attempt to view the commotion that had only increased in size and volume since the guards rushed into the fray. As she met the king's eyes, she spotted movement behind him. Then some unreadable emotion flashed on his face, his body shuddering violently.

She gasped, clutching him as he collapsed, a knife lodged firmly in his back. She fell with him, unable to hold up the king's dead weight. Her eyes glistened with tears. Her mind swirled with horror and disbelief. She held his gaze, unable to look away as the light disappeared from her grandfather's eyes.

As if from somewhere far away, chaos erupted as the crowd took note of the king's fate.

Tarquin yelled, "The king, the king's been murdered. Catch the villain, you fools!"

The guards attempted to close in around them while simultaneously trying to find the man who'd stabbed the king.

An old man burst through the crowd, his pristine white robe and imposing bearing marking him as a Palisade Mage. "I'm a healer. Let me through," he said calmly, slipping between the guard and crouching down beside her.

She shook her head, blinking furiously, her mouth opening and closing soundlessly. The mage's wrinkled hand pried her fingers from the king's shoulders, then he rolled him onto his stomach.

Kayda pulled herself into a seated position, watching the mage as he set his hands on her grandfather and examined the wound.

After reaching into a pouch on his belt, he pulled out something small enough to hide in his fist. Then he spread his hand on the king's wound and pulled the knife from his back. He closed his eyes, his palm covering the wound tightly.

Kayda held her breath, watching. A tremor tingled over her skin. It was there and gone in the space of a heartbeat.

The mage opened his green eyes, staring into her own and smiled weakly. "I've done what I can. The rest is up to him."

"Thank you," she whispered. She reached for her grandfather and gasped at the wound. The skin was perfect and unmarred, as if the knife had never been there. Hope erupted in her chest. She stared into the mage's face. "You've healed him. Bless you!"

The mage shook his head slightly. "I've healed the body only. We have to wait and see if his soul returns." He turned his attention to the guardsmen surrounding them. "What are you men waiting for? Get the king and princess back to the keep."

A wagon appeared, surrendered willingly from some folk in the crowd. The guards made quick work of lifting the king and carrying him to the back of the cart. By the time they held him aloft, dozens of people had offered their blankets to cushion the wooden boards. Their tear-stained faces crowded around the guards, and the sound of wailing reverberated as the masses wept for the fallen king.

Kayda allowed herself to be moved, still in a state of disbelief. An armored man ushered her into the back of the cart to sit beside the king. She searched her grandfather's ashen face. His eyes were closed, his features slack. His scarlet suit was covered in dirt and grass, soaked with a dark stain that could only be from his blood. As the cart began to move, pulled by a brown mare and driven by a set of armored men, she grabbed her grandfather's hand and squeezed it tightly.

"We'll be back home soon, Grandfather. You're going to be fine." She stroked the back of his hand with her thumb. The panicked thudding of her heart slowed as they made their way closer to the keep.

It had all happened so fast. There'd been no time to think, but now that she had a moment to reflect on the attack, one image returned to her, and her mouth dropped open.

She'd seen the face of the man who'd stabbed her grandfather. The stranger—it was him! The same man that had been engaged in a whispered conversation with Tarquin this morning just tried to assassinate the king.

She dropped the king's hand, wringing her own together as the implications of that fact dawned on her. Tarquin had been involved. Her stomach turned. She didn't have any proof, but she *knew*. All those secret meetings she'd happened upon, all his suspicious behavior, it had all led to this.

If only she'd told her grandfather like she'd planned that day in his chambers. Her heart pounded again, and she snapped her eyes closed, dizziness washing over her. Tarquin was behind this, and she was the only one who knew... What was she going to do?

The wagon jostled violently, and her eyes shot open as she bounced off the side of the wagon. "Hey, take it easy." She steadied herself before she fell on top of her grandfather.

The two guards up front didn't respond, and Kayda's eyes bulged when she spotted where they were headed. "Why aren't you heading for the Keep?"

Her gaze locked on the tower. It grew closer with every passing instant as they sped straight for it.

"Take us to Kings Keep." She crawled on her hands and knees to the front of the wagon. She grabbed the man's shoulder who steered the reins, her hand closing on the cold metal of his armor, and she jostled him—hard. "Listen to me. We need to go to the Keep!"

The driver sat unmoved, her attempt to grab his attention as effective as a child screaming at a storm cloud. But the second man swiveled to face her, his features shielded by his helm, so all she could see was a set of piercing brown eyes glowering at her. "The tower is more secure. You'll be safe there, my lady." His gauntleted hand rose, aiming for her fingers that still clutched his companion's shoulder, but Kayda snatched her hand back before he touched her.

"No." She slammed her fist against the wooden slats, then pointed to the Keep. "Take us to Kings Keep. That's an order."

"We are following orders. Prince Tarquin's orders." He spun forward again, and Kayda sat back, covering her mouth with her palm.

No... it couldn't be true. The guards were under orders from that sneaky bastard, and she was about to be locked up in the tower. She reached instinctively for her skirt pocket. The one where she kept the tinderbox Izora had gifted her. But her hands only slid over the smooth silk of her ceremonial dress.

Damn. She had no pockets, no tinderbox, and no way to call forth the flames. Even if she had, she couldn't summon. What would she do? Kill the guards and steal the king? There was no way she could leave him, not now.

Even if she succeeded, she'd have nowhere to go. The sad fact was Kings Keep was all she knew. Except for the occasional jaunt in the countryside or sightseeing trip, she'd spent her entire life here. And there was no one she trusted enough to take them in. She grimaced, realizing she had little choice but to go with the guards and hope her inaction in this moment didn't destroy what chance she had of stopping her brother.

The tower loomed above them. She crawled back to the king and grabbed his hand. "Don't worry, Grandfather... I'll think of something," she whispered. "I'm going to figure out what he's up to and stop him." She cupped a hand on his face, eyes filling with tears, her jaw set firmly with determination. "I'll find a way to make him pay for what he's done... I swear it."

Chapter 13

Smoke and ash filled the air. Conall slowed to a stop, panting in the forest just outside the farm. He gripped the side of his chest. His lungs burned, and the taste of metal lingered in the back of his throat as he swallowed breath after gasping breath.

They'd made it to the farm in record time, running at full speed through the forest. It was a miracle neither of them had stumbled in the fog-shrouded underbrush. Now, they were here—and it was too late.

He fell to his knees as he caught sight of the wreckage for the first time. Fire had torn through the entire house, leaving smoldering debris in its wake. His heart, still racing from the run, wrenched. It was gone. His home was gone.

Shadow sidled up beside him. Conall draped an arm around him, accepting the comfort he offered. He sucked in another gasping breath, resting his cheek on the soft gray fur on Shadow's back as he tried to wrap his mind around the loss of his home. All those hours in the cave recovering, all the miles he'd trekked, all the pain he'd endured... it had not been enough to save his home.

He closed his eyes, shutting out the devastation in front of him, and said a silent prayer for his sister. She was probably sitting at a neighbor's house right now or out tending to a sick child in town. There was no reason to assume she'd been in there when the fire blazed through. She would show up any moment, just as surprised as he was to see the farm in ashes. He opened his eyes, refusing to believe otherwise. She had to be all right.

"I have to go check things out. I need you to stay here, Shadow."

"Are you sure?" The wolf's muscles stiffened below his cheek as Shadow tensed. *"What if Gael is there?"*

"I'm sure. The barn is still standing. If the animals are in there, you'll only spook them. Besides, this is a farm town. With all the livestock here, the people don't have a great fondness for wolves. If anyone happens by, they're likely to shoot first and ask questions later." He took to his feet, exhaling through his mouth and adjusting the pouches on his belt. *"I'll be all right. Wait here. I'll be back as soon as I get some answers."*

"All right, brother, I'll be right here waiting. Call for me if you need me."

Conall nodded and set off across the grazing field on a straight course for the barn. The building still stood, but it was empty. The doors were thrown wide open, and the noise of animals was gone.

He walked into the shadowy interior. The familiar musty scent was absent, overpowered by the smoky bonfire that had been his home. It was a good sign. Lark had probably set the animals free, then set off with Sunny to bring them round to a neighbor's house.

He sighed as he spotted the worn wooden loft ladder, still standing. He climbed, careful not to put any weight on his aching shoulder. Gazing upon his things, a small weight lifted off his chest. He dug through his trunk for a change of clothes and grabbed his second-best bow and quiver off the wall, where it hung waiting.

It took only a moment to replace his filthy clothes with a brown tunic and wool trousers. Then he stood there—the familiar heft of smooth wood in his hands, his clothes free of bloodstains and shredded holes—feeling refreshed and better prepared but still at a loss for what to do next.

He spotted a crumpled piece of parchment lying on the loft floor near the ladder. As he bent to pick it up, Shadow's voice rose in his mind. *"Conall, someone is coming."* Stuffing the paper into his pocket, he crouched down on the loft floor. He nocked an arrow and aimed his bow at the barn door.

"I saw you heading in there, boy," a weathered voice called out. "We don't take kindly to thieves in these parts. You better drop whatever you're stealing and show yourself before I send for the magistrate and you end up losing a hand."

Conall let his bow arm relax. He knew that voice. "Barrow, it's me, Conall."

The bewildered face of his closest neighbor peeked through the barn door. He looked the same as he always had, his white hair unbrushed and wind-tossed, dirt-dusted overalls covering his lanky frame. Conall climbed down the ladder, holding his bow in his left arm.

When he turned around, Barrow gaped in surprise. "Conall? Blazes. It is you!" He pulled him in for a hug. "We all thought you were dead. I'm so glad to see you."

"What's happening? Do you need my help?"

"No, stay where you are. It's just my neighbor," he told his bondmate as he returned Barrow's embrace. The old man squeezed his shoulder a bit too tightly, and he grimaced. *"Maybe he'll have some answers."*

"You thought I was dead?" Conall stepped back a few paces.

Barrow threaded a hand through his messy locks. "Gael came into town a few weeks back. Told everyone how you'd fallen to your death while out trapping in the forest." He set his tanned hands on his hips, brown eyes searching him intently. "A few of us didn't believe him. We demanded he take us out there to see where it happened."

"And he did?" Conall's brow furrowed. That would've been risky. If anyone spotted him there pierced with an arrow, Gael's story would be revealed as a lie.

"He didn't want to at first, but the magistrate convinced him. A few of us trekked out there the next day. All that was left when we got there was a trail of bloodstains and the tracks of a wolf nearby on the streambed. We all figured you'd been dragged off into the woods." Barrow's wrinkles deepened as he frowned. "I'm sorry we didn't look harder for you."

Conall stared at the ground, shaking his head. They'd been out there searching for him? He must have been in the cave, fighting off the fever that had nearly killed him. A bitter smile crossed his face, there and gone in an instant, before he returned his attention to Barrow.

"It's all right. You couldn't have known I was out there." Conall aimed for the open doorway and took a few steps in that direction before Barrow stopped him.

"What happened out there in the forest, Conall? Was what Gael said the truth?" Barrow's bushy brows knitted together. "Did you slip and fall?"

"Yeah, I fell." Conall pulled the neck of his tunic to the side, revealing the red puckered flesh of the still healing wound on his left shoulder. "But not before that lying bastard shot me."

"Blazes." Barrow leaned closer, examining the wound. His mouth dropped open, and his eyes bulged. Then his jaw snapped shut, and his brows furrowed as he met Conall's eyes again. "Well, he got what was coming to him, at least."

"What do you mean?" Conall headed outside.

Barrow kept step with him, nodding at the wreckage as they stepped out into the daylight. "The fire caught in the night. Everyone was in town, watching some traveling show and camping on the village green before heading to Flamesmoat for the Harvest Festival. I decided to stay home for a little peace and quiet. I happened to speak to Gael earlier in the afternoon. He told me he was skipping the feast this year, too. And, well, I was out in my field stargazing when the fire started. I watched it all from a distance."

Barrow glanced down at the ground before looking back at the smoldering remnants of the building. "It started in the kitchen. Then the rest of the house—it was the strangest thing—it sank right into the ground like the floorboards collapsed and it all tumbled into the cellar." He clasped Conall's shoulder. "By the time I made it here, the place was completely engulfed... No one made it out."

The words pummeled Conall like a punch to the gut. He closed his eyes, scrubbing at the lids with his fingertips. There's no way Gael would have let Lark go camp on the village green alone. And no one made it out...

Gael and Lark were gone. He clasped his head in his hands, pressing his fingers into his temples. No... not Lark... please, not her.

"I'm so sorry to be the one to tell you, Conall." Barrow rubbed his back gently.

Conall dropped his hands at his sides and stared ahead blankly. It couldn't be true. If only he'd just climbed that damn ridge like he'd planned, maybe he would've made it back in time. Now he'd never see his sister again.

Barrow continued, "I came to make sure I hadn't missed any animals. They were out to graze when the fire rolled through. I brought them all to my farm. Was planning to sell them and send the money round Mage Keep to your sister, but I suppose now you'll be wanting them back."

Blinking rapidly, Conall whirled to face his neighbor. Did he hear that right? "Lark is at Mage Keep?"

Barrow nodded. "She left the same day you had your fall. Went with that chubby sister of Gael's into Flamesmoat before traveling to Mage Keep." He chuckled. "Gael was plenty steamed about that when he found out... He kept shoving her letter in everyone's face, jabbering on about the mages stealing her youth or some such nonsense. Was why he didn't want to take us into the forest to look for you. He was dead set on setting off for Flamesmoat after her, instead."

Conall clutched his chest, his lungs full enough to burst. Lark was alive! And she'd left Gael a letter. He smiled and pulled the crumpled parchment out of his pocket, smoothing the paper, revealing the word written on the sealed envelope.

He sighed. There was his name written in his sister's unmistakable handwriting. "You have the animals at your farm. Is my dog Sunny with them?" Conall folded the letter carefully and placed it in his pocket, his smile fading as Barrow clasped his hands together, frowning.

"I'm sorry, son. I haven't seen your dog."

Conall swallowed, his heart crushed. She must've been inside with the only master she had left, Gael. Poor Sunny. She should've been with him, not that murderer.

Tendrils of smoke escaped from the charred remains of his home. His stomach clenched. He would never again tousle Sunny's golden fur or feel the warm weight of her against his side as he slept. He gritted his teeth, his hands curling into fists at his side.

"What now?" Barrow asked. "Should I bring the animals back? Will you rebuild?"

He blinked repeatedly, trying to focus. The house might be gone, but the land was still his. He'd better decide what to do with it. One thing was certain. He wouldn't be around to take care of the animals anytime soon.

"You were willing to sell the animals for Lark... would you mind doing the same for me?" Conall raised a brow.

"Sure, I could handle it. It's the least I can do after how Lark and your mother saved Leda and my new grandbaby last winter." Barrow pulled a worn leather coin purse out of his pocket and dumped the contents into his hand. "This ought to cover about half of it. Come on down the road to my house, and I can fetch you the rest."

Conall shook his head, holding out a hand for the coins. "Thanks, Barrow, but I want to head into town, tell the magistrate what happened here, and let him see I'm not dead before I leave for Mage Keep."

He was going to see his sister. He hadn't forgotten Gael's warning. She deserved to know the truth. And he had to tell her the facts of what had happened with him and her beloved step-father.

The coins landed in his palm, clinking together before he dropped them into his belt pouch. "I wouldn't want to travel with too much coin on me. Mind if I pick up the rest when I get back?"

"No, won't be any trouble. Tell the magistrate I witnessed the fire, and he can come find me if he has any questions. I'll keep an eye on the farm for you while you're gone." The old man took another long look at the smoldering rubble. "So, you are planning to come back and rebuild?"

"Yes, I'll be back. You can count on it." Conall joined his neighbor in staring at the destruction as a snippet of conversation from earlier came back to him. "Hey, you said earlier the house sank, didn't you?"

Barrow nodded.

Conall stepped closer to the wreckage, pulling the neck of his tunic over his face to shield his nose from the smoke wafting in the air. The fiery debris' heat rose to greet him.

"Yep, this side of the house." Barrow walked beside him, peering at the part of the house sunken much lower in the ground than the other half. He coughed, then shielded his face with his sleeve. "One moment it was there, and the next, it was halfway buried in the ground. One of the most bizarre things I ever saw... But if the floorboards were on fire, and the whole section dropped into the cellar—well, that would do it, I suppose."

Conall tilted his head, pursing his lips. "Yeah, that's the strange thing, Barrow. We didn't have a cellar."

The door to the Greenvale Inn slammed shut behind him. Conall trudged away from the inn, headed for the forest trail that would lead him to his sister. He'd just finished telling the magistrate his tale. He sighed deeply, shading his eyes from the midday sun.

All the gory details would be known throughout town in a matter of days. Although he'd tried to relay his tale quietly, the acoustics in the inn made the feat impossible. And with practically everyone in town away at Flamesmoat for the annual Harvest Feastival, the few stragglers who stayed behind had gone quiet as he spoke, leaning in close to discover how he'd returned from the dead.

His eyes adjusting to the light, he lengthened his stride. At least it was over and done with now. He could rest easy knowing that although the farmhouse lay in ruins, the land would be there waiting for him when he came back from Mage Keep.

The inn door creaked open and shut. Hurried footsteps followed. "Hello. I couldn't help but hear you were headed for Mage Keep. Care for some company?" inquired a female voice behind him.

Conall slowed and turned to examine the young woman walking toward him.

She smiled, her sun-kissed, white cheeks a pretty pink. At first glance, she appeared to be close to his age and was attractive despite her plain traveling clothes, with long brown hair pulled into a simple ponytail and bright blue eyes. He didn't recognize her, which was strange, as their small farming town wasn't a place that typically had many visitors.

"You're going to Mage Keep?" he asked, stopping to await her answer.

"Yes, I'm on my way back. Just passing through this little town after completing an errand for my mother." She stuck out her right hand, still looking at him directly. "I'm Ereni."

His gaze jumped to her hand, then back to her face before he grasped her hand and shook. "Conall."

Her grip was firm and her hands soft as she shook back. "So, what about it? Shall we travel together?" She dropped his hand and strode forward, toward the trail he planned to use. She wore sturdy leather boots and had a knapsack strung around her shoulders as if prepared to leave that instant. "I was planning to leave today, and it looks like you are as well. It would be nice to have a little company." She cocked her head sideways, peering at him.

Conall walked, too, keeping pace with the girl as he considered her proposition. It would be nice to have some company to help stave off the loneliness he felt without his family and friends. And she'd said she was headed back, so it sounded like she'd been there already. It couldn't hurt to learn some inside information about the keep before they arrived. But what about Shadow?

"Brother, there's a girl here that wants to travel with us to Mage Keep... Do you have any objections to her joining us?"

"I won't eat her, if that's what you're asking."

Conall couldn't stop the chuckle that escaped him. Ereni looked his way, eyebrows raising.

He cleared his throat. "My hound is waiting for me in the woods." It was his turn to raise his brows. "You're not afraid of big dogs, are you?"

Her face lit up, her arms swinging as she entered the trail. "I love dogs."

Conall led the way to his bondmate. He was curled up below a star oak, resting in the shade. When they neared the tree, Shadow rose to his feet, leisurely stretching and staring at Ereni.

He had to give her credit. She didn't balk at his size or the wild intelligence of his stare. The only sign of her surprise was the slight hitch in her voice when she spoke next.

"You weren't kidding. You keep big dogs in Greenvale, I see."

Conall shrugged. "Not Greenvale. Just me. This is Shadow."

She knelt down, offering her fist. "Hi, Shadow. I'm Ereni."

"Go on." Conall slid his gaze from Shadow to Ereni's fist. *"I told her you're my hound."*

"Your hound?" Shadow snorted and backed up a pace, shooting him a glare. Then he padded forward, gave her fist a single sniff, and sat on his haunches.

Her gaze lingered on the gray fur above Shadow's head. For a moment, he was certain she would pet him, but she retracted her hand and stood. "You two ready? Mage Keep is this way."

They walked, the late summer breeze humming through the leaves. The wind and the shaded trail made for a comfortable hike, despite the lingering heat.

She edged closer until they strolled side by side, tilting her head toward him. "I couldn't help but overhear your story in the inn."

He winced, staring down at the dirt path. "Yeah. Kind of crazy, I know."

She nodded, her brows sinking as she concentrated on him. "Sounds like you've been through a lot. And now you're going to Mage Keep to tell your sister?"

"That's the plan."

The mention of Lark had him tapping his pants pocket, sighing as the fabric crinkled beneath his fingers. He'd been so busy planning what he'd say to the magistrate on the way into town he hadn't opened her letter.

They spent the afternoon walking and chatting. When the sun sank down behind the trees and they stopped to make camp for the night, he pulled the crumpled parchment out of his pocket and unfolded it.

"What's that? A goodbye letter from your sweetheart?" Ereni perched on a fallen log, digging through her pack.

He shook his head. "It's from my sister."

He scanned Lark's elegant handwriting from where he sat on his bedroll, next to a small campfire. Shadow was off hunting, leaving them alone in a clearing surrounded by trees, a short distance away from the trail they'd hiked all day.

"What's it say?" she asked.

He scrunched his nose and glanced over, spotting parchment sticking out of her bag. "You've got a letter in your pack. Are you gonna read it to me?"

She chuckled and pulled a shiny red apple out of her pack, then cinched it closed. "If I did that, I'd have to kill you."

Conall rolled his eyes before dropping his gaze back to the letter. "It doesn't say much. Just that she's going to Mage Keep, and she'll write to me as soon as she gets there." He folded the letter again and stuffed it into his pocket.

Ereni pulled a knife from her belt, sliced the apple in half, and handed him a portion.

He accepted the fruit and nodded to her bag. "What about yours?"

She shifted on the log and crossed her legs. "I don't know. It's for my mother." She sheathed her knife, then spun the apple half over and over in her hands.

"Was that the errand you mentioned? Your mother sent you to deliver a letter?"

"Mm-hmm. She's not just my mother. She's my boss, too."

He cocked a brow.

She bit her lip, looking down at the dirt. "My mother is Sade Prim. Leader of the Palisade Mages."

Her mother was the mages' leader? He took a bite of the apple, taking his time chewing to let his shock subside. A smile tugged at the corner of his mouth. "So, you're like a princess mage, then?"

She shook her head once. "No. More like a lapdog." She smiled sheepishly. "Not that I mind, actually. I've always loved to travel."

"You'll get along with my sister. Lark's always wanted to travel, too."

Her smile widened. "If she's anything like you, I imagine I'll like her just fine." She bit into her apple and leaned back, stretching out her legs.

The tips of his ears warmed. Was she flirting?

He stole another glance at her. She made a pretty picture, reclining on the log, smiling slightly as she chewed, relaxed and open. It wouldn't be the worst thing in the world if it were true.

He cleared his throat. "Funny that your mother wouldn't send someone else to be her letter carrier. You don't see a lot of young girls traveling alone through the forest."

She snorted, her eyes twinkling with mischief. "That blade's not just for cutting fruit. Don't get any ideas."

Conall gulped. Not flirting, then. He watched her, lounging in the clearing, slowly chewing on her apple. How far could he trust her?

"Can I ask you something?"

She swallowed. "Sure."

"My stepfather... He told me the Palisade steals youth from mages."

She narrowed her eyes and sat up straight, crossing her legs again. "And?"

"Is it true?"

"In a way. I wouldn't call it stealing. The initiates know what they're giving up. It's not exactly a secret, but it's not something the minstrels sing about either."

So, it was true. He scratched his jaw, the bite of apple weighing down his stomach like a stone. "I don't get it. Why would anyone make that sacrifice?"

She shrugged and stared at her feet. "It's the way it's always been. If you want to be a mage, you have to pay the price." She glanced his way. Her gaze softened, and she reached over to squeeze his knee. "Don't worry about your sister. She won't be forced. Maybe she won't even go through with it. Not everyone does." She pulled back her hand, offering a small smile. "It'll take us weeks to travel to Mage Keep. I'll tell you all about it while we travel. You'll see it's just a place like any other, magic or not."

He exhaled, a small weight lifting off his shoulders. It sounded like no matter what, Lark would have a choice. He turned toward Ereni, gazing at her inquisitively. "What about you? Will you go through with it?"

She rubbed her arm, gazing into the fire. "My family can trace our talent all the way back to the first mages that helped conjure the Palisade." She sighed. "It's always been my fate to be a mage."

Shadow reappeared then, a freshly killed hare dangling between his teeth. Conall let the conversation drop, but he didn't miss the fact that she hadn't answered his question. It must be hard having to live up to her mother's expectations.

In a way, he could relate. All these years, his father's last words to him hadn't ceased echoing in his ears. "Watch over your mother and the new baby," he'd said that fateful day before he'd left for the ocean journey he'd never returned from. Conall spent his whole life seeking to fulfill that request.

His gaze lifted to the sky before returning to his new companion. He sent her a smile. Maybe together they could satisfy their loved one's expectations. At the least, he'd have another friendly face to talk to.

Ereni smiled back, licking her lips. "You gonna skin that hare, or should I?"

Chapter 14

A late summer breeze blew through the clearing, raising goose-bumps on Lark's tanned arms and whirling the brown wool of her skirt around her legs as she strolled toward the colorful wagon.

Whisper sat tethered to his perch, sunning himself with the last rays of daylight. Sunny watched Lark's passage across the clearing from the back of the plain wagon Lark and Tiora had taken ownership of, while happily chewing on a stick.

Nearby, the rhythmic *thunk* of knives hitting wood echoed. Tiora did her best to stand perfectly still and smile without flinching as the twins took turns throwing knives with expert precision dangerously close to her limbs. All three of them glittered in their multicolored garb.

Every night when they stopped to rest, Dausius monopolized all of Lark's time, teaching her the lyrics and melodies to dozens of beautiful songs from his homeland. Tonight, he'd let her off easy, only asking her to practice on her own before disappearing into the woods on some mysterious errand. But instead of repeating the same tunes over and over, she headed for Whisper.

She could finally examine the gorgeous hawk up close. Maybe it was to be expected, since she shared her name with a songbird, but she'd always loved birds. Her mother claimed a meadow lark landed on the window sill the moment she gave birth and serenaded them. The bird's feathers were a perfect match for the brown curls she'd been born with, so her mother thought it only fitting to name her after the bold songbird.

It led her to become a little obsessed with the delicate creatures. She'd learned the names and songs of dozens as a child. But though she'd dreamed of owning a bird one day, she'd had to content herself with viewing them from afar, until now.

She smiled as she walked to within a pace of the wagon and stopped to admire Whisper. He gazed back at her, then tucked his pointed beak into his chest, scratching his glossy brown and white feathers.

"He likes you." Aren appeared between two trees and sauntered up beside her.

Lark flinched but stopped herself from gasping out loud. "Do you think so?" She stole a glance at Aren. He'd taken off the oversized hat since they stopped in the clearing and donned the long leather glove on his right arm. "How can you tell?" She tore her gaze away from his handsome face, focusing on Whisper.

"He's preening. Hawks don't let down their guard to take care of their feathers if someone has them on edge."

Whisper lifted his head from his chest, looked at her again, then with great agility proceeded to turn his neck, scratching the long, brown feathers on his back with his beak.

Lark giggled. "I wish I could scratch my back like that."

"Do you want to see something?" Aren strode to the front of the wagon and rustled around in the open bed.

Lark lost herself for a moment, admiring the cut of his shoulders. The muscles of his back bunched and released through his silk shirt as he bent over. She gulped and forced her gaze away as it wandered lower, stealing a glance at his trousers. Lowering her face, she prayed the tan she'd acquired these last few days on her otherwise light skin, along with the shaded, late afternoon sun, would be enough to disguise the blush warming her cheeks as Aren turned around.

He held his right arm out stiffly. On his leather glove was a hooded bird, much smaller than Whisper.

All thought of her burning cheeks faded. She lifted her chin, leaning close, and traced the bird's features with her gaze. Feathers of gold, brown, and white covered its body and wings, with a few small, fluffy white feathers peeking out from beneath the bottom of the hood. Its clawed feet clutched the leather glove, its head pivoting in all directions. Sensing the bird's nervous energy, Lark reached out to stroke its chest.

Aren pulled his arm out of reach before her fingers connected with the silky-looking feathers. He sent her a small smile. "Most birds don't like being touched. You wouldn't want to lose a finger." The bird seemed even more restless now, digging those sharp talons into the leather gauntlet.

"I'm sorry. She's just so beautiful. I don't know why, but I thought if I touched her, I could calm her down."

Strangely, while she'd been speaking, the bird stood perfectly still, as if intently listening to her voice. The moment she quieted, the bird was back at it again, twisting and twitching under the hood.

"I found her this morning. She's only a few months old, still learning how to fly. You can see she still has some baby down on her neck.

Are you familiar with falcons?" Aren asked, holding his arm steady despite the bird's movement. "Or did you guess she's female?"

Lark shrugged. "Just lucky, I guess." She peered at the falcon again, still itching to touch her, though she kept her hands plastered to her sides. "Can I see her face?"

Aren shook his head. "It's not a good idea to take off her hood while she's so agitated. Though I wonder…" He shifted his weight, leaning closer. "Could you sing?"

Lark's gaze darted to Aren's face, her stomach fluttering. He'd heard her sing before. Dausius would often call him over to accompany her on his lute as she practiced around the campfire each night. For some reason, the request felt much more intimate with just the two of them there and him staring at her so closely.

"Are falcons fond of singing?" She dropped her gaze back to the beautiful bird, sucking in a nervous breath.

"Can I tell you something?"

Aren's softly spoken question drew her gaze again. She nodded.

"That first night we met, Meital and I… well, we're both light sleepers."

Lark's stomach twisted. First from the image of Aren and Meital sleeping together. Then, as the meaning of his words sunk in, it twisted even harder from the memory of what had happened that night.

Aren glanced at the ground, leaning away slightly. "We both woke up when Pax… did what he did to Tiora." He grimaced, then met her eyes again. "After we realized what was happening, we woke up Daus, but by that time, it was over. We tried to convince him to come up with a plan to free you both. But he hadn't heard what we had… He said it was too dangerous."

He frowned, his Adam's apple bobbing as he swallowed. "I thought Meital and I would have to handle it alone—until you started to sing.

I took one look at Daus' face, and I knew he heard it, too. You have something special, Lark. I don't know if you've ever noticed, but when you sing, the whole forest listens. All the owls, the crows, the songbirds, they go quiet. It's... kind of amazing."

Lark's cheeks burned again. She'd always known she could sing. It was a talent she shared with her mother. But this was the first time anyone had ever called her voice amazing.

She studied the falcon still wriggling on Aren's arm and drew in a deep breath. "I guess it can't hurt to try." She cleared her throat and sang.

The effect was immediate. As Lark sang the first words to one of the songs Dausius had taught her, the falcon stilled. Her head swiveled toward the sound, and her whole body, from the tip of her tail to her wings and talons, relaxed.

Lark felt lighter than air. She kept singing with a smile peeking through between words.

Aren was smiling, too. He pulled the black hood free, revealing the falcon's face for the first time.

The bird's stare fixed on Lark, and a rush of something—some incredible, indescribable feeling—filled her as she locked eyes with the bird for the first time.

She kept singing, studying her, those black eyes staring back at her hypnotically. Her voice burst forth from her effortlessly; the words rolled off the tip of her tongue. The song she'd practiced only a scant handful of times sprang forth like it had been written for her.

It was as if, for the first time, she wasn't just singing with her voice. Something inside her soul sang, too.

From the corner of her eye, she caught movement. She broke eye contact with the bird but continued the song as Dausius returned from the woods. He wore his multicolored tunic, his arms loaded with fruit. Apples and berries overflowed from a small basket he carried in his dark brown arms. His expression made Lark blush yet again. His eyes were wide and a grin split his face from ear to ear as he hustled toward them, his beaded hair clinking musically.

"Brilliant, gorgeous, transcendent even," he exclaimed as Lark sang the final word to the ballad. "You are going to make us famous, my dear." He ambled to the back of the wagon and placed the basket of fruit on the wooden boards. "I saw these beauties growing wild and couldn't resist gathering a few." He plucked a shiny red apple from the top of the pile and bit into it with a loud crunch. He closed his eyes briefly, letting out a tiny moan, his lips puckering.

Dausius opened his eyes and finally took note of the falcon. "Well, who do we have here?" He strolled toward the bird. "Another new addition to the show?" He quirked a brow in Aren's direction.

"I'm not sure yet." Aren pulled the hood over the falcon. She squirmed around, agitated again. "My father always said female birds weren't worth the challenge. Too smart for their own good. This one seems anxious, too. I might set her free, once I'm sure she can fly on her own."

Lark's heart skipped a beat. "No, you can't." She grabbed his arm and looked up at him imploringly. She stared, unblinking, as he returned her gaze, then dropped her hand from his arm and backed up a step, dropping her gaze to the ground. "Just give her a chance. Please?"

She glanced back at Aren's face, and his expression softened. "All right. I will." He smiled. "Maybe you'd like to help with her training?" he added, cocking a brow toward Dausius. "If you don't mind your new star spending some time with us animals?"

Dausius looked back and forth between the two of them, crunching away on his apple. His face was full of amusement, like a child munching on popcorn while watching a play.

Lark bit her lip, staring at Dausius while he chewed.

He finally swallowed, swinging the half-eaten apple around as he performed an exaggerated bow. "By all means. You heard the girl sing... I don't have much else I can teach her."

Lark's face lit up, and she bounced on her toes, nodding emphatically. "I would love that."

Aren's smile deepened. "Would you like to give her a name?"

It came to her instantly, sliding off her lips breathlessly. "Muse."

Dausius paused with the apple—only a core now—in front of his lips. A peel of laughter burst out of his mouth, spraying tiny chunks of yellow fruit in the air. He laughed so loud it echoed around the clearing. Mazen and Meital halted their practice, sending curious glances in their direction.

"I think you better get used to working with females, son." He thumped Aren on the back and wiped a tear from the corner of his eye. "Our star needs her Muse." He turned to Lark, winked, and tossed the core into the woods.

Chapter 15

Movement outside the window caught Kayda's eye. A hawk landed on the sill, folding broad, brown and white checkered wings into its sides. It swiveled its head to stare inside the glass.

She imagined what the bird must be seeing. A plain, freckled girl, sitting on the cold stone floor in a crumpled red dress. Her long red hair spilling wild down her back, darkness encircling her tired, brown eyes.

An old man, his pale skin yellow and sickly. The strength he'd always exuded slowly ebbing as he lay unmoving on a cot, wrapped in the multi-colored blankets of his subjects.

The hawk looked in for a moment, then turned its head and flew away.

Kayda sighed. If only it were that easy for her to leave.

A full day and night had passed since she'd been brought to the tower and locked inside one of the top floor's bare stone rooms. She spun away from the window and clenched her hands together in her lap. She was going to go mad in this place if she didn't escape soon.

The tower was home to the castle guard. They lived and worked in the bottom levels of the converted prison. Those floors had been full of noise and life as they led her inside. Several men paused their activities to peek at her as she traversed the building, trailing along behind the soldiers who carried the unconscious king.

From what she'd glimpsed during their hurried passage through the halls, they'd renovated the space into something much warmer and more welcoming than the old prison had been. Weapons and armor of all kinds festooned the walls, with detailed scenes of battles painted in the common areas.

But the tower's top floors had been unoccupied for countless years. Despite the thorough cleaning she'd insisted on when they arrived, their room still felt barren and cold, no matter how hot the hearth in the corner blazed.

The room they were in belonged to the former warden. While technically not a prison cell, it was serving the same purpose for her and the king. The door remained locked, and no matter how much she begged and cajoled the men who brought food and drink every few hours, she could convince no one to listen to her pleas for release. They were all steadfast in their commitment to keeping them safe and following Tarquin's orders.

Tarquin...

She shuddered, remembering his treachery. There was no doubt in her mind he'd been involved. Every moment that passed without him appearing to check on her grandfather's condition made her even more positive about his betrayal. She should be out there, finding the proof she needed to implicate him in the king's assassination, not forced into hiding.

Kayda's shoulders drooped. Proving her brother's involvement seemed impossible when she couldn't even convince the guards to let her leave a single room. Why would they listen to her, a mere girl, rather than the prince who'd trained with them daily, year after year?

She scratched her thigh. At the least, they could send her a change of clothes. Her ceremonial dress had not been designed for comfort.

Her attention was drawn to the hearth fire. She itched to summon. She could burn down the door, set fire to anyone who got in her way, and be outside in the fresh air before they knew what hit them.

Kayda tore her gaze off the flames. No. She wouldn't have all those deaths on her conscience. The guards were only doing their jobs. Following the prince's orders was protocol for them, with the king incapacitated. The only person who could override him was her father, but he was probably too busy staring at the bottom of a bottle to even notice she was missing.

She walked away from the window to the cot where her grandfather rested. The guards had sent the castle healer up to examine the king. He'd echoed the mage's assessment, insisting all they could do was wait and hope the king would recover. He ordered her to keep a close eye on him and to call for him if he showed any improvement, but so far, there had been no change.

She let out a shaky breath, looking down at her grandfather's prone form. If only he would wake up...

Her stomach buckled. She couldn't do this alone. She couldn't shake the feeling that she wouldn't be enough to stop Tarquin.

The steady clunk of footsteps sounded in the hall outside. They were muted at first but steadily became louder until they reverberated throughout the silent room and stopped outside the door. The sound of a muffled conversation followed, brief enough that she barely had time to wonder who was speaking before the lock clicked and the door swung open, revealing the familiar face of Izora framed in the doorway.

Kayda raced forward as Izora stepped into the room. They both threw their arms open wide and collided together, clasping each other tightly. After a moment, Kayda pulled free, the soft press of cloth brushing along her back as Izora's arms slid off her.

"I brought you some fresh clothes, Princess." Izora placed a large bag into her arms. "I'm sorry I didn't come earlier. Those fools downstairs wouldn't let me up."

"It's all right." She smiled for what was likely the first time since she'd seen her grandfather's stabbing. "I'm just glad you're here now. I'm going crazy locked up in here, not knowing what's happening."

Kayda carried the bag to the far side of the room, where a second cot had been set up with a curtain dangling down from the ceiling. She pulled the curtain closed, dropped the bag on the bed, and dug through it.

"Tell me what I've missed while I dress." Kayda breathed a sigh of relief as she spied one of her favorite dresses in the bag, along with more clothes and the little tin tinderbox.

"I don't know where to begin. It's been madness." Izora's boots tapped in rhythm as she paced the wooden floor. "Utter and complete madness. There's been rioting in the streets. The guards are spread thin, keeping a constant force around this tower and trying to help the local forces to keep the peace. If the Guard Captain hadn't gone out this morning to help in Southmoat, I don't even know if they would've let me in to see you today."

Kayda frowned as she listened, while shucking off the crimson silk gown and sliding on new undergarments. "I don't understand. Why wouldn't they let you see me from the start? You've been my nurse since the day I was born." She slipped into the simple turquoise frock and fastened the buttons lining the center between her breasts.

"Tarquin's orders, apparently. You and the king are not to be disturbed under any circumstances." Izora punctuated the statement with a derisive snort. "From what I gather, the Guard Captain had to be persuaded to even let the castle healer in. That's how serious he is about following that idiot's orders to the letter."

"Why is the Guard Captain in charge?" She circled the curtain, feeling much lighter in her clean clothes. "Where's Tarquin?"

Izora leaned close and pitched her voice low. "No one's seen him since the feast. He took off in pursuit of the villain who stabbed the king. Left with an entire contingent of the guard and headed east into the forest. None have been back, except for a lone rider bearing a letter for the Guard Captain that detailed the prince's orders."

"Am I to be stuck in here until Tarquin returns?" Kayda turned to her grandfather, praying for the hundredth time he would open his eyes. "I don't know if I can do it, Izora." Her voice broke. "I can't watch him die."

Izora was there in an instant, wrapping her arms around her. Kayda inhaled her familiar floral scent, comfort enveloping her as tears rolled down her face and wetted her nurse's tunic. It had all gone so wrong, so quickly. Her entire life unraveled in an instant as the knife pierced her grandfather's flesh.

In the warm embrace of the only woman she'd ever loved, Kayda let herself feel the pain and loss she'd shoved deep down inside. She grieved for her grandfather. For herself. For the suffering the entire kingdom experienced and she could do nothing to fix. She let the agony surface from deep within her soul where it burned, and she wept.

Izora held her, rubbing her hands tenderly along her back, and said nothing until she ran out of tears. Then Izora broke their embrace but remained close enough to touch. She pulled a finely crafted silk handkerchief out of her skirt pocket and wiped the tears off Kayda's face. "You can handle much more than you give yourself credit for, Kayda. Just like your mother. She had the heart of a warrior, like you. Born of the sand."

Kayda shook her head gently. What was Izora going on about? Her mother was the daughter of traders.

Izora finished wiping away the moisture but kept one dark hand on Kayda's face, tipping her chin up and staring into Kayda's watery eyes. "Don't give up hope for the king. He's strong, too. Just like his granddaughter."

Izora pitched her voice low, speaking in a hushed whisper. "I'm working on getting you out of here. I have a plan, but I don't have all the pieces in place yet." She glanced away, her gaze darting to the window. "I don't know if they'll let me visit you again, so on the day I have all the pieces ready, I'll send you a signal at dusk. You'll see it from your window."

Kayda's heart jumped. She searched Izora's face, backing up a step. Her old nurse was going to sneak her out past a whole building full of guards? It sounded too good to be true. "But how?" she asked, her voice just as quiet.

Izora smiled and tucked the handkerchief back into her pocket. "You didn't think I've spent over fifteen years of my life here without making a few friends and earning a few favors, did you?" Her smile dropped, and her face turned serious. "There's too much for me to tell you right now. Just know I have a few friends within the guard. On the night I send the signal, the door to this chamber will be left unlocked, and you can walk out with no resistance. I'll be waiting for you once you get outside."

She opened her mouth to ask Izora a few more questions, but before she got out a single word, the lock clicked on the door. Kayda snapped her mouth shut as the door swung open and a gruff voice called in, "Time to go."

Izora pulled her in for a last hug goodbye. "I'll see you soon," she said as they parted, then strode out the door.

The door closed behind her with a *click*, and Kayda marched across the room to the window. She caught sight of a hawk, perhaps the same one as before, circling the woods nearby. The lone hunter zeroed in on its prey before plunging down for the kill.

As the bird disappeared into the tree cover, she smiled. A few more days, and she would be out there, too, hunting for Tarquin. She flexed her fingers and stared through the glass as the hawk swooped into sight again with a small bird clutched in its talons.

When the signal came, she would be ready to fly.

Chapter 16

Applause echoed all around Lark, bouncing off the walls inside the modest country inn. She stood next to Aren, their shoulders pressed together, crammed into the corner behind the scores of townspeople who'd gathered to watch the show. He finished plucking the strings of his lute as clapping thundered around them.

Dausius hopped up from his seat. "Thank you. Thank you all. You're too kind." He grinned and squeezed through the crowd to stand beside them. "We'll be back with more entertainment after a quick break."

The applause died down at his announcement, and the crowd thinned. Lark picked her way through the throng to the table the rest of their group shared. She sank down on the hard wooden bench beside Tiora. "I don't think I'll ever get tired of this."

"That's easy for you to say. You don't have to stare down the sharp end of a knife at every performance." She giggled and elbowed Meital, who sat beside her and offered a wobbly grin. "I can't say it's the worst job I've ever held, though."

Lark slung an arm around her shoulder and squeezed gently. The silk of their matching multicolored tunics slid against her wrist. They were full members of the show now, matching outfits and all.

Lark's gaze trailed along the faces in the crowd. Seeing the pure enjoyment on their faces as she sang—there was nothing quite like it. She'd always sought to help others. She'd spent her entire childhood helping her mother as a healer. This was still helping others, in a way, but it was so much more *fun*. And didn't she deserve a little fun in her life after everything she'd been through?

Aren leaned across the table. "Busy in here. I'm gonna grab a drink from the bar. Can I get something for you?"

Lark nodded. "Water would be lovely."

Mazen rose from the bench. "I'll go with you. We can grab a pitcher and some glasses. Maybe some ale to go with it." He grinned.

They left together, leaving her with Tiora and Meital. Dausius was a few tables away, chatting merrily with some townspeople.

"Rot and decay," Meital muttered.

Lark turned to her, raising a brow. Meital stared at a pair of young men headed their way. It seemed a table of three young women alone was easily interpreted as an open invitation. Aren and Mazen hadn't even worked their way through the crowd to the bar before the strangers descended on them.

The larger of the two, a beefy fellow with straw-colored hair, spoke first. His gaze zeroed in on Tiora, and he licked his lips like a glutton staring down a delicious morsel. "It's been a long while since our little town has had any ladies so fetching as you three."

Tiora dropped her gaze to her lap, her shoulders tensing. Lark's eyes widened, and she tried to think of something clever to say. Something pleasant and innocuous that would send them on their way.

"You're too kind, sir," Meital said smoothly. "But I'm afraid we're all spoken for."

Lark nodded in agreement, but one look in the man's glassy brown eyes had her stomach sinking.

"Is that so?" He wobbled a bit before leaning closer, a flagon of ale clutched in his left hand. "I don't see any rings."

Meital smiled and flicked her long brown braid over her shoulder as she reached behind her back. Her hand slid back into sight with a blade resting across her knuckles. "Look again."

The man's companion's freckled arm shot out, gripping his shoulder, his brown eyes wide. "Shouldn't we be getting ba—"

The big man shrugged off his friend's hold and leaned closer, trying to catch Tiora's eye. "What about you? Where's your ring, beautiful?" The ale on his breath wafted across the table and sent a prickle of revulsion up Lark's throat.

Tiora twisted her hands in her lap, her gaze flicking up and back down.

Meital didn't wait for her answer. She stabbed her blade into the wooden table directly in front of the man. Her voice was a dagger drenched in honey, sickly sweet and deadly sharp. "Here it is. Would you like to see the rest?" Another blade appeared in her hand, flashing silver. "I'd love to show them to you up close."

Dausius rushed up to the big man's side with a wide grin. "Fellas, have a drink on me, hmm? Let's go grab a round at the bar." He twirled the pair and launched into a story, his voice pitched low as he ushered them away from their table.

"You certainly have a way with words, Meital." Lark grinned.

Meital shrugged, making her blades vanish as quickly as they'd appeared. "I guess you could say so." She nudged Tiora with her elbow. "You all right, Ti?"

Tiora nodded, offering a smile that didn't quite reach her eyes. "Yeah, thanks."

Lark gave Tiora's hand a gentle squeeze. Would things ever be normal again for the two of them? Times like these, normal seemed so close and yet so far all at the same time.

Soon Aren and Mazen returned with drinks. They spent a pleasant quarter hour chatting and laughing. The room buzzed with merriment, and some of the villagers stopped by with a kind word or the occasional tip.

Then Dausius joined them with an indulgent smile and a wink for the twins. "I was ready to regale the crowd with a tale, but I'm afraid I need a rest after handling that mess. You're up next."

Mazen splayed a palm on his chest with a laugh, brown eyes twinkling. "Don't look at me, Daus. I wasn't even here."

Meital stood, her lips curling into a smirk. "I was getting bored, anyway. C'mon, Ti."

Lark settled back to watch as the twin's knives sailed through the air. The crowd curled back, giving them room at the front of the building, none eager to stand too close to the sharp blades.

As the room quieted and all eyes fell upon the trio, Lark couldn't help but overhear a pair of voices talking quietly behind her between the *oohs* and *aahs*.

"Haven't you heard? The king's been stabbed," declared a woman, her voice raspy and tinged with sadness.

Lark's heart skipped a beat. Not King Quinton?

"No. Surely that's only a rumor?" replied a man.

"I heard it straight from my cousin in Flamesmoat," the woman continued. "He was there at the Harvest Festival when it happened. He saw it all with his own eyes."

"Did they catch who did it?" the man asked.

"No. It's such a shame." She *tsked* softly.

Lark leaned forward in her seat and rubbed her temple. Aren reached across the table, grabbing her glass and refilling it from the water pitcher. He quirked a brow. "Something wrong?"

The twins chose that moment to pull off their final trick, and the crowd roared with applause. Lark sent Aren a small smile and shook her head. Now was not the time. She'd share what she'd overheard with the group later.

Lark plopped down beside Sunny atop a pile of hay in the barn behind the inn. Dawn was not far off. They'd just wrapped up their last performances for the night, leaving a crowd still buzzing with excitement and a portly innkeeper grinning with undisguised glee.

She groaned. "I feel like I could sleep for a week."

Tiora sank down beside her and yawned. "Me, too."

Dausius stuck his head in the horse stall. "Have a good long rest, girls, you earned it." His beaded hair tinkled gently as he swung around and raised his voice. "That goes for all of you. I've arranged it so we can stay and play one more night at this inn before moving on."

Lark hopped up and caught Dausius at the door before he disappeared into another stall to rest. "Wait. I overheard some news in there. They're saying the King of Dracwood's been stabbed."

Aren whirled around, his eyes widening. He abandoned his efforts to tend to the birds and strode closer. "The king's been stabbed? Are you sure?"

Dausius frowned. "I heard much the same, I'm afraid. From what I gather, he's been locked away since it happened, with no word on his fate."

Mazen's hand stilled as he brushed down one of the horses. "What does that mean for us?"

"I imagine once the news spreads, there'll be even more folks in need of entertaining." Dausius' gaze flicked over them all. "We've an important job to do, my friends. It's not all fun and games. People need folk like us more than ever in such trying times." He smiled. "Get some sleep. We're back at it again tomorrow night." Then he disappeared into a stall, closing the door behind him.

Lark slid the door to their stall closed, joining Tiora and Sunny atop the fragrant hay pile. She closed her eyes, her fingers tangling in the soft golden fur on Sunny's back.

Dausius was right. They were doing important work. Not as important as healing, but useful just the same.

Lark sighed. Was it so bad for her to take a few months of her life to enjoy traveling the world with these amazing people, learning new skills and bringing smiles to people's faces? There would still be time for her to become a mage. She hadn't forgotten about her calling. She would receive the training she needed one day. But did it have to be now?

She kept telling herself it would be all right. That she'd earned the right to a little pleasure in her life after all the hardship she'd been forced to endure. She'd lost everything. The father she'd never met. Her mother and brother. Her home.

She snuggled closer to Sunny, holding tight to the last physical remnant of her former life. No matter what else happened, she could never go back. She'd never again feel her mother's warm embrace or hear Conall's laughter. The memory of all she'd lost still haunted her, especially in quiet moments like this.

Was it wrong to grab the one thing in her life that brought her joy? The Wandering Bards might not be changing the world, but they weren't hurting it either. And she couldn't discount the role they'd played in saving her and Tiora. Didn't she owe it to them to at least help with the performances until they reached Mage Keep?

It couldn't hurt to spend some time getting to know this incredible group of people. Deep down, she knew a few months spent on the road living the life of a traveling entertainer was no crime. But a small part of her kept nagging her to give up this foolish dream and become a mage like she'd always envisioned.

Lark forced the questions aside as sleep dulled her thoughts. She fell asleep with the memory of applause echoing in her ears and a smile on her face.

Chapter 17

The sun sank behind the tallest trees to the west. Conall dragged his feet, his pace slowing. "I think we ought to find a place to camp soon."

"Sure. Maybe we can find a stream or a river. I've been sweating like crazy." Ereni tugged the neck of her brown tunic.

The day had been particularly hot. One of those early fall days that hung onto the remnants of summer. He would kill to submerge himself in a river or to splash some cool water over his face and neck.

"Any sign of a river nearby?" he asked, careful not to show any sign of his silent communication on his face.

Conall still hadn't told Ereni about his bond. He couldn't think of the words to explain without sounding crazy. And every day that passed without him bringing it up, the more it built up in his mind, like a snowball let loose to roll down a hill, gaining mass with every rotation. Would she believe him when he told her? Or would she be angry he hadn't mentioned it from the start?

"No, but there's something else," Shadow replied. He was a few paces ahead of them on the trail, just out of sight. *"A town."*

Ereni gasped. She'd spotted a signpost sticking out of the trail with an arrow leading down a well-worn footpath to the north. "It's even better than a river." She smiled, standing on tiptoe and peering between the trees. "We can stay the night at an inn."

Conall rubbed the back of his neck. "I don't know. What if they don't allow pets?"

Ereni shrugged. "Then we'll sneak him in." She tugged his elbow, towing him toward the footpath. "C'mon, it's been nearly a week since we left Greenvale. I'm dying for a bath and a proper bed, aren't you?"

Well, it would be a shame to pass up a good night's rest and a chance to clean up. He grinned, keeping pace with Ereni down the trail. "C'mon, Shadow," he called over his shoulder.

"We're going to spend the night indoors for a change," he added through the bond.

"Do you think that's wise?"

"Just stick close to me. We'll say you're my hound."

Shadow snorted, catching up to them on the path.

"It worked with Ereni," Conall added. *"And she'll be there to back me up."*

Shadow made no other complaint, so he let the matter drop. They'd be all right. What's the worst that could happen? They'd be asked to leave and have to spend another night camped outdoors?

The little town nestled in a large clearing in the middle of the woods. A handful of wooden houses rested alongside an empty building that vaguely resembled the Church of the Dragon in Flamesmoat—only on a much smaller scale—and a large wood and brick inn and stable.

They turned straight for the inn, ignoring the stares of the few people who ambled about on the neatly swept dirt streets. As they approached, they were met with a lovely sound spilling out from behind the inn's walls. One he vaguely recognized.

"Is that a lute?"

"Sounds like it." Ereni grinned. "What luck! I hope you're not too tired for a dance or two." She winked, sweeping past him and shoving open the door.

He held back the frown that threatened to spread at her request. He'd never been much of a dancer. Then the image of her smiling in his arms, cheeks flushed as they took a turn on the floor, rose in his mind, and he shrugged. He could probably stand a dance or two.

Conall followed her inside. The room was so packed he couldn't even see the musician through the crush of people dancing. Live music must be as much of a draw for the people of this village as it was back in Greenvale.

Fresh stew bubbled on the hearth, filling the air with a delicious aroma. Conall breathed deep and followed close on Ereni's heels as she slipped through the throng, headed for the bar. Shadow walked by his side, eliciting a few gasps and wide-eyed glances from those he passed.

Ereni slapped a handful of coins on the bar. That was enough to grab the innkeeper's attention. "We'd like rooms for the night, please. And some of that stew you have boiling."

The innkeeper leaned over, his bald head glistening with sweat. "We've plenty stew for ya, but I'm afraid I've only one room to let tonight."

Conall's stomach sank. Only one room?

Ereni glanced at him briefly. "We'll take it."

The innkeeper nodded, pocketing the coins. "Will ya be wanting the stew brought up to the room, or will ya be eating down here?"

"Oh, I think we'll stay and enjoy the music while we eat," she said.

Just then, the lutist began to sing. Conall grimaced. Ereni shot him a look, then grabbed the innkeeper's sleeve before he bustled off. "On second thought, we'll eat in the room."

The innkeeper laughed. A hearty belly rumble that sent his jowls jiggling. "I understand. Too bad ya weren't here a few days past. We had a full show in here. Let me tell you what, that lass could sing circles around this fellow." He chuckled once more, rounding the bar. "Follow me, then. I'll show ya to your room."

The innkeeper caught sight of Shadow and gasped. "Blazes. I didn't see your—dog standing there." He backed away warily. "Don't think I can house him in the stable. The horses wouldn't like it."

Conall stepped forward, pulling a coin from his belt pouch. "He can stay with us in the room. He's house trained."

The innkeeper frowned but accepted the coin, then turned aside with a nod. "All right, but damages will be extra."

He led them up a wooden staircase to the third floor. The door swung open to reveal an attic room with two large windows hanging open on opposite walls to let in a cross breeze. A large bed sat in the center, the only piece of furniture except for a single chair and a tiny table tucked into the far corner.

They crowded inside. Shadow curled up beside an open window. *"Awful cozy in here. Sure you don't want me to meet you outside of town in the morning?"*

And be alone with Ereni and that single bed... What would she say, if he sent Shadow away? *"No, stay."* Conall ducked his head to avoid bashing it on the low roof.

"I'll send up a girl with the stew. Enjoy." The innkeeper spun on his heel to leave.

"Wait." Ereni stopped him with a hand on his sleeve.

Conall drew in a breath. Was she about to call off the whole thing? They couldn't spend the night together in this tiny room, could they?

But she smiled, another coin winking in her fist. "Where can a lady get a bath in this town?"

The innkeeper frowned. "You'll be needing much more coin for that here, my dear. We've only got the one well. How about a bowl of hot water and a washcloth? I'll have the maid set up a screen for privacy."

Ereni sighed. "I suppose that will do. Thank you, sir." She tossed him the coin, and then he was gone, closing the door behind him.

Conall shucked off his bag and sank down on the bed. "Are you sure you're all right sharing a room? Shadow and I can camp outside."

She waved a hand and pulled off her bag, settling down beside him. "It's not a problem. We've been camping together for days. All that's different is we're indoors." She shrugged. "We're not even really alone. Shadow's here with us."

Conall nodded. Seems he'd been right to ask Shadow to stay with them. He couldn't argue with her logic. Still, he had to admit to being flustered, knowing she wasn't the least bit uncomfortable sharing a bed with him. There were times the last few days when he could've sworn she was flirting. There'd been countless little quips and side-eyed glances. And now this. Was she happy to allow it because she knew nothing would happen, or was she hoping something *would* happen?

There was a knock at the door. A trio of maids piled in. The first two carried trays. One held two bowls of fragrant stew, and the second, two bowls of steaming water. The last carted a slatted wooden screen and an armful of towels. They settled the bowls on the table and the towels on the chair, unfolded the screen, and left.

No sooner had the door closed than Ereni hopped up off the bed with her pack. She grabbed a bowl of stew and handed it to him. "Here, eat. I'm going to clean up first."

She disappeared behind the screen, leaving him alone on the bed, trying his best not to picture what she was doing back there.

The screen did its job. He couldn't see a thing behind it except for the top of her head peeking out above it. But he could hear everything. The *thud* of her boots hitting the floor. The gentle *pop* of buttons being unfastened.

Food. He scooped up a bite of stew and stuffed it into his mouth. The sound of his chewing dampened some of the noise distracting him.

"Mighty hungry tonight, I see." Shadow's voice sounded amused. *"Careful you don't choke."*

Conall glared at him, not bothering to respond.

He kept shoveling in bite after bite, chewing methodically. But though he was hungrier than he'd been in ages after a full day of walking, the stew sat like a stone in his stomach. As the splash of water sounded behind the screen, he strode across the room to the window.

He placed the bowl on the floor beside Shadow. *"Here, you can have the rest."*

"What are you doing?" Ereni called out from behind the screen. Her voice sounded a bit off. Breathless.

"Nothing." He returned to his spot on the edge of the bed. "I was just passing Shadow the last of my stew."

"Oh." Water splashed again. She was dipping the washcloth back in the bowl. Then came the gentle dribble as she rang it out. Next, she'd be sliding it across her skin. "You like it?"

Conall's heart skittered. "Huh?"

"The stew. How's it taste?"

"It was fine." He tugged the neck of his tunic. "Hot."

He caught movement in the corner of his eye. Her bare arm snaked out from behind the screen to grab a towel off the chair.

He exhaled slowly. At least that was over. The light in the room was dim, the sun well on its way to being fully set. Soon they would be sleeping, then back on the road again in the morning. Back to normal.

A moment later, she reappeared and lifted her bowl of stew off the table. She wore a fresh change of clothes. Brown trousers and tan tunic, the long sleeves rolled up to her elbow, her feet bare.

The bed sank as she settled beside him cross-legged and scooped up a bite of stew. She paused with the bite halfway to her lips. "Go on." She nodded to the screen. "Your turn."

Conall gulped. He'd forgotten he'd be expected to wash up as well. He stood, keeping his neck bent to avoid smacking his head on the ceiling, and rounded the screen.

He grabbed the second bowl of water. The wood vessel warmed his hands as he settled it on the floor beside him. Then he cast his gaze about for a washcloth.

"Where did you find the washcloth?" he asked.

"It was atop the pile of towels. I think they only brought the one. I hung it on the screen for you."

Conall gulped again and lifted the damp square of fabric. He tried not to picture where it had just been. Sliding across her skin. Everywhere on her skin. He closed his eyes and exhaled.

He had to get this over with. Fast. He tore off his clothes and got to work, scrubbing his skin with the cloth. Surely, he'd never washed as quickly in his entire life. Within a few moments, he reached out to grab the towel off the chair. Then his stomach sank.

Shit. His bag. He'd left it sitting on the floor beside the bed. He eyed the sweaty pile of clothes he'd just shucked off.

He sighed and wrapped the towel around his waist. "Ereni, could you do me a favor?"

"Depends what you're asking," she replied. Was it his imagination, or did her voice sound different again? Deeper, almost husky.

"I left my bag on the floor. Could you hand it to me?" He stuck his arm out the side of the screen, his hand open. He listened to the soft tap of her bare feet on the wood. Then came the slide of cloth on his hand as she settled the strap against his palm. "Thanks," he said, his voice a hoarse whisper.

He waited for the sound of her footsteps to retreat before he dropped the towel and dug out a change of clothes. It was nearly fully dark now in the little room. He slid out from behind the screen and took careful steps on the wooden boards until his toes tapped the bottom of the mattress.

He sank down on the edge, sitting upright on the side. "Maybe I should sleep on the floor. I've got my bedroll."

Silence greeted his statement. Then movement on the mattress. "Don't be silly," Ereni said, finally. "There's plenty of room. I scooted over for you."

"All right." He laid down stiffly, keeping close to the edge. If she was fine, then so was he. They were both adults. Fully clothed. No reason this had to be awkward. They were only going to sleep.

He smiled as his head sank into the plush pillow. It was much nicer than the hard ground beneath his bedroll. He closed his eyes, his muscles relaxing as his breathing slowed.

"Conall?"

His eyes shot open in the dark. "Yeah?"

"Sorry, were you sleeping?" The bed shifted as Ereni turned. Her breath wafted against his face.

"No." What could she want from him now? Together in bed. In the dark.

"I thought you might like to hear another story about Mage Keep."

"Oh." Of course, that was all. But he couldn't stand the thought of her whispering voice sliding across his ear. He shook his head. "Can you tell me in the morning?"

"Sure." She shifted again, turning away.

He sighed and closed his eyes again.

"Can I ask you something?"

His eyes popped back open. "Hmm? Sure."

"What will you do after you find your sister?"

He slid an arm behind his neck. "Go back to Greenvale, I suppose. Rebuild the farm. Marry eventually and have a few kids. I know it's not as exciting as traveling the world and all that, but it's what I've always planned."

"No, it sounds lovely." She sighed. For a moment he was sure she'd ask him more, but then she said, "Goodnight, Conall."

"Goodnight."

He took a deep breath, trying to find the peace he needed to slip off into sleep. But though the bed was soft against his back, and Ereni remained on her side of the mattress, he couldn't stop his thoughts from turning over in his mind.

Why was she so curious about his future? Did she want something more from him? He couldn't help but wonder if she felt even a tiny sliver of the attraction he felt for her. If he reached across the bed and touched her, would she recoil? Or would she welcome his embrace?

As he listened to the soft sound of her breathing, he realized it was not a question he would answer tonight. Finally, his thoughts slowed, and sleep found him.

He awoke sprawled out on his side on the edge of the bed with a warm weight pressed against his back. He looked down and spotted an arm wrapped around his waist, the fingers slack. Ereni. He sucked in a breath, and her fingertips grazed his shirt, pressing gently against his skin.

What was she doing? Had she rolled against him as she slept? He should slip out of bed. Get ready for the day. But as the soft rise and fall of her chest pressed against his back, he closed his eyes and lay still. His skin tingled as the warm wash of her breath glided across the back of his neck.

Another moment, and he'd get up. Just one more moment.

Ereni stiffened behind him. Her hand slid off his waist, and she rolled away. Then the bed rose, and her feet tapped on the floor.

He lay still, his eyes closed, trying not to let the fact that she'd immediately gotten up bother him. He'd let her think he was still sleeping. That he hadn't awoken and caught her holding onto him and then just remained there like a fool.

After a moment, he stretched and made a show of yawning, long and deep. "Good morning."

"Good morning." She sat on the single chair, lacing up her boots. "Let's see if they have some breakfast downstairs before we hit the trail." She smiled.

He sat up. Nodded. He grabbed his boots and shook off the last vestiges of the attraction that lingered in his mind. He could tell by her actions this morning nothing was going to happen between them. When she'd awakened to find her arm draped over him, she couldn't bolt up fast enough.

In the cold light of day, he had to face the facts. Ereni was just a girl he'd met on the road. After they made it to Mage Keep, he'd probably never see her again. He had to stop imagining feelings from her that didn't exist.

"All right," he said. "Let's go."

Chapter 18

The light of dawn spilled in through the high tower window. Kayda rubbed the sleep from her eyes. Her gaze was immediately drawn to the bed where her grandfather rested.

She crept across the cool stone floor. Her chest ached as she stared down at his prone form. It was five days now since he'd been stabbed. Five whole days of him lying unmoving on the lonely cot. How much longer could he last without food and water? She knew the answer to that question—she wished she didn't.

Her chin quivered, and she turned aside to cross the room to the cold hearth. She crouched down and poked at the coals, then threw more wood on the pile and coaxed the flames back to life.

She settled down beside the fire. She might as well spend some time practicing. It would be a shame to lose all the progress she'd made training with Izora. And at least it would give her something else to concentrate on, besides her poor grandfather.

Reaching out her hand, she took a deep breath. She emptied her mind. Pictured the flames taking shape before her eyes. A wave of cold spread across her skin as her talent responded, and the fire materialized in the air, floating at eye level. She made the flame grow. She made it dance. Sent it to the ceiling and flying across the room.

Then Kayda glimpsed movement out of the corner of her eye. The flame disappeared, and she gasped.

It was the king, sitting upright in bed. She raced over.

"Grandfather?" She crouched down in front of him and stared into his cloudy eyes. "Grandfather, you're awake." She sat next to him on the bed and took him into her arms, squeezing him tightly.

Yes! He was awake. He was finally awake. Her heart soared, so full of relief she almost squealed aloud. All those days and nights waiting—he'd finally pulled through.

But something was wrong. He didn't return her embrace. She loosened her arms, peeking up into his face. He stared at the ceiling, his eyes glassy and unfocused.

"Grandfather?" She gripped his shoulder and shook gently. "Grandfather!" She shook a little harder. "Grandfather, please, say something." He didn't respond. Tears pooled in the corners of her eyes.

The healer. She would call for the castle healer. He'd know what to do.

She rose from the bed and strode to the door. She slid her fingers against the knob. It didn't move. Damn. For a moment, she'd forgotten she was a prisoner in this blazing room.

She banged on the door instead. "Help us. We need the healer. The king is awake."

Footsteps sounded in the hall outside. The door opened, revealing the face of one of the guards who'd been bringing food and drink every few hours. He stuck his head inside, his eyes wide as he caught sight of the king sitting upright on the cot.

"What are you doing, man? Call for the healer," Kayda demanded.

The guard nodded and slammed the door shut without a word. The lock *clicked*. Kayda rubbed a hand down her face. It was too much to hope he'd be lax and leave it unlocked.

How long would they be? She prayed the healer would come soon and break her grandfather out of this stupor. She wrung her hands, returning to his side.

He must be starving. And thirsty. She rushed across the room and grabbed the pitcher of water she'd been left last night. Water trickled into the wooden cup as she poured. She lifted it with a shaky hand and returned to her grandfather's side.

Could he even drink in this state? There was only one way to find out.

She raised the cup to his lips. "Here, Grandfather. I brought you some water," she whispered, tilting the cup toward him. For a moment, she was certain nothing would happen. That the water would come spilling out the side of the cup, wetting his face and neck. But when the cup brushed against his lips, he opened his mouth and drank.

Kayda smiled gently. If he was drinking, then there was hope. He would live. They could nourish his body and give his mind the time it needed to heal completely.

Soon, he'd drained the cup. She returned to the table and lifted a half loaf of bread left over from last night's dinner. The crust crunched beneath her fingers. It might be a little stale, but it would do until she could call for something fresh.

She walked back to the cot, broke a tiny chunk off the loaf, and lifted it to her grandfather's lips. He opened his mouth dutifully, like a baby bird ready to be fed. She watched his throat work as he chewed and swallowed.

"It's all right, Grandfather. The healer will be here soon, and we'll get you all fixed up." She patted his hand where it rested, slack in his lap, and kept feeding him.

The castle healer arrived as she was feeding the last bite to her grandfather. His dark cloak billowed around him as he slipped into the room and shut the door behind him, a wide smile on his weathered face.

"Sire, it's good to see you awake." He strode across the room before he noted Quinton's blank stare. When he did, the smile fell from his face. "Has His Grace spoken yet?"

Kayda shook her head. "He's been like this since he woke. He'll eat and drink if you feed him, but he hasn't said a word. He just keeps staring. Do you know what's wrong with him?"

"Hmm. I'm not sure. We'll figure it out. Don't fret." He set his bag down and leaned over, examining the king with his shrewd gaze.

The door opened again, revealing the Guard Captain. The hulking man barreled in, his dark brow dampened with sweat. He slammed the door behind him, shoving his lanky brown hair out of his eyes. "I heard the news. The king lives?"

Kayda rose to her feet and met the Guard Captain in the center of the room. "He's awake, yes. Eating and drinking. Perhaps now we can return to Kings Keep? I'm sure the king would recover much faster in his own bed."

The captain's brow furrowed, and his gaze fell to the ground. "I'm afraid I can't allow it, Princess. Not without orders." He met her eyes. "But now that the king has awakened, we will of course follow his wishes to the letter."

"I'm afraid that won't be happening today," the healer stated, not looking up from his examination. "The king is not yet speaking."

The Guard Captain grimaced. "Well, then I'm bound by duty to keep you here under my protection." He turned to leave.

"Wait." Kayda grabbed his sleeve. "My father. Did you call for him like I asked?"

The captain spun to face her, his eyes hard. "Prince Gideon has not answered. He's been holed up in his rooms since the king's attack." His face softened. "I'm sorry, Princess."

Kayda sighed. Was it too much to ask for her father to take even a tiny smidge of responsibility? Even in the face of the king being attacked? Her heart sank as she realized she would remain a prisoner in the tower, even now, after the king had awakened.

Her gaze slipped to the window as the Guard Captain left the room. At least she still had Izora to count on. And now that her grandfather had awakened, she could be sure she'd not be leaving him here to die all alone when she escaped.

She turned back to the cot. The healer gathered his bag and stood.

"You can't be leaving already?" Her voice rose on the final word. She clutched her chest. "Can't you fix him?"

"My lady, I will try. I must go retrieve some more things from my chambers. Take heart, my dear. This is a good sign. The king lives." He sent her a small smile and retreated from the chamber, leaving her alone again with the silent king.

Kayda sank back on the cot beside her grandfather. She lifted his hand from his lap and gave it a gentle squeeze. "Grandfather, can you hear me?" she asked gently. "Please, I need you to come back. I need your help. I can't do this all on my own."

Her words had no effect. Her grandfather stared, unfocused, at the wall.

She laid her head on his shoulder and smiled. It would be all right. He was alive. At least he was alive.

Chapter 19

F ire crackled, shooting sparks into the night sky. Conall basked in the campfire's warmth, his belly full and feet aching slightly from the day's exertion.

A *crunch* sounded beside him. Shadow was busy with the bones of their latest kill, cracking them open to suck the marrow from inside.

Conall's eyelids drooped. He yawned as he relaxed on his bedroll and watched the stars winking in the sky through a hole in the forest canopy, which shone with fall colors splashed among the green leaves.

A feminine moan made his eyes shoot open. Ereni was seated opposite him with the fire between them. Her fingertips kneaded the bottom of her bare left foot. One sturdy boot sat next to her, standing straight up and empty with a long, tan sock folded neatly atop it.

Conall heard something strange in his mind. *"Did you just snicker at me?"* he asked Shadow.

"Told you." Shadow glanced at him, then his gaze changed direction, his long snout pointing across the fire. *"This proves it."*

"Don't be ridiculous." He shot his bondmate a sideways glare.

Shadow kept trying to convince him Ereni was interested in him. But he couldn't be right. If anything was going to happen between them, surely it would've happened back in that little inn.

He glanced across the fire again. She still held one slender foot in her hand, her half-lidded eyes staring off into the darkened trees surrounding the small clearing they'd stopped in for the night.

"She's not even looking at me."

The thought had barely escaped his mind before she moaned again. Her eyelids lifted lazily, blue eyes connecting with his own. Her slack mouth curved upward in a smile of pleasure.

Conall gulped.

Shadow snickered again. *"You still have a lot to learn."* He rose from his spot, arching his back and stretching his muscles before standing fully. *"I'm off to hunt."* He disappeared into the darkened trees.

Ereni's fingers stilled. She dropped her naked foot to the ground and stretched out her booted right leg to roll up her trousers. "So, are you going to sleep while Shadow hunts? Or would you like to hear another story about Mage Keep?"

Ereni had been true to her word. She'd told him much about the keep in the time they'd traveled together. Her stories of growing up with the mages did a great deal to ease his misgivings about his sister joining their ranks.

She clearly looked back on her childhood fondly, regaling him with tales of pranks she and the other children pulled on the mages that had him laughing and blushing despite himself. And according to her, the mages took it all in stride. She described them like one big family, all taking great pride in molding the next generation of mages.

The *clunk* of a boot hitting the ground broke his train of thought. He gazed back across the fire and watched her pull the sock from her leg slowly. Well... he definitely wasn't tired now. "What story do you have for me tonight?"

"I think I've told you all the good ones from when I was a child. Would you like to hear about how I became a seer for Mage Keep?"

"Sure."

The sock was off now. She folded it methodically and placed it neatly atop her boot then stood both boots next to each other before she spoke. "I'm sure you know magic talent is inherited. In most families, it skips a generation. Sometimes even two. But some families, like mine, are blessed with magic that doesn't skip."

Ereni folded her leg, readying her fingers to perform the same action on the bottom of her right foot. Then she seemed to change her mind. She stretched out both of her feet instead and wiggled her toes near the fire.

"It was always assumed I would grow into my powers one day. What I didn't realize was I had been born with a special talent. One so rare that even at Mage Keep no one recognized it until a chance encounter when I was eight years old."

Conall's interest was piqued. He tore his gaze from her delicate little toes and looked at her face.

Ereni stared at the fire, her features relaxed.

What talent could be so rare?

"I'd spent my whole life knowing I was different. Destined for greatness, if you will. I thought what I saw, all mages could see. I mean, why wouldn't I?" She scoffed, shaking her head gently. "Really, it was like spending your whole life viewing a world full of color, only to one day discover the rest of the world could only see in black and white."

"I'm not sure I follow..."

She glanced at him, a lopsided smile crossing her face before she stared back into the flames. "Sorry, it's a little hard to explain. For me, when I look at someone with talent, I can see something—a glow."

Conall's stomach clenched. She could see talent?

"My whole life at Mage Keep, I always knew who'd inherited talent and who'd been skipped. But I didn't realize it was anything special." She stared at the fire, leaning back on her bedroll. "Until one day, we had a special visitor come to the keep. King Quinton. My mother introduced me, and I asked her why he glowed red, and not blue."

Her stare bored into his, and she lifted a brow. "We've been traveling together for weeks. Were you ever planning to tell me?"

Conall sat up and rubbed the back of his neck, grinning sheepishly. "I haven't told anyone yet... I'm still trying to wrap my head around it myself, actually."

Her brows lowered, but she didn't smile, only stared back at him with a flat expression.

"So, you've known this whole time? When I walked into the inn that day back in Greenvale—you saw me glowing red?"

She gazed at the fire again. "Yes, and no... Shadow glows red." Her blue eyes connected with his once more. "You glow purple."

He quickly connected the dots. "Red and blue... you're telling me I can summon?" His gaze dropped to the forest floor, his brow furrowing. It made sense, in a way. His grandmother had been talented. His sister was talented. But the revelation still crashed around him like a shock wave. "I can summon," he repeated. His mouth went dry, and he shook his head slowly.

Ereni stood and walked toward him, her bare feet leaving prints behind in the loose soil. She lowered herself and sat in front of him on his bedroll, folding her feet to the side, resting an elbow on her thigh.

She lifted her ponytail off her chest and tossed her long brown tresses over her shoulder, drawing his gaze to her tunic.

His heart picked up speed. The top three buttons were undone, revealing the creamy skin beneath.

"There's something else you need to know about being a mage."

Conall sucked in a breath, lifting his gaze from that enticing bit of flesh to look into her eyes. She was so close. His fingers itched to touch her. Was Shadow right? Did she want him to touch her?

"What should I know?" he asked, his lips parting.

She dropped her gaze to the bedroll. "Since talent is inherited, we're all strongly encouraged to have children before we become full-fledged mages." She took a deep breath, her breasts lifting.

He fought to pull his attention away from her chest as the meaning of her words struck him. Her eyes drifted back to his, her gaze earnest. He gulped.

"I've always thought I would be one of the few who took my vows without a child. But now…"

Conall's mind raced. Shadow was right! But she didn't just want a quick diversion in the woods. She wanted a child. With him. He'd always pictured his future with children, but this was so sudden. Blazes. They'd never even kissed. He gulped again.

"Tell me, what are you thinking?" Her eyes darted back and forth across his face.

There she was, vulnerable, open, willing to share her life story with him. In the weeks they'd spent together, he'd grown to care for her. She'd done a great deal to banish the loneliness that plagued him when he thought of his family. She was sweet and funny. Beautiful. He'd never considered himself an impulsive man, but as gazed into her eyes, he made the decision instantly.

"Brother, can you find somewhere else to sleep tonight?"

The snickering was back, louder than before. *"Already done, little brother."*

Conall reached across his bedroll and pulled Ereni into his arms.

A yawn stretched Conall's face, but he didn't let it slow his pace through the dense forest. Despite averaging less sleep the last few nights—which he didn't regret in the least—they'd kept on schedule during their days of traveling and almost made it to Mage Keep. Shadow was somewhere up ahead, scouting. He expected to hear him announce through their bond at any moment that he'd sighted their destination.

Conall pushed a breath out through his teeth. He should be ecstatic right now. He was on the cusp of finding Lark and finally setting his mind at ease. She would be safe and happy, thrilled to see him. And now that he knew about his own talent, he might even do more than stop for a visit. He might have cause to stay.

Perhaps that was what had his stomach quivering nervously as they approached. It was a lot to consider. Unlike Lark, he hadn't spent years of his life dreaming of becoming a mage. He always had simpler dreams for himself. Settling down on the farm. Maybe a wife and children, one day.

He'd certainly complicated matters in that regard. His gaze drifted to Ereni as she strode beside him, her pale cheeks pink from exertion. He sighed, then found himself smiling. He could get used to complicated.

She caught him staring and sent a grin in his direction. With her eyes lifted from the forest floor, she didn't see the root sticking up that tried to send her tumbling to the ground. Conall caught her elbow and steadied her.

"Thanks." She straightened her brown tunic after planting both her feet firmly on the ground. "Do you mind if we took a break, just for a moment?"

"All right." He spied a large rock to the left of where they stood. He seated himself upon it, patting the smooth stone beside him in invitation.

Ereni settled beside him. "You know, I always thought I kept a pretty fast pace, but you and Shadow are a challenge to keep up with."

"Sorry." He frowned. "You should've said something earlier. We could've slowed down."

The smile never left her face as she reached for her waterskin. "Oh, I'm not complaining. It just reminded me of something..." She lifted the skin to her mouth and took a long drink.

"What's that?" He admired the graceful curve of her neck as she swallowed.

She finished her drink and reattached the skin to her belt. "I read a book, once, about bonding magic. Did you know bonds don't just let you hear each other's thoughts? You share certain physical attributes as well."

"Really?" His mouth dropped open. "That's incredible."

"I'll have to see if I can find it again in the keep library. There was a chart in it that listed all the different enhancements bonding pairs had reported." Her gaze lifted skyward, her head tilting sideways. "I can't remember them all, but I remember each animal brought unique skills to the bond."

"Do you remember what skills wolves enhance?"

"I'm pretty sure sense of smell was one of them. And increased stamina."

Enhanced sense of smell? He couldn't recall noticing anything different with his nose lately. As for the second thing she'd listed. "Well, that explains a few things." He smiled at her mischievously.

She laughed and poked his side with her elbow. "That's what made me remember. You certainly have the stamina part." She grinned shamelessly. "You know what else is great, too?"

"What?"

"The skill humans bring to a bond is always the same. The bonding animal's lifespan is lengthened significantly. Doubled in most cases."

"Really? That's great news."

It had crossed his mind that wolves had much shorter lifespans than humans. Doubling Shadow's years still wouldn't give them as much time together as if he were human, but he would take whatever he could get.

It was strange to think they'd only been together for a few short months. Shadow was already such an integral part of his life. The thought of one day going on without him... He shook his head. He didn't even like to think about it.

"You all right?" Ereni asked, gazing at him closely.

He forced the thought away and sent her a smile. "Yeah. You rested enough?"

"Yes, I'm ready." She rose from the rock and held out a hand to help him to his feet. He took it, his fingers tingling as they slid across the soft silk of her wrist. He stood but didn't release her hand and pulled her close.

Her blue eyes fluttered closed as she tilted her head upward. Conall drew in a breath through his nose, concentrating on the gentle aroma he could sense surrounding her.

They drew closer. Her breath warmed his skin. Was that lavender in her hair? His lips curved into a tiny smile as they brushed her petal-soft lips. Maybe that whole enhanced sense of smell was working. Her tongue collided with his own then, and all thoughts of magic fled his mind.

Shadow interrupted the haze of desire swirling inside him a moment later. *I found it. Mage Keep is not far ahead.*

Conall broke the kiss and stepped back, putting distance between them. "Shadow says the Keep is just ahead." He tugged his sleeves, composing himself.

Conall, something seems off about this place... Hurry.

His eyes widened as he received Shadow's warning.

Ereni didn't miss his change of expression. "What is it?" she asked, already in motion, heading for the Keep.

"I'm not sure. He said to hurry." They exchanged a look, then both took off running.

Chapter 20

The morning air was cool and crisp. The woods were awash with yellow, orange, and red, which joined the vibrant green of the forest canopy. The wind tousled Lark's brown curls, and leaves crunched beneath her feet as she strolled by the river's edge.

She tensed her fingers within her new leather gauntlet. Her gaze was drawn upward as Whisper and Muse took to the sky, searching for prey. She'd grown to love these early morning outings. Watching Muse learn to hunt brought her a thrill unlike anything she'd experienced.

Every day traveling with the Wandering Bards was a pleasure. It was like the world had seen fit to reward her for her past suffering with the experience of a lifetime.

She spent her nights singing in small towns all over the countryside, reveling in the applause and pure pleasure on the faces in the crowd. Her days, she spent traveling with a group of people she'd grown to love who treated her like family. And best of all were mornings like these, where she watched Muse fly, full of grace, strength, and cunning.

She stole a glance beside her at Aren. He kept step with her on the riverside, occasionally prodding a bush or tree with a long stick, hoping to flush out prey for the birds. His oversized hat shaded his pale face from the morning sun.

He'd been so patient and kind, helping her learn the basics of falconry, but there was still so much she didn't know about him. Of all the performers in the group, he was the most mysterious. While the rest of the group were happy to share stories of their lives prior to joining the show, he'd yet to share anything but the barest details of his past.

"So, I've been wondering something..." She blurted when her curiosity became too strong to bear. "When Daus introduces Tiora and the twins, he always tells the story of where they're from. He's been making a big deal about me being from Dracwood, too... but with you, he says nothing."

"And you're wondering why that is?"

"Yeah. Are you on the run or something?'

He laughed. "No... I'm from Doln."

She blinked. "Oh."

"That reaction is why he doesn't mention it. Raimire and Joria are exotic and exciting to the people here. But your people and mine aren't exactly on the best of terms."

"Might have something to do with the whole slavery thing..."

He tipped back his hat so he could look her in the eye. "I haven't traveled as much as some, but I've seen enough to know that there are good and bad parts of every country. I know you had an awful experience with slavers, Lark. But really, Doln is a lot different than the people here imagine it to be."

She raised a brow, noting the serious look on his face.

Her trip through Southmoat had proven there were bad parts everywhere. But while slavery surely existed in some form in Dracwood, it was hidden, relegated to the seedy parts of large cities. It must be so strange to live in a land where it was accepted by rulers and common folk alike.

She decided to at least hear him out. "How so?"

He readjusted his hat, covering his face again. "Well, most slaves are treated well."

Lark scoffed. "Really?"

"It's a tradition from the days when both sides of the country were ruled by competing clans. There's Minsport on the Magus River's western side and Gransea to the east. The chiefs on both sides would kidnap high-ranking members from rival clans and try to convert them to their side. It was worth the ultimate bragging rights if they could convince one of the kidnapped clan members to pledge their loyalty to the new clan chief. Once that happened, they'd become a full member of the new clan, no longer considered a slave. But if they held onto their loyalty, chances were good their home clan would save them in a future raid."

"That's not how it works anymore, is it?" She looked away as the memory surfaced of being squeezed in the back of the wagon with Tiora that first night. She shuddered, remembering the terror that had overcome her when she discovered she was headed for Doln's borders. "Now they want slaves from other lands instead."

"You're right. The clan chiefs squashed their rivalry centuries ago, and stealing rival clan members fell out of favor. Slavery was around there for so long it became a big part of the culture. These days, having a foreign house slave is fashionable, like a status symbol. Some clan chiefs even favor slaves as wives. But you'd be hard pressed to find one who's treated poorly. It's a manner of honor in Doln to treat all those who work in your household with respect and honor."

"I still don't like it. Keeping someone against their will is wrong, even if you treat them nicely." She frowned. "Not that I don't find that part a bit hard to believe."

"Well, you'll believe it when you see it. We're planning to take the show to Doln next spring. I'll introduce you to a few slaves in Clan Chief Aundrea's household, and you can ask them all about it, if you're still interested."

Lark swallowed, not sure what to feel about the prospect of visiting the county she'd escaped being sold to. "You know slaves?"

"Sure. I grew up as a member of Clan Chief Aundrea's house. My father was Clan Huntsmaster. And my mother was music teacher for the clan's children."

"Well, that explains how you ended up talented at falconry and the lute." She raised a brow, tilting her head. "But if it's so great there, then why did you leave?"

"Wanderlust, I suppose." He grinned, adjusting his hat for more shade as they circled a bend on the riverbank, the splash of some aquatic creatures echoing in the distance. "All of you have such interesting tales about your lives before joining the show. I'm afraid my life was boring in comparison. I wasn't orphaned and made to live by my wits on the streets like the twins, nor am I a healer, like you. I never had to make a horrible choice to save my family, like Tiora. I'm just a guy who lived a normal life with loving parents until I woke up one morning with an itch to see the world."

Could that be why he never spoke up when everyone was talking about their pasts? He was worried about being boring? She stole another glance at him, then returned her gaze to the sky. He wasn't boring at all.

"Help, someone, please help!"

Lark stopped in her tracks, scanning for the source of the desperate voice shattering the calm morning.

Aren caught sight of him first, staggering up from the riverside. He raced ahead as soon as he spotted the panicked child. "What's wrong?" Aren approached the boy, steadying him as he tripped in his haste to reach them.

Lark arrived on his heels, scanning the boy for injuries. He had to be less than ten and wore plain homespun clothes. His trousers were soaked from the waist down. His face and hair were splattered with mud.

"Please, mister, you gotta help him." His voice cracked, and he gestured wildly behind him. "My little brother, he fell in the river."

Aren didn't hesitate. He shucked off his hat and leather gauntlet. In a few short steps, he reached the river's edge and dove into the water.

The boy spoke again, and the sorrow in his voice broke her heart. "Please, Lord Dragon, let him be okay."

"It's all right. Aren will find him. Just you watch." She crouched down, and brown, terror-struck eyes stared back at her. "I'm Lark. What's your name?"

His lip quivered. "Kaleb," he whispered. "I knew I shouldn't let Nico come with me." Tears spilled down his face, leaving tracks on his mud encrusted cheeks. "He begged and begged, promised to stay out of the water. I should've never let him come. It's all my fault."

Lark held him as he cried. She stared at the river, searching for any sign of Aren or the boy. It was taking too long. Her stomach wrenched as she watched the deep, placid water.

Aren surfaced downriver. Lark jumped to her feet, spotting the boy clutched in his arms. "C'mon, he found him."

They raced forward, meeting Aren as he struggled out of the water and placed the unconscious child gently on the muddy riverbank.

Kaleb fell to his knees beside his brother and grabbed his shoulder, shaking his lifeless form. "Nico—No!"

Tossing her own gauntlet on the ground, Lark knelt and pushed him aside hastily. "I'm a healer. Let me look at him."

Kaleb backed away on his hands and knees, his face screwed up with pure anguish. "Please, you have to save him!"

Nico was much smaller than his brother, perhaps only five or six. His pale face had already taken on a bluish tinge.

Lark placed a hand on his breast and felt nothing. The steady thump of his heart was absent and his chest still. She prayed it was not too late to save him. She grabbed a handful of mud from the riverbank.

Closing her eyes briefly, she placed her mud-filled hand on his chest. Her heart pounded out of control; her entire body filled with anxiety and doubt. Lark took a deep breath. She'd done this before; she could do it again. She let out the breath and wished.

For a moment, she thought nothing would happen. Then she felt it. The tingling tremor of energy flowed through her body. A pulse rose from his chest to vibrate her palm. Then another. His heart had started.

But one look at his face, still that unnatural blue, banished the smile that threatened to escape. He still wasn't breathing.

"Help me turn him on his side," she said to Aren, who crouched on the other side of the boy.

Together, they rolled him sideways. Lark climbed on her knees, holding him steady with one hand and beating on his back with her fist.

"What are you doing to him?" Kaleb's voice was wobbly, full of distress.

"He breathed in water. We have to get it out." She thumped over and over. His body quaked with the force of her fist; his blue face darkened into purple. She held her breath, her heart pounding with each blow she landed on his back.

Finally, he coughed, spewing a huge mouthful of water into the air. She smiled as she tilted his face downward so he could finish expelling the water on the muddy ground.

She'd done it! He was breathing. For one blissful instant, she rejoiced. Then, she glanced up at Aren, and the relief vanished. He looked green, his stare locked on the back of the boy's head.

She followed his gaze, and her stomach plummeted. How had she missed that? Nico's head was caved in from behind, covered with a huge, jagged laceration. Blood gushed from the wound, and bits of white bone peeked through his dark hair.

Her mind spun and bile rose in her throat. She couldn't fix that.

Kaleb cradled his head in his hands, crying silently. Her chest ached. She had to try. She had to at least try.

She grabbed another fist full of mud and slathered it on the head wound.

"Is that going to work?" Aren whispered, staring at her incredulously.

"I don't know," she admitted.

Her mind raced with thoughts and memories. The baby, Pax... her mother. She closed her eyes, praying and wishing with everything inside her for this to work the way it had worked before. But doubt kept forcing its way to the surface. Her mother's face returned to haunt her, looking exactly the same as it had the day she'd held her as she took her last breath. She waited for the vibration to fill her. But deep inside, she knew. She didn't have it in her to fix this child, the same way she couldn't save her mother.

She opened eyes flooded with tears. Nico's wound was unchanged. Cold mud and warm blood mingled in her palm and gushed between her fingers. Her chin quivered, and she gently lowered his head to the ground, the rise and fall of his chest already slowing. It hadn't been enough to save him.

Kaleb lifted his head. The grief and pain on his face stabbed her like a knife through her breast. "Is he... is he going to be all right?"

Lark wet her lips, tears burning a hot trail down her face. "I'm sorry, Kaleb. I'm so sorry."

"Kaleb, Nico?" A man's voice reached them just before he emerged from the woods. The man was tall and muscular, dressed in simple homespun clothes like the boys.

"Father..." Kaleb leapt to his feet and raced into the man's arms, crying hysterically, anguish pouring off him like a flood.

It took the man a moment to notice Nico lying dead in the mud, but when he did, he gasped, his face contorting with pain. "Oh no, not my boy." His gaze jumped around the scene. Lark's heart tore apart as she watched the realization dawn on him that what he was seeing was real. "Who are you people?" he demanded. "What's happened to my son?"

She opened her mouth to speak but found herself unable to form a single word in the face of his anger. Tears flowed freely down her face. Her lungs burned.

Aren stood. "We heard your son call for help. I managed to pull Nico from the river, but his wounds were too much. I'm so sorry, sir."

She shook herself out of her stupor, reaching again for the boy. "I'll try aga—"

"No." The man's harsh demand made her retract her hands. "You've done enough."

The man stared at them again. Aren soaked to the bone. Lark covered in mud, blood, and tears.

He let out one gasping sob, clutching Kaleb tight. Then he set his mouth in a grim line and gently set Kaleb aside. "It's going to be all right." He stared down at the boy's tortured face. Then, he plodded forward and picked up Nico's small, battered body from the muddy ground. "Thank you for trying," he said as he approached where Aren stood. "Let's bring Nico home," he said to Kaleb, then disappeared back into the trees.

Kaleb's eyes met her own one last time. She knew with absolute certainty his face would be burned into her memory forever. He dropped his gaze, then trudged off after his father into the woods.

As the boy's back retreated into the woods, his shoulders slumped, his body shuddering with the force of his grief, something inside of her snapped.

She had allowed herself to forget her purpose. She'd ignored her calling. No longer. She couldn't keep letting the thrill of singing and the camaraderie she felt with the performers stop her from becoming a mage.

She rose to her feet and retrieved her leather gauntlet from the ground. Her hands closed on the rough fabric. It would be so easy to slip it on. Slip back into this life she loved. A life that let her forget all about the people she'd killed and the ones she'd not been strong enough to save. Her gaze lifted to the sky where she could still see the pair of birds circling the woods in the distance, and she clenched the leather, painting it red and brown with the muck on her fingers.

Her heart breaking once more, she walked forward and thrust out the gauntlet, placing it into Aren's hands. He stared down at the glove, then met her eyes. "Lark... I—"

She shook her head, the words tumbling out before he said anything to change her mind. "I have to speak to Daus."

Chapter 21

Dusk was upon them. Kayda sat beside the window, her legs curled beneath the skirt of her favorite turquoise dress, watching the clouds light up with color from the setting sun.

The first few days after Izora's visit, she'd watched the sunset with bated breath. Her stomach churning and nerves on edge as she waited eagerly for the promised signal. Then days stretched into weeks. She was beginning to think the signal would never come.

She glanced sideways to where the king sat staring blankly out the window. Was he admiring the colorful sky? Could he even see at all? She sent a small smile in his direction and wiped a tiny bit of spittle from his chin with a handkerchief.

The king hadn't awakened from his stupor. He spent every day like a statue. Staring blankly. Never talking. Content to sit or stand in the same position for hour upon hour, unmoving.

The healer tried countless things to snap him out of it. Bleeding, potions, and tonics by the dozen. But nothing had worked.

Now, she spent every day taking care of him. Feeding him like a child. Leading him to the privy and from bed to chair and back again.

She kept telling herself as long as he was up moving and eating, there was hope. But every time she looked into his dull blue eyes her heart ached. His body was alive, but his mind was gone. She didn't know if she'd ever see him smile or hear him call her "little red" again.

Her gaze returned to the window. Where was the signal? Had she missed it somehow?

Every night, she cursed herself again for not taking the time to question Izora more carefully about what to expect. If she'd missed her chance... Her chest squeezed at the thought.

No, she just had to be patient. Izora would come through. She had to.

The sun dipped down below the horizon at last. The last rays of daylight lingered as she stared out at the castle, resigning herself to another day as nursemaid and prisoner. She leaned back and was on the verge of turning away from the window when she saw it.

There was a light high up on the keep. It flashed erratically, as if someone held a torch out an open window and flailed it about in all directions. She gasped as it dropped. The flame careened down the side of the stone keep, twisting end over end before sputtering out on the ground.

Her heart sped up. Finally!

She rose to her feet, her wooden chair skidding against the stone floor in the silent room.

This was it, the moment she'd been waiting for. She would leave this tower and put an end to whatever fiendish plot her brother had become embroiled in.

She told her feet to move, but they remained fixed in place. Her gaze slid to her grandfather's face. She bit her lip, her hand raised to her throat that'd suddenly gone dry.

Was she insane to leave him here? He was already lost inside his own mind. Was she really going to leave him alone in truth?

She strode forward, crouching down and looking at her grandfather face to face. His foggy eyes stared blankly ahead, not focusing on her, even when she was close enough to smell his stale breath.

"I'm sorry, Grandfather. I... have to go. I'll do my best to set things right, I promise." She started to say more but backed away, wiping the corner of her eye with her sleeve.

What was the use? He wasn't listening.

She stood once more, her gaze glued to the door. A few steps later, she stopped before it, her hand shaking as she reached out to turn the knob.

Wait—her bag.

She raced to her bed and shoved aside the dangling curtain, fishing out the sack Izora had brought her from beneath the cot. It took only a moment to strap the bag to her back, then she was back at the door.

She grabbed the knob and the smooth, cold metal turned beneath her fingers. She smiled. But before she could shove the door open, she heard a terrible sound—the steady *clunk* of footsteps in the hall headed toward her.

Her heart sank. If only she'd left at the first sign of the signal, she would be outside already. Blazes, she was so stupid!

She let the knob go slowly, praying whoever stood in the hallway didn't notice it twisting from the other side and backed away from the door. She just had time to shuck off the bag and shove it beneath her grandfather's cot, out of sight, before the door swung open.

Kayda's jaw dropped. "Father?"

After weeks of begging the guards to speak to him and dozens of letters, he had to show up now? Right when she was poised to leave?

Prince Gideon lingered in the doorway. Like the rest of the men in the family, he was tall, blond-haired, and blue-eyed, but unlike Tarquin and Quinton, the years had not been kind to him. His pale skin was yellow and sallow. His body was no longer muscular and trim but bulged with fat, making the black tunic and trousers he wore appear a few sizes too small.

He stepped forward, his stare fixed on the king's back where he sat by the window. Then he swung to face her, his face flat and unreadable as he strode inside, closing the door behind him.

He walked straight to her, grabbed her upper arms, and stared down into her upturned face. "I'm so sorry, Kayda. I've been worse than useless for years. But I'm here now. You don't have to be alone any longer." He pulled her close, embracing her tightly.

Kayda held herself stiffly in his arms. She steeled herself for the sour stench that would surround her—but it never came. She pushed free from his embrace and searched his face. His eyes, so often bloodshot, were clear tonight. His cheeks were missing their familiar rosy hue, and his voice had not slurred in the slightest.

"Did you stop drinking?" Her brow furrowed.

Gideon's stare locked onto her own. He nodded. "Yes. It was the hardest thing I've ever done, but when I heard about the attack on Father..." He glanced at the king's back again, then refocused on her face. "I locked myself in my room and ordered my man to keep me there, no matter what, until I was off the stuff. I should have done it long ago, Kayda. I'm so, so sorry. All those years wasted—I want to do better. I will do better."

His face burned with intensity, but Kayda shook her head in disbelief.

Her entire life, she could count on one hand the number of times her father had said so many words to her at once. And he'd never apologized. Who was this man standing before her?

Her eyes filled with tears. "Why didn't you? We could've been so much more if you'd only cared enough to try."

He frowned at the floor. "I don't know. My life... just didn't turn out the way I expected. I should've faced my problems, dealt with them. But I drowned them instead."

"What problems? You're a prince." She narrowed her eyes and backed away another pace.

"I know it sounds crazy. I should've been able to be happy... but I just... couldn't." He sighed and met her eyes. "I wasn't always this way. Growing up, knowing the royal talent had skipped me, I could handle that. When it skipped your brother—that's when everything went to shit."

His face screwed up, and he shook his head. "I couldn't get it out of my mind. He should've had it. Bonding magic skips a generation in our family, but it always comes back... always. I couldn't stop thinking that his mother had been untrue. She denied it, of course, but I just knew. It was the only explanation that made sense. When she got sick later that year and died, I was glad." He laughed, a single joyless sound that echoed through the room. "I was glad to be rid of her lies. Glad to remarry and try again. She'd robbed me of my birthright. Bringing the next royal with talent into the world. But then the rumors started..."

Kayda's mind roiled with uncertainty. She'd heard the rumors. Everyone had. When Tarquin was born without talent and his mother died of a mysterious sickness a few short months later, it didn't take long before people began whispering that her death hadn't been natural. That Gideon had poisoned her.

When she first heard the story as a child, she'd brushed it off, not inclined to think so poorly of her father at the time. But she'd remembered, her view of the man forever colored differently thereafter. It was always there in the back of her mind, unanswered. Was her father a killer?

"It's not true. I swear it." His gaze sought out hers, full of fervor. "It might as well have been, though, for all the trouble it caused me. No one would allow their daughter to marry me after that. Father and I searched for years in Dracwood before we accepted that we'd have to look elsewhere for a bride. By that time, I wanted nothing more to do with it. I would've rather let the bloodline die than force some unwilling foreign wife to bed me. But my father convinced me..." He scowled. "For duty."

Kayda's stomach turned. She was more similar to her father than she realized. She knew all about the pressures that came with keeping the royal bloodline alive.

"Your mother—she was a sweet girl, but she didn't marry me by choice. If it hadn't been for the trade deal that Father negotiated with her family, then she wouldn't have had anything to do with me. But we did our duty. And then there you were."

He sent a rueful smile her way. "You don't know the relief I felt that day when the seers announced your talent. But your mother died during childbirth." His upper lip curled back. "The rumors flew again. I started drinking. I couldn't stand to see the veiled accusation on everyone's faces, and the drink, it let me forget. After that, it became a way of life for me. I'd done my duty. Who cared if I drank myself to death?"

Tears stung her eyes. "Who would care? I did. Your daughter."

He flinched, but she refused to lower her voice or temper her emotion.

"I needed you, and you ignored me. My entire life, you acted like I wasn't even there. How do you think it made me feel, knowing you'd rather drink yourself into oblivion than spend time with me?"

He raked a shaky hand through his hair, staring at the floor again. "I know. I'm so sorry, Kayda. If I could go back and do it all over, I would. I would be the father you deserve. Please... just tell me what I can do to make it right?"

Her gaze shot to the fireplace. It would be so easy to call forth the flames. Part of her wanted it. To watch him burn.

No. She balled her hands into fists and looked away. "Let me leave. I don't want to be a prisoner in this blazing room any longer."

His gaze raised from the floor, and he nodded. "Done."

"And don't let him die." Her arm shot out, pointing directly at the king. "Don't you dare." She stepped closer and stared straight into his eyes, her voice laced with venom. "If Grandfather isn't still breathing when I return, you won't get the chance to drown yourself again when all the rumors start."

His eyes bulged, and he backed away a pace, staring at her strangely. She expected him to say something, to chide her not to speak to her elders in such a way, but he only nodded again.

Kayda spun on her heel, knelt down to retrieve her bag, and fled the room before he could change his mind. She stormed through the tower in a daze, disappointment and anger boiling in her veins. Maybe one day she could forgive her father for his faults. Not today.

Chilly autumn air hit her face as she emerged outside, cooling her rage. She inhaled deeply, the fresh air a welcome relief after the stuffy tower room. Spinning around slowly, she gaped at the scenery. She spent so long in that single room, staring out the lone window toward Kings Keep. She finally escaped, only to be greeted with the night's darkness.

As she turned east, she was met with a strange sight that sent a shiver up her spine. The full moon perched there in the sky, blood-red. From where she stood, it appeared to hover over the path to Mage Keep.

"Kayda!" Izora stepped out in the moonlight from a shadowed alcove in the brick tower, her black-hooded cloak blending into the darkness. "What took you so long? Did someone stop you on your way out?" She grabbed her elbow, towing her toward Northmoat. "Never mind, it doesn't matter. There's no time. We have to hurry."

"Why are we rushing?" she asked as they sped up. "Please, you have to explain what's happening."

"Do you remember the mage who healed the king?"

Kayda nodded. She would never forget that kind man's face.

"His name is Vespen." Her voice became increasingly labored, but she didn't slow. "He's waiting for you outside the Royal Grounds to take you to Mage Keep."

"Mage Keep?" She stopped and shook her head vehemently. "No, I have to find Tarquin. I didn't have time to tell you when you came to see me. He was involved in the attack on the king."

Izora tugged her arm again, starting her moving. "I don't doubt it. That boy is always up to no good. No one's heard from Mage Keep for days now. Something's happening there, and I won't be surprised to find out that fool is behind it." She jolted to a stop, panting. "I can't go with you, child. I'd only slow you down. Go find out what's happening at Mage Keep. I'll stay behind and keep an eye on the king."

"My father is with him now. He promised to keep him alive."

Izora's face blanched, all the color draining from it in an instant. "What did you say? Your father..." She gasped, a hand on her breast.

"Izora, what's wrong? Are you okay?"

She pulled in another breath, struggling for air. "That man is not your father."

The words struck her like a slap to the face. "What are you talking about?"

Izora shook her head, her white curls bouncing beneath her hood. "There's no time. I have to get back, and you have to go. The Sade Prim, Delyth, she can tell you everything when you reach Mage Keep." She clutched her tightly. "I love you, my princess," she whispered before she let go. Then she hurried off, disappearing into the darkness.

Kayda stood silently, trying to wrap her head around Izora's shocking revelation. Gideon was not her father? How could that be true? She almost raced after her to demand an explanation. How could she reveal something like that and just leave?

Then, a commotion started somewhere nearby. The unmistakable clash of violence resounded in the night, and she jogged off toward Northmoat. She'd been given this chance to set things right. She wouldn't waste it.

Her bag bounced on her back as she sprinted toward the light of the blood-red moon. The sounds of fighting faded as she approached the edge of the Royal Grounds, and her stomach sank. That meant Kings Keep was under attack. She stopped, turning around to stare in the keep's direction as a cold sweat broke out on her skin.

"Princess," said a voice behind her. "I'm glad you made it."

The mage from the feast, Vespen, rode up to greet her. He was seated atop a black stallion and held the reins of a chestnut mare in his hands. He'd exchanged the white robes for dark brown traveling clothes, and he perched upon his steed with that steady expression Kayda remembered so clearly.

"It's too late. If you head for the mages, we're all doomed."

Kayda gasped, immediately realizing what the voice meant. She raced forward and placed her hands on the second horse. *"Are you my bondmate?"* She rubbed the horse's silky mane as Vespen stared at her. *"I'm bonded to horses just like Grandfather?"*

"A horse?" Laughter filled her mind. *"No, I'm definitely not a horse. But I am your bondmate. I need you to find me."*

"My lady, we have to go," Vespen said.

She ignored him and dropped her hands from the horse, backing away. *"Where are you?"*

"Hard to say. Underground somewhere, in the darkness."

A locked door flashed in her memory. Instinctively, she knew. Her mind raced. She had to get back in the keep.

"I have to go back." She looked up at Vespen as she backed away slowly.

He frowned. "I promise you, whatever you left behind, we can replace. We have to leave now."

Kayda shook her head. "No, you don't understand. My bondmate is back there."

His eyes widened, and he dismounted. "No, *you* don't understand, Princess. We needed a distraction to secret you out of the city. If you go back there, you'll be walking into a battle."

She gulped but refused to let the news dissuade her. "It doesn't matter. I have to go back. I have to do this."

Vespen stared into her eyes for what felt like ages. Then he drew a breath in through his nose and crouched down to grab fists full of soil, stuffing them into his pockets. He rose, setting his shoulders back and staring straight forward. "All right. Let's go find your bondmate."

Kayda smiled, her heart overflowing with gratitude. Then she squared her shoulders and shoved aside the anxious fluttering in her stomach. *"I'm coming to find you."*

Chapter 22

Mage Keep was a ghost town. It was no surprise something spooked Shadow when he first set eyes on the sprawling compound.

"Is it ever deserted like this, in the middle of the day?" Conall asked, glancing at Ereni.

She shook her head and frowned. "No, never. Even if there was a mandatory meeting called, there should be someone outside keeping watch."

"I don't like this. I have a bad feeling..." Shadow stood stiffly, staring at the empty keep.

Conall gulped. *"Me, too, brother. But my sister's in there."*

He studied the landscape. Mage Keep nestled at the bottom of a ridge, leaving the back half inaccessible from their position. It was surrounded by great swaths of farmland on all other sides, with a slow-moving river to the north. They were hidden in the woods on the outer edge, but to reach the keep, they would have to traverse a huge, empty field.

He sighed. If they'd arrived a few weeks ago, they might've had some options, but with harvest completed, there was no chance of using the crops for cover. He could see no other way to stealthily approach.

Even waiting for nightfall would be a gamble unlikely to pay out. They were due for a full moon tonight, and the sky was clear and cloudless.

He unslung his bow from his shoulder, the familiar weight a comfort in his hand. "I'll head in first. You two can wait—"

"If you think I'm going to wait in the woods like some helpless maiden, you're sorely mistaken," Ereni said with a huff. "That's my home. We go together."

He considered debating, but one look at her face assured him she would not be swayed. "All right, then we leave Shadow here as backup."

"There's no livestock here." Ereni waved a hand. "Bring him. If there's trouble waiting for us inside, we'll need all the help we can get."

He gazed again at the deserted compound. She was probably right. It's not like Shadow could sneak in any easier to rescue them if something happened. "Together then."

He exchanged a glance with Shadow and nodded toward the keep. *"We go together, stay sharp."*

"Always." Shadow edged forward.

Conall followed, gritting his teeth as he exited the tree line. There was no movement from the keep. No arrows shot at them. No blasts of fire or eruptions of magic disrupted the eerie stillness. Just the gentle plodding of their footsteps in fresh-turned earth.

Still, he couldn't shake the sensation of being watched. His gaze slid from building to building, expecting an ambush at any moment. It wasn't until they'd crept past several mismatched buildings, each one as silent and empty as the last, that he was certain they were not alone.

A gentle breeze carried a scent to his nose. The foul scent of unwashed flesh.

"Someone's here." He grabbed Ereni and shoved her behind him. At the same time, he reached into his quiver, pulling out and nocking an arrow.

"Drop it," said the gruff voice of an unseen man. "You're surrounded."

Shadow growled, the fur on his back standing on end.

Conall's head jolted all around as he searched for cover. There was a building they'd just passed that might work. Heart pumping, he shuffled sideways, his bow held at the ready, preparing to jump back.

Then the whistle of a dozen arrows flew through the sky and thudded into the ground by their feet.

Shadow's growling intensified. He hopped back, an arrow landing just shy of his snapping teeth.

"I said drop the bow," the same voice yelled, "and calm that hound, or the next round of arrows won't miss."

"They have us surrounded. Calm down, Shadow." Conall scowled. His gaze darted all around as he tossed his bow on the packed dirt road between buildings. Shadow sat down by his side, tucking his tail beneath him.

"All your weapons. You, too, girl."

Conall shucked off his quiver and pulled his hunting knife from its place on his belt. He tossed both down. Ereni stepped forward. Her knife clattered against his own before it landed in the dirt.

Only then did the gruff voiced man reveal himself. He was large, middle-aged, and balding. He charged forward, muscles rippling, and whistled.

The sound had barely cleared his pursed lips before a dozen men revealed themselves, pouring out between buildings, a few vaulting down from the rooftops.

"Restrain them. Put them in with the others," said the leader.

Several men sauntered forward with swords, spears, and bows aimed at them. They wore plain clothes but handled their weapons with the familiarity of constant use.

Were they mercenaries? What could they possibly want at Mage Keep? And why had the mages allowed themselves to be captured? It was all so strange.

A short man with a pocked face approached Shadow, and a growl rose in his throat. The man retreated a step. "That ain't no hound." His eyes bulged, and he trained his bow directly at Shadow's face. "Blazes. That's a wolf."

Conall's heart jumped into his throat. He inched between the man and Shadow, swallowing as the arrow targeted his chest. "He's trained. He's no threat to you."

"Relax, Lonan." The leader said to his man as he marched toward them, a long rope coiled in his hands. Then he turned to Conall. "Here, you tie him up. Round his neck and muzzle." He shoved the rough rope into his hands.

Conall knelt, catching a glimpse of Ereni glowering at a stocky man as he tied her outstretched hands. How were they going to escape now? He uncoiled the rope and gazed down at Shadow's face. *"I'm sorry, they want me to tie you."*

"Do what you must. We'll think of something, little brother."

He wrapped the rope around Shadow, leaving a long length free to hold like a leash. Then he stood, handed the rope to a waiting man, and stuck out his own hands to be tied.

Lonan slung his bow on his shoulder and got to work with a rope. "C'mon then," he said as he finished.

The rope bit into Conall's flesh so tightly he had no chance to slip free. A group of six men formed up, their weapons held at the ready, and led them away from the leader, further into the keep.

Ereni gasped as they rounded a corner to reveal a large building in similar bondage. Its ground-level windows were boarded with freshly cut wood tacked on from the outside. The door was barred with an iron bar and locked. Lonan detached a key from his belt as they approached, and Conall's stomach turned.

Lonan ushered them in. Ereni went first, her steps quickening as she caught sight of the huddled folk within.

Conall paused, gazing in awe at the massive building. The interior was far grander than he'd expected. Huge wooden tables that could comfortably seat hundreds were lodged in neat lines along the walls. High ceilings shone with massive glass windows, illuminating walls painted a dazzling white. Each of the four walls displayed a brilliantly wrought tapestry depicting mages using one of the four elements.

A shove on his back set him in motion again. He stumbled forward. Shadow followed by his side after the man holding his makeshift leash tossed the lead to the ground and pulled the heavy door closed, sealing them inside.

Ereni had already reached the center of the room. She embraced an old woman wearing the long, white robes the mages favored. Conall approached the pair and scanned the rest of the room, desperately seeking one familiar face in the crowd.

There had to be more than a hundred people staring at them. At least three quarters of them were old and wearing the white robes. The rest were young adults and teens, who wore plain clothes. His heart sank. Lark was not among them.

"What's going on here, Amora?" Ereni pulled free of the old woman's embrace and frowned. "Who are these men? Where are my mother and the children?"

Amora wrung her hands together, her brow furrowing. "Ereni, I'm so glad you're here. We've been stuck here for days. It's been absolutely wretched not knowing what's going on. What did you see on your way in?" Her wrinkled hands tugged at the bindings on Ereni's wrists.

"All we saw was empty buildings before those men ambushed us. Who are they? What do they want?"

Amora's stare fixed on Ereni's hands as she released the final loop of rope. "They're castle guards, from Kings Keep."

Ereni raised a newly freed hand to her lips. "No." Her eyes widened like a hare caught in a trap before she whirled to face him and began loosening his bonds.

"They came last week, with Prince Tarquin." Amora glanced at Shadow but made no move to free him. "You know it's not unheard of for the royals to visit. We welcomed them, invited them in for a feast. It all seemed perfectly normal... until it wasn't. A few of the guards offered to put on a demonstration for the children. Sword fighting. Turns out it was merely a ruse to separate us. Once they had the children, they used them as leverage to herd us all in here like cattle. They threatened us, said if any of us summon or try to escape, they'll kill them."

Ereni finished untying his hands. Her face flushed and her jaw clenched as she listened to the tale. He couldn't imagine what she must be feeling. He wanted drag her into his arms, but he suspected she wouldn't appreciate it with all the mages eyes on them, so he settled for sending her a sympathetic smile before he knelt down to free Shadow.

Ereni spun back to Amora and crossed her arms. "And my mother?"

Amora shook her head. "No one has seen her since that first day. The prince took her with him. What he wants with her, or with any of us, he didn't say. We keep waiting for something to happen. So far, nothing." She turned and stared at him. "What about you, Ereni? Who are your companions?"

Ereni offered a small smile and raised her voice, projecting her answer to the whole assemblage. "I'm so sorry everyone has been through this. I'll see it all gets sorted out, I promise. This is Conall of Greenvale and his wolfhound, Shadow. He is seeking his sister, Lark."

Conall finished removing Shadow's bindings. He stood and thrust out a hand. "Pleased to meet you."

Amora shook his hand, her grip firm and warm.

"I don't see my sister here, now. She left me a letter a few weeks back, said she was heading here for training. We have the same curly brown hair and hazel eyes, but she's a few years younger than me and about this tall." He lifted a hand to the height of his shoulder. "Have you seen her?"

"There's been no one here by that name, I'm afraid." Amora gazed at him intently. "I can recall no visitors in the last few weeks who share a resemblance with you, either. You are welcome to inquire among the rest of the mages, but I don't think you'll find her here."

Conall swallowed, his chest aching. The fear that had subsided when he learned of Lark's intentions to travel to the mages assaulted him once more.

Where could she be? He had no other clues, nothing to go on except for the letter she'd left him. Would he ever find her?

Even worse, now they were caught in the middle of some strange standoff. His mind raced as he examined the sad and fearful faces of the assembled mages. Some sat in small groups, their gazes downcast, eyes ringed with dark circles. Others paced mindlessly or stared dejectedly out the tall glass windows.

They'd been separated from their families just like he had. He had to do something to help them.

"What's going on? Where is your sister?" Shadow sat by his side, looking at the gathered mages, seemingly unbothered by the attention despite rarely being around so many people before.

Conall closed his eyes and pressed his fingertips against his eyelids. *"Sounds like she was never here."* His hand drooped back to his side. *"But those men, they're holding the young of this keep hostage. We have to help them."*

Footsteps pounded outside. The door opened a moment later, and two men carrying food and drink barged in. Several others shadowed them with weapons drawn.

Conall scowled as he saw what was on offer. Was this what he had to look forward to now? Stale bread and ale spread between too many mouths to be satisfying.

His head pounded. How long would they be stuck in here, waiting on the royals to play their political games?

From the corner of his eye, he spied movement. Ereni glided forward, showing no fear even when the guards pointed their weapons straight at her. "Take me to my mother," she demanded.

He clenched his fists, staring a hole in her back. What was she doing?

"I don't have orders to move you, lady," said the same stocky man who'd tied Ereni's hands earlier.

"My mother is the Sade Prim, and I have an urgent message for her. You would be wise to allow me to see her."

The man frowned, then heaved out a sigh. "I'll take you to the prince. He'll decide what to do with you."

Conall started forward, ready to protest, but Ereni sent a hard glare his way and shook her head from across the room. He stopped moving, his nails digging into the palms of his hands as he watched her wrists being bound. Then she was led through the door and out of sight.

Amora squeezed his arm as the iron bar clanged back into place, echoing through the silent Hall. "It's all right. She'll get things sorted. She promised."

He looked down at the old woman and forced his hands to relax. "I hope you're right."

Conall's thighs burned, the muscles in his legs and calves straining as he climbed up the steep rise to the top of the ridge overlooking Mage Keep. He stepped carefully, aware he might not catch himself with his bound hands if he were to fall on the uneven ground.

Beside him marched Shadow and four mages, all bound in similar fashion, and the six guardsmen who'd collected them from the hall. They'd stormed in with a list of names, ordering them to follow but not saying why or where they were heading.

It shocked him when the guards read off their names. Ereni had done it. In the short time she'd spent with the prince, she'd convinced him to let them go. This had to be part of her plan. There was no other way those guards would even know who he was. He hadn't given them his name, or Shadow's.

Eventually, the ground leveled off. Conall was the first to round the summit. He found himself on the top of a flat rise that overlooked both Mage Keep behind them, and a large swath of coastal plains ahead of them. He glanced around, admiring the unspoiled land's majestic beauty, until his gaze was captivated by an unexpected sight.

It was just before dusk, but tonight, the moon chose to grace the land with an early appearance. The entire surface shone a bright, bold red. He couldn't stop the uneasy shiver that slid down his spine. It was like he was face-to-face with an ill omen hovering in the sky before him.

He didn't have long to stare. Amora crested the rise a moment later and gasped aloud. Conall turned as she raced forward and stopped next to a woman seated on the rise's far side. She wore a white robe, her hands were bound, and she had a pair of guards watching over her as she sat stoically gazing into the distance.

He stopped mid-stride as he caught sight of the woman's face. He didn't need anyone to tell him he was looking at the Sade Prim, Delyth. Although her hair was gray instead of brown, the familial resemblance was uncanny. This woman was undoubtedly Ereni's kin.

"Sade Prim, I'm so glad you're all right." Amora knelt, her face lit with joy. "What's going on? Do you know why they've brought us here to the Palisade?"

The other three mages hastened over and crowded around the pair. Their leader didn't speak. Her stare was fixed on the horizon.

Conall walked forward more slowly as he took a second look at the shoreline. He'd missed something with his first glance. He squinted in the fading daylight and spotted a ship moored offshore, along with what appeared to be a camp full of people on the beach. From this distance, the details were unclear, but the unmistakable sight of smoke rose above their campsite. Someone was out there.

A gasp stole his attention. Amora had noticed the scene. She stared at the shoreline, her mouth agape. "They're in the Abandoned Lands? We have to stop them!"

"You'll do nothing of the sort," proclaimed a new voice behind him.

He spun around in time to see a tall blond man cresting the ridge with more guards surrounding him. From his fine silk attire and pompous air, he suspected he was looking at Prince Tarquin. "Say hello to my good friends from Joria. They're going to help me build a port here as soon as you mages take down that blasted wall."

"You have no idea what you're asking, Prince Tarquin," said a woman's voice behind him.

An icy chill spread through his chest. The prince wanted to build a port? Here? Conall backed up, turning sideways so he could watch both parties speak from where he and Shadow stood in between them.

"You've already doomed those men to death," continued Delyth, "don't doom us all." She rose to her feet and tore her gaze from the shoreline, surveying everyone with her steely blue eyes.

"You mages and your silly superstitions." The prince strode forward, smirking. "Those men have been camped on that beach for a week. They've trekked all over the land and found nothing. No creatures jumping out to spook them. No monsters descending on them in the night. There's nothing out there to be afraid of."

Delyth stepped forward, staring at the prince. Until she veered alongside him and Shadow. Her head flicked to the side, studying them both. Conall swallowed, meeting her gaze and seeing something in it he couldn't quite name, but it made his stomach sink all the same.

Delyth's head snapped back, her gaze refocusing on Tarquin. "Where is my daughter?"

Tarquin's smile widened. "She said you were smarter than most. I didn't believe anyone so easily taken in with ghost stories and legends could be, but I see I'm mistaken."

Conall's stomach climbed into his throat. Why was he being evasive? Where was Ereni?

Then he spotted movement coming up the ridge behind him. He smiled. It was Ereni, hiking up to join them, with several young people from the hall following closely behind her. They walked freely with no bonds and no guards trailing them.

She'd done it. He knew she would find a way to free her people.

Something was wrong. The smile fell from his face. His gut ached, a terrible wrongness eating a hole inside him.

She crested the ridge and walked, not toward her mother, or even him. She strode up to Tarquin and stopped beside him, entwining her arm with his. "Hello, Mother."

Conall's head spun. What was she doing with the prince? She hadn't greeted him. She hadn't even looked at him. After everything they'd been through. All those days traveling together. All those nights...

He sucked in a breath through his nose. His jaw clenched tightly as his gaze flicked away from her traitorous face and down at her stomach. He was going to be sick.

Shadow sidled up beside him, brushing against his leg and standing at attention. A growl rose from his throat, no less menacing despite the rope wrapped around his muzzle.

Conall lifted his gaze back to Ereni's face and found her staring back at him. Those blue eyes he'd spent long hours staring into were full of indifference. Those lips he'd kissed, slack and emotionless. His heart wrenched, pain stabbing behind his ribs. He wanted to scream. But all he could do was stare back dumbly in shock.

"Why?" Delyth approached her daughter, her eyes flashing. "You've read the journals. You know what's out there. How could you be a party to this?"

"You're right, I've read them. That's exactly why." Ereni dropped Tarquin's arm. "The Palisade was never meant to last this long. It's weakened us for centuries. Enough is enough." She walked past her mother, striding closer to the edge of the ridge overlooking the coast. "If there is something out there, we must stand and fight while we still have strength." She closed her eyes, her lips parting and her chest slowly rising as it filled with air. She exhaled, opening her eyes.

Conall backed away, the hair on his skin standing on end. A massive wall materialized, blocking the shoreline and gleaming strangely. The Palisade. His breath caught as he stared up at the colossal structure.

Ereni turned, spreading her arms wide. "Take a good look, my friends. You will be the last people to set eyes on this sight. Tonight, the Palisade falls."

Cheers erupted behind him, but he didn't turn. His gaze was glued on her. He watched the smile slowly spread across her face and cursed himself for a fool.

Chapter 23

Lark hopped down from the back of the wagon and wrapped a brown woolen blanket around her shoulders against the chilly night air. She paused, her hand snaking out from beneath the blanket to pat Sunny's head.

"Don't get up, girl," she whispered. "I'll be back in a little while."

The yellow mutt wagged her tail lazily and rolled over, closing her eyes.

Lark sank down on a log next to the remnants of the evening fire. She sighed, halfheartedly poking a stick at the dying embers of a log that had once been nearly as big as the one she sat on.

Everyone had gone to sleep hours ago. She'd tossed and turned for ages, but finally gave up trying. Her mind was on edge tonight and sleep elusive.

Her eyes lifted and instantly widened, mirroring the shape of the full moon. The silver orb had darkened tonight to a brilliant crimson-red.

How strange. A prickle of unease crept across her shoulders.

"Couldn't sleep?"

Lark gasped, clutching her chest beneath the blanket. "Aren? I didn't know anyone was still awake."

He strode forward and crouched by the fire, the corner of his mouth lifting in a smile. "I couldn't sleep either." He grabbed a few twigs and tossed them onto the log, coaxing the fire back to life. "Care for some company?"

"Sure." She scooted over and tightened the blanket across her shoulders. Her fingers tangled in the rough cloth as Aren seated himself beside her.

His eyes lifted to the sky, his ice-blue irises reflecting the red moonlight. "Wow. That's not something you see every day."

Lark tilted her head, her brown curls spilling over her shoulders. "Do you think it means something?"

"Where I'm from, they have a saying. Blood-red moon, tides changing soon."

"Well, that's certainly ominous." Her knees trembled.

"Think that's what's keeping you awake?"

"Maybe. No." She rolled her shoulders. "Daus says we'll reach the turnoff for Mage Keep tomorrow morning."

Aren shifted. His thigh pressed against her leg, sending a frisson of electricity across her skin. "You know, we'll be back this way in a few short months. Maybe you could—"

She shook her head, closing her eyes. "No. I've waited long enough."

Kaleb's grief-stricken face flashed in her memory. Once she reached Mage Keep, she wouldn't fail anyone like she'd failed him. Never again.

It was like she'd been blessed with a deep well of water, but no tools to bore down to reach it. She couldn't keep clawing through the dirt with her hands, praying to stumble across a geyser.

Aren's hand landed on her knee. "Lark, you can't blame yourself for what happened to Nico."

She opened her eyes. Her fingers released the rough cloth and slipped out to give his hand a gentle squeeze. "Please, I don't want to think about that right now. Can we talk about something else?"

Her thumb lingered on the smooth skin of his wrist. She drew in a deep breath, tempted to link their hands together, but she slid her fingers back inside the blanket instead. "What about you? Will you travel with the show much longer?"

Aren lifted his hand from her knee. She shivered, regretting the loss of his warmth.

"Yes, I will." He brushed his fingers through his hair, tousling his light blond locks. "I'm afraid my wanderlust has only grown stronger since I left home."

She smiled up at him. "Is that so?" They were alike in that. The more time she spent traveling, the more she craved it.

He leaned closer, speaking in a hushed whisper. "Can I tell you a secret?"

She nodded.

"In Doln, there's a legend about a hidden land, somewhere beyond the Orrdon Ocean. A paradise full of white sand beaches. The sea so clear, you can look straight down into the water and watch the fish swimming between your toes."

She giggled at the imagery, and Aren grinned.

"My friends back home never believed the stories. They said it was just a myth. A foolish tale to keep the kids entertained while the blizzards raged in the winter." He wrinkled his nose, smiling down at her. "One day, I'm going to set sail and find out the truth of it."

"That sounds amazing." She could picture him on the bow of a ship, that oversized hat of his hiding his face from the sun. "I wish I could join you."

"Well, then you shall. I'll swing round Mage Keep and collect you before I set sail." His grin widened, and he slung an arm around her shoulder, giving her a squeeze. "I'll be getting into plenty of scrapes that could benefit from a healer's touch on that voyage. You'd be a welcome addition to my crew."

Lark smiled back, but she couldn't match Aren's enthusiasm.

When his gaze flicked down to her face, his smile dropped, and he pulled her closer. "Hey, tomorrow, when you go to Mage Keep, it's not goodbye. At least, not forever. We'll meet again. We'll have more adventures together. I promise."

Lark snuggled closer to Aren's chest, watching the flames flickering in the moonlight.

"I wish you would reconsider." Dausius huffed out a dramatic sigh. "The show won't be the same without you."

Lark stood at a crossroads early the next morning. The road before her led to the show's next performance. And the one behind her led to Mage Keep.

"I've made up my mind, Daus. Thank you for putting up with me for so long. And for saving me."

His lower lip quivered. He pressed a palm against his chest and made a show of breathing in and out deeply.

She cocked her head to the side and smiled. Always so dramatic. She was going to miss that. Her heart swelled. She was going to miss them all.

Suddenly, his face lit up. "I almost forgot." He squeezed her arm gently. "I have something for you. Don't move, I'll be right back." He spun around, his beaded hair tinkling musically as he made a beeline for his wagon and scrounged around in the back. "Where is it? Where is it?"

Lark raised a brow, shoving her hands into her dark blue dresses pockets as she waited. Daus was notorious for misplacing things. She might be waiting for a while.

Mazen and Meital stood on the far side of the wagon, chatting among themselves. They'd already exchanged their goodbyes with her. Both expressed regret that she wouldn't be staying for longer.

And Aren. He'd been so sweet last night, not pushing her to stay. Telling her their adventures weren't over. But she couldn't help but worry he'd regret wasting so much time teaching her to handle birds of prey only for her to leave.

She exhaled, shifting her weight from one foot to the other. She would miss those mornings with him and Muse a great deal. But she'd made her decision.

Aren caught her staring and sent her a crooked grin from across the road. Then he whistled, holding out a gauntleted arm to catch Whisper, and strode into the forest.

"I think he's going to be heartbroken for a while." Tiora walked over and joined her, staring at the woods where Aren had disappeared. She wore a golden-brown dress today, the color a perfect match for her eyes.

"Aren? Surely not." She scoffed, her gaze dropping to the dirt road.

"All that time you two spent together, alone in the woods every morning. Don't tell me you didn't realize how much he's in love with you?"

Her gaze shot to Tiora's, and a frown spread across her face. "Don't be silly, Ti. Anyway, he told me about Meital. He's got her to comfort him."

"He told you what about Meital?" Tiora crossed her arms.

"How on the night we all met, they were sleeping together. And that they both woke up and heard me singing."

Tiora laughed. "He told you he and Meital? Lark, that's not true."

"What? Why are you laughing?"

Tiora squeezed her shoulder. "Meital... I've grown to know her very well since becoming part of her act." She smiled fondly, meeting her gaze. "She's not sleeping with Aren."

Lark rolled her eyes, shaking off Tiora's hand. "You know women aren't always willing to admit when they're with someone, for modesty's sake."

Toira shook her head, her smile never wavering. "No, no. She's not being modest. People don't even care about modesty where she's from the way they do here." Her gaze flicked to the sky, as if she were gathering her thoughts, before her brown eyes connected with hers again. "Meital..." She dropped her voice, speaking in a whisper. "She doesn't sleep with men. Any man."

"Oh." Lark's eyes widened. She thought back to that conversation with Aren. Had he said he and Meital were sleeping together? Or had he said something vague, and she'd just assumed? She grimaced. "I suppose it's possible I misheard," she admitted, a pit forming in her stomach.

Tiora sighed. "Well, we'll see you again. You know Daus won't pass by Mage Keep in the spring without checking in on you. Maybe things will be different with you and Aren next time."

Lark lowered her head, her shoulders sinking. She was right, there was the future to look forward to, but it didn't stop her from feeling any less of a fool in that moment.

"Ah ha, I found it!" Dausius jumped down from the colorful wagon, waving something in his hand. With a few steps, he stopped in front of her. He bowed, his body finally stilling enough for Lark to get a clear look at the gift. It was a book with a brown leather cover. "This is for you, my dear." He extended it with a flourish.

She took the book with a grin, her hands sliding over the smooth leather. The pages glided open with a whisper, revealing page after page of handwritten words. No, not words. Songs. The lyrics to every song he'd taught her filled the pages.

"Forgive me if my handwriting is a bit wobbly. It's not easy writing in the back of a moving wagon."

Her eyes welled up as she smoothed the yellowed parchment. "You made this... for me?"

"Songs for my songbird." He chuckled. "Oh, don't cry," he added, as he met her gaze. "It's all in self-interest, I swear. One day, when you decide you've had enough of spells and magic, you'll open this book. All the songs will come flooding back, and you'll return to us." He pulled her in for a quick hug, smashing the book between them. When they pulled apart, his eyes were full of tears.

"Thank you, Daus."

He stared down at her, his expression earnest. "Don't forget. We're going to stay in Bogsmouth for an entire week before leaving for Raimire. You have until then to change your mind and come find us." He sniffled and pulled out a huge, multicolored handkerchief and wiped his eyes. "Oh, I can't bear it any longer." He spun on his heel and waved the handkerchief in the air. "Farewell." Then he disappeared back into the wagon.

"Never a dull moment with Daus around," Tiora said with a giggle.

Lark turned to her friend, and saw her eyes were red rimmed, too, despite her laughter. Her chin wobbled. "I'm going to miss you, Ti. I wish you could come with me, but I know you're excited to see your family again when the show goes to Joria."

"I'm going to miss you, too. One day, when you're a mage, you'll have to come visit Joria with me. I'll take you swimming in the Peat River, just like we talked about." Tiora pulled her in for a hug, clutching her tightly. "Daus is right. The show won't be the same without you."

"Anyone can sing. You'll find someone to replace me soon enough."

Tiora pulled away, frowning. "We might find another singer, but they'll never replace you, Lark." She bit her lip and turned away. "Go on then. Go become who you're meant to be." She met her eyes one more time before drifting back to the wagon.

Lark swallowed. She took one last long look at the wagons before pulling her pack from her back. Carefully tucking Dausius' gift next to her mother's spell book, she cinched the bag closed. She whistled, watching both Sunny's and Muse's bodies perk up at the sound from where they sat on the back of the colorful wagon.

Her stomach sank. If only she could bring them both. She'd decided to leave Muse with Aren. She didn't know what life would be like at Mage Keep, but she doubted she'd have time in her days for flying Muse like she deserved.

But Sunny was getting old and was happy to lie around all day. Dausius told her he'd seen a few hounds around the keep on his last visit, so she was taking the chance of bringing her. Really, she just couldn't stand the thought of parting with the dog. She was the only reminder she had left of her brother.

"Sunny, c'mon, girl."

Sunny rose, stretching and yawning, before hopping down from the wagon. Lark ruffled the yellow fur between her ears as she stopped beside her, tail wagging.

She had one more goodbye she needed to offer. She took a few steps closer to Muse's perch. The falcon's eyes trailed her movements, her body still as she rested in the wagon bed. Tears gathered in the corners of her eyes. For some reason, this goodbye was the hardest of them all.

"I'm sorry I can't take you with me, Muse. I can't give you the care you deserve at Mage Keep. Aren—he's promised to take great care of you." Her voice trembled, and her final words were a choked whisper. "We'll meet again, my friend. Goodbye."

She whirled around, using her sleeve to catch the tear that trickled down her cheek. Then she walked with Sunny down the path to Mage Keep. When she peeked back, the path had curved, and all sight of the wagons and her friends was gone.

Lark inhaled the fresh autumn air, but it didn't help calm her nerves. The pit in her stomach had only grown larger. She had to admit she was afraid of what the future held.

All her life she'd longed to become a mage. She'd watched her mother, Rhea, struggle to live up to the legacy her grandmother left as a healer.

Lark had been too young to meet her grandmother, Simone, but she had her to thank for the talent she possessed. According to her mother, Simone had just enough talent to make her healing spells work, but little enough that the mages turned her away from training.

Her mother had possessed no talent and couldn't match any of the miracles Simone performed while making a name for herself as a healer in Southmoat, but she didn't let that stop her. She spent her whole life learning herbal lore, finding ways to heal with the earth, just as surely as Simone healed with magic.

Lark had vowed to continue her family's mission. The power she'd been born with was much stronger than her grandmother's. Once she was trained, she could live up to the legacy of the women in her family. When she came across another poor child on the brink of death, she would be ready. She would make her mother proud.

She looked forward, steadily plodding down the forest path. Half a day's walk to the keep, Daus had said. She was almost there.

She needed this. On her own, all she'd used her powers for was death. Her head sank, her gaze drifting to the leaf strewn dirt footpath. Would the mages even allow her to train after learning she'd used her talent to murder?

Despite the question, she didn't regret her actions. Pax had been a beast. She would kill him a hundred times over for the pain he'd forced on Tiora.

And her stepfather Gael. A part of her wanted to cry when she thought of what she'd done to him. But then she remembered all he'd been party to. Stealing their home. Selling her into slavery. Killing Conall. Anger and hurt spread through her just thinking about it, paining her like a wound left to fester.

He deserved the death she gave him.

Did that make her irredeemable?

Lark was so lost in thought that at first, she didn't notice the forest coming to life all around her. It was the screeching bird cries that finally made her notice the strangeness surrounding her.

All the creatures in the forest were on the move. Squirrels and hares sped past, squeaking and squealing as they hopped through the underbrush. Birds took to the sky, a cacophony of sounds filling the air as they squawked noisily.

She gulped, realizing where they were all headed. Away from Mage Keep.

From somewhere ahead, a howl tore through the air, sending shivers down her spine. Sunny stopped in her tracks, her ears perking up and her fur bristling.

"Turn around."

Lark shook her head. That was only fear talking. She buried the fear deep down and stepped forward. She'd made her decision. She wasn't going to let anything stop her from becoming a mage. "C'mon, Sunny. Something's happening at the keep. Maybe we can help."

Sunny whined, her tail tucked between her legs, but she followed.

"Run. You have to run!"

She took another step, ignoring the voice. She was done being afraid.

A blur dropped down from the sky and streaked past her eyes. She jerked back, her legs wobbling as she staggered on the uneven ground.

"Muse?" Her brows shot up as the bird slowed and landed on a low branch in the forest beside her.

"Don't you ever listen? I said run!" She hopped along the branch, her wings flapping nervously.

Lark gawked at Muse, rubbing a hand on her temple. *"What the blazes? I'm going mad."*

"You're not crazy. I don't know how or why, but I can talk to you now. There's something happening where you're headed. I can see it from the sky. Something evil has been unleashed, and it's spreading. If you don't turn back, you'll be killed."

Her head spun. Could it be... was this bonding magic? Was she really talking to Muse?

A second howl split through the sky. Sunny cowered and backed away down the forest trail.

"See. She feels it, too. We have to go!" Muse bounced on the branch and spread her wings, her stare glued to where she and Sunny stood on the trail. *"Turn around, you stubborn girl!"*

"No, I can't turn around. I'm almost there." She cursed under her breath. *"What if we can help them?"* She lifted her foot, taking another step forward.

"Stop. You can't help them. Not from this."

Footsteps thundered up the trail. She whirled around, her chest thudding in time with the footfalls as she waited for the person making them to appear.

"Aren?" Her heart skipped a beat. She didn't think she'd see him again for months.

He skidded to a stop. His short blond hair was wind-tousled, and his pale skin was red with exertion. "Lark. I was searching for Muse." He paused, panting. "She took off like she spotted a blizzard brewing. I'm not surprised she found you."

"You can make eyes at each other later. We have to move."

Lark swallowed. "I... Something strange is happening. Muse, came to warn me."

Aren's brow furrowed. "She came to warn you?"

"Yes, I can hear her in my mind."

His gaze flicked between them, then he nodded. "Bonding magic."

"You don't think I'm crazy?"

"No, it makes sense. The way you are with her. The way birds quiet when you sing. I believe you."

Lark smiled, warmth blooming in her chest.

"C'mon. We have to go. Now. If you won't run to save yourself, then do it for them. Save your friends back at the wagons. Save Aren. They're in

danger, too." Muse rose into the sky, hovering for a brief instant before lifting into the air. *"Run."*

"What's she saying?" Aren gazed at Muse in flight, his head tilted and lips parted slightly.

"Run. We need to run." She sucked in a breath, her feet glued to the spot. She couldn't abandon her mission. Not again.

Aren strode forward, grabbing her hands. "Lark, I know you mean to be a mage, but you can't go to Mage Keep now. There are more people in this world with talent that can teach you. Come with us to Raimire. I'll help you find someone to teach you. I promise." He dropped her hands but didn't take his eyes off her.

She stared back, her mind racing. He could be right. She knew little about the world beyond her own country. She had a choice. She could race headlong into danger, hoping to find a mage still alive after facing whatever mysterious evil that had Muse and the rest of the forest animals fleeing, or she could run to warn her friends and try to find someone, somewhere, who could guide her in the future.

Lark searched herself, taking stock of her own feelings. She had to admit she could sense it, too. Something was wrong. It was there just beyond her grasp, wriggling across her shoulders, like a pair of eyes watching her from the woods.

She drew in a deep breath. There would not be a repeat of that day so long ago in Flamesmoat. She'd had a goal that day, the same as she had now. She'd ignored the voice that whispered something was wrong. Not today. Today would be different. She remembered the promise she'd made to herself in that tiny, barren warehouse back room. It was time for her to trust her own instincts.

She took off running. Sunny and Aren followed, all three of them with an eye on the sky, watching as Muse led them away from the keep and whatever evil had been awakened.

Chapter 24

"You arranged this as a distraction? What were you thinking?" Disgust tinged Kayda's voice as she stared at the battle spread out before her in the blood-red moonlit night. Hundreds of people swarmed Kings Keep, like scurrying mice fleeing floodwater.

The castle guards were spread thin, struggling to keep up with the sheer number of invaders. As she watched, a pair of guards were overwhelmed, crushed under the mass of bodies that poured in relentlessly. Yet others held their own, using their skill and superior weapons to spray blood through the air, hacking limbs, felling the enemy, one after one, mercilessly.

Bile stung the back of her throat as it dawned on her. There were no skilled warriors among these attackers. The common people of the city were attacking, and they were being slaughtered.

Vespen turned to her, his white hair lit vibrantly by the full moon. "You misunderstand, Princess. We arranged nothing. We merely used an inevitable event to our advantage."

Kayda shook her head. "What do you mean, inevitable?"

"Flamesmoat has been simmering with anger for weeks. Their beloved king was attacked and imprisoned. The castle guard beating down any who speak or act against them, filling the prison in Southmoat full to bursting. It was only a matter of time before their rage boiled over."

Her heart sank. She needed to get in the keep. But how could she countenance slaughtering her own people to clear a path?

She could see no way around it. There was an immense crowd surrounding the back entrance, kept at bay by a half dozen guards on the ground blocking the way. They would have to pass through a hail of arrows raining down from archers posted high on the keep walls to even make it that far. Then somehow, they would need to convince those guards to pause their bloodlust long enough to let them inside.

She gulped. "Please tell me you have a plan?"

"I'll get you to the doors, my lady." Vespen reached into his pockets, pulling out fistfuls of soil. "Stay close to me. Keep up with my pace, no matter what." The soil flew from his hands and scattered through the air in all directions.

A tingling sensation slid over her skin. At first, Kayda stared in confusion, wondering how the flying debris could help them, but then the dirt took shape and formed a sphere around them. She grinned, admiring the ingenuity of the earthen shield.

"Let's go." Vespen started forward. The sphere moved in sync with him, large enough to protect both of them, so long as they stayed within a few paces of each other.

Before long, they were in the middle of the fray. "Make way," Vespen shouted at the top of his lungs. All around them, people leapt aside, fear and shock painting their faces as they spotted the magical shield barreling toward them.

Most people had a healthy respect for mages, and they backed away reverently. Most, but not all. Kayda winced as a tanned man approached them, his face full of rage, a wooden cudgel held menacingly above his head, aimed at them.

Vespen saw him, too. The man swung the cudgel, his battle cry ringing hoarsely through the air. A clump of soil broke free from the shield and flew through the sky to strike him between the eyes. He staggered backward, his cry and assault interrupted, dropping the cudgel to scrub his face.

A rain of arrows flew through the sky. Her heart lurched as silver death winked in the air, coming closer. The shield kept them protected. The arrows hit the top and ricocheted off harmlessly.

But the rest of the crowd was not so lucky. Bodies fell all around her. Cries of agony filled the night.

A man beside them was struck in the eye. Droplets of his blood passed through the shield. His warm, wet blood sprayed Kayda's face before his lifeless form crumpled to the ground.

"Move!" Vespen took advantage of the confusion to shove his way further through the crowd.

Kayda buried the urge to vomit and tore her gaze from the dead man's body, panic driving her feet to move. She had to keep up with Vespen. Keep up or die.

All around her, people fell. She forced herself to ignore the screams and the gore. Death did not touch them beneath their shield. They were safe amid the madness.

Yet with every arrow turned aside, every projectile Vespen sent to displace another maddened attacker, their shield shrank. By the time they neared the door to the keep, the few paces of space they'd started with was gone. They stood shoulder to shoulder, the sphere reduced to a dome hovering close to their faces, the debris no longer protecting their legs.

Luckily, they didn't have far to travel, and the rain of arrows was no longer a threat this close to the handful of guards that held the door. She spotted one ahead. His metal armor was painted red with blood, his body never resting. His swung an axe and wielded a shield he used with just as much vigor, deflecting blow after blow and shoving folk back violently.

The guard spun sideways. His axe slammed into the chest of the man ahead of them with a wet *thud*. He lifted a metal-clad foot and kicked the man in the stomach, dislodging his axe. The kick sent the man tumbling into them, his dead weight rebounding off the remnants of the earthen shield. The rest of the debris fell to the ground, leaving them exposed.

The guard finally paused. Though she couldn't see his face below his helm, surprise was evident in his body language and clear in his voice. "Princess Kayda?" He sprang back in motion immediately. He snatched her away from Vespen and shoved her behind him. "Get her in the keep, now."

Kayda refused to retreat. "Vespen!" Her arm shot out as she desperately searched for the mage in the crowd. Her heart dropped to her feet. He was gone, already lost in the seething mass of people.

A second guard appeared a heartbeat later. His arms wrapped around her waist like a vise and he towed her away from the crowd and opened the keep door. He tossed her inside.

Tears stung her eyes as she landed hard on her behind on the cold stone floor. The door slammed shut, leaving her alone in the dimly lit corridor.

Her breath came flooding in gasps, chest heaving. She scrambled backward, her back smacking the corridor wall. The solid mass at her back helped calm her. She couldn't fall apart now. She clutched her chest, forcing her breath to slow. This wasn't over. She had to get moving.

She rose to her feet. Her heart was heavy as Vespen's face flashed in her mind. She took a step toward the door, the muffled sound of the melee outside reverberating in her ears.

Kayda turned from the door. No matter what guilt she harbored for Vespen's fate, she could do nothing to save him. She rushed through the keep in a daze, her familiarity with the building steering her feet while her thoughts jostled all around.

Somehow, she ended up in the library, the dusty tomes overpowering the scent of blood lingering on her skin. She snatched a candelabra from the wall and placed it on the floor, her shaking hands coaxing the hearth embers back to life.

Glass shattered with a crash. Screams and clashing steel roared in her ears. She couldn't move. She was transported back into the battle, watching from below the shield as death rained down from the sky and bodies fell all around her. Her breath quickened, her heart pounded as the wounded were trampled by their fellows. The dirt ran red and squished beneath her boots.

"No." She clutched her chest. *"Make it stop."*

She saw the man beside her, the one destined to catch an arrow in the eye, still alive and moving toward the keep. Only this time it was not some random man—it was Vespen. Her soul screamed as the arrow lodged in his skull. Vespen's hot blood splattered across her face. His body crumpled to the ground. *"Please, make it stop!"*

"You're not in battle any longer, my friend. It's over."

The calm voice snapped her out of her daze.

"It's over and you have to find me."

She shook her head, listening. Though the clamor from outside had not calmed completely, it had lost some of its intensity. It wasn't over, but her part in it had ended. She had work to do.

"Yes. Yes, you're right. I'm coming." She lit the candelabra and rose to her feet.

Soon, she found herself standing before the locked door in the forgotten basement chamber. The one that called to her. It called to her still.

This is where she would find her bondmate. She could feel it in her bones.

She turned the knob. The metal was no longer smooth but rough and rusted. Nevertheless, it held fast. She had no skill as a lock pick, but she did have one advantage. The door was wood.

She smiled, cupping her hand around one of the candelabra's three flames. She drew in a deep breath, a chill sinking into her skin. Then the door burst into flames.

She backed away. The water-damaged bottom ignited quickly. The top took a moment to catch before finally succumbing to the flames. While the fire ate away at the wood, a problem arose she'd not anticipated. The chamber was slowly filling with acrid smoke.

Kayda coughed, holding the sleeve of her tunic to her nose. It became harder and harder to breathe. Her throat felt raw, and her eyes stung, but she waited, watching smoke curl through the air as the door burned.

She could take it no longer. Letting out a hacking cough, she concentrated on the wooden door. She pulled at the flames, forcing them to move. Fire floated toward her, leaving the door a pile of crumbling ash at the bottom and smoldering char above.

With a thought, she extinguished the floating flames and strode forward. Using her boot, she tamped down the smoking ash on the ground. Then she bent, and lifting the skirt of her turquoise dress with one hand and the candelabra with the other, she carefully shimmied through.

She stood and smoothed her skirt, a lightness in her chest as she took her first breath from the other side of the door. Then she shivered, holding out the candelabra. Smoke curled through the air in the darkened tunnel. The walls, floor, and ceiling were made of packed dirt and stone. She could see no end of it. It appeared to go on forever.

Her heart sped up. Was she really going to do this? March into a darkened corridor that could lead anywhere? What if the walls collapsed, burying her beneath the castle? No one would ever find her.

She sucked in a breath, setting off another round of coughing. She staggered away, heading forward. At least she would leave behind that blazing smoke. She had to believe the walls would hold. Finding her bondmate was all that mattered.

The tunnel curved and wound through the earth. She walked for what felt like forever. Eventually, she rounded a bend and gasped as she spotted a problem. There, before her, sprawled a pile of stone and dirt that almost completely blocked the tunnel.

A small opening sat at the top of the piled rubble. She clambered up the rough stone and lifted the candelabra, squinting into the darkness. It appeared to lead somewhere. If she lay down on her stomach, she could squeeze through.

There was one problem. The candelabra was too tall to fit. She extinguished two candle flames, trembling as the darkness crept closer. Plucking the single lit candle from the center of the holder, she shoved the candelabra into the bag she'd slung over her shoulder.

There was only one way this would work. She would have to push the bag ahead of her while holding the candle, and then shimmy down the narrow passage on her stomach like a worm wriggling through the dirt. She gritted her teeth and put her plan into action.

Her bag was nearly too big for the small opening; it blocked much of the tunnel ahead of her. Her stomach roiled with discomfort. Only being able to see the scant bit of space between her and her bag was maddening.

Dust rose to choke her with each movement. She squirmed along, trying her best to ignore the sharp rocks stabbing at her belly and legs.

Before long, her entire body was inside the hole. She slid further. Would her next move cause another rockfall? The jungle people of Raimire buried their dead. She shuddered. Thankfully, she'd been born where cremation was the norm.

Time seemed to slow, the way it always did when she was doing something detestable. She tried to stay calm, to remind herself that every tiny lurch forward was one step closer to freedom. One step closer to finding her bondmate.

Then she felt it. The tickling of an insect crawling across her back. Panic overcame her. Immediate and visceral panic.

"Ahhhh!" Kayda shoved forward, heedless of the rocks stabbing her. She slammed her back along the top of the tunnel wall. Dust and debris rained down in a cloud. She had to knock it off. She had to escape.

Her heart hammering, she tossed her bag forward—and it slipped out of her grasp as it fell. Finally! Her breath flew out in a rush. The passage opened ahead. She scrambled forward. She clutched the edge of the opening and pulled herself free.

She tumbled straight down and landed with a jarring *thunk*, her head slamming into something hard. Pain screamed at her. She lost the candle, and the light snuffed out, leaving her shrouded in a darkness so complete it stole her breath.

Blazes.

She grappled in the dark, searching for the candle or her pack but finding only rock and dirt. Then she remembered the crawling sensation on her skin and snatched back her hands. Kayda curled into a ball, terror seizing her. She swept her hands all over herself, frantically trying to rid herself of the crawling bugs.

Get them off. She had to get them off!

She couldn't do this. She needed to see. She needed fire.

All of Izora's warnings came flooding back. Never summon without a source. Remember the cost. The terrible cost.

She didn't care. She would go mad if she had to spend one more instant in this unending black. She gulped a steadying breath and summoned.

Ice filled her veins as a fist-sized ball of fire appeared floating in the air in front of her. Relief washed through her, along with a wave of exhaustion. If she'd been standing, she would have fallen, but luckily, she was still curled on the floor. She wobbled instead, her eyes heavy and her body as weary and spent as a newborn babe.

She struggled to push through the exhaustion. Her teeth chattering, she forced her eyes open. She skimmed her gaze over her body and almost wept with relief. No bugs. Then she shifted her focus beyond the flame and shuddered.

She perched atop a pile of rubble on the tunnel's right side. To the left lay a huge, deep hole in the floor. She gasped, staring down into the cavernous pit.

Her bag was nowhere to be seen. It must've fallen, lost in the earth. Her clothes and food were gone. Worse still, her treasured tinderbox. She exhaled shakily. It could've been worse. She could be the one who'd vanished into that gaping maw.

White wax winked in the corner of her eye. Carefully, she crawled toward it, away from the hole. As her fingers wrapped around the skinny taper, she said a silent prayer of thanks. Pulling the floating flame toward her, she lit the candle with it and extinguished the flame.

The worst of the exhaustion lifted immediately. Her skin warmed. But a bone deep weariness lingered as she stood.

She shook her head. Couldn't be helped. She'd needed fire in that moment as surely as she needed air to breathe. Without it, she could've joined her bag in the pit. A little fatigue was a fair price to pay.

Kayda continued her trek through the tunnel, the light of her single candle barely enough to stave off the shadows. Her weary body dragged her down with each step. She needed rest. Sleep. But she pressed on, sheer determination keeping her feet shuffling forward when all she wanted to do was sink down and close her eyes.

At long last, she stopped before a doorway. Another door loomed there, identical to the one she'd burned at the start of her search. The thought of having to breathe in that choking smoke again started a phantom tickle in the back of her throat. She reached out, twisting the knob.

It turned. She bowed her head and sighed. Then she pushed.

Inside was an enormous chamber. She couldn't see the entirety of it with the scant light of her single taper, but she could sense the size of it nonetheless.

The trickling of water whispered in the distance. A musky scent assaulted her, the odor pungent after so long spent with only moist earth surrounding her.

And from deep within, she sensed something else. Movement. There was someone inside.

She crept forward cautiously. "Hello?" she called out.

"Ah, you made it." The voice in her mind sounded pleased. *"Come in, quickly. I need your help."*

Though she squinted in the dim light, she couldn't see her bondmate yet. She walked a few steps farther into the chamber, her pulse racing.

This was really happening. She was about to meet her bondmate.

Her foot connected with something on the dirt floor. Her gaze slid to the ground as it skidded away.

She gulped. A bone.

Another step. Another. Then her jaw dropped, her eyes blinking furiously.

She must be dreaming. Surely, she'd laid down in the tunnel and let the exhaustion lull her into a dream-filled slumber. This couldn't be real.

She stared into the room, her heart hammering madly. And from the shadows, a creature of myth stared back, eyes red as the flame of her candle.

Her bondmate was a dragon.

Chapter 25

Night had fallen as they waited on the ridge. The red moon rose high in the sky over the Abandoned Lands. Conall and Shadow sat with the five old mages off to the side, under guard.

The pulsating wall glimmered in the moonlight as the young mages and the castle guard roamed up and down from Mage Keep. They carried up boxes of all shapes and sizes. And weapons. So many weapons. For someone convinced there was nothing to fear beyond the Palisade, the prince certainly wasn't taking any chances.

Conall grimaced and rubbed his hands to warm them, ignoring the twinge of pain that shot out from his tightly bound wrists.

He wished they would get on with it. He still wasn't sure what part he had to play in this whole debacle, but he was cold and angry and sick of waiting. If Ereni was so set on the wall crumbling, then let it. He just wanted to get off the ridge and as far away from Mage Keep as possible.

He tore his gaze away from the hypnotic Palisade and found his stare drawn back to her. She talked with Prince Tarquin on the other side of the ridge in hushed tones. He swallowed hard as Tarquin placed a hand on her back and smiled down into her face.

Blazes, he'd been so stupid! How could he have trusted a girl he'd only known a few weeks with so much of himself? His stomach churned with disgust. He deserved this. Every awful feeling roiling within him. He would never make that mistake again.

"Brother, look. I think they're ready."

Shadow was right. The path from the keep was empty, the ridge crowded with everyone milling about among the stacked boxes and weaponry. Anticipation was heavy in the air.

Ereni strode forward, staring at the men standing guard over their group. "Stand them up and bring them forward toward the wall." She spoke in a commanding tone, her voice clear and unwavering. "The wolf and my mother stay."

His heartbeat surged as the man behind him grabbed his elbow and shoved him up onto his feet. Why was he being led to the Palisade? He was no mage.

"You don't have to do this, daughter," Delyth said from the ground. "It's not too late to change your mind."

Ereni ignored her, turning her back and strolling up to where he stood with the four mages, a handbreadth away from the pulsating wall of magic. "To break the Palisade we need four mages. One strong in each of the four elements." She strode between them, her gaze flicking between them as she spoke. "When all four mages join together with one strong in bonding magic"—her stare slid to him, and his stomach burned—"then, and only then, will the magic be broken."

That was why she needed him here. It all made a sick kind of sense now. She had never cared for him at all, only for his magic.

He shook his head. Suddenly, he wanted nothing to do with her plans. "I won't do it."

Ereni quirked a brow, her lips curling into a twisted smile. "Won't you?"

Shadow growled. The guard beside him held the rope leash in one hand and a sword at his neck with the other.

Ereni continued, "You might want to reconsider that, or you'll be searching for a new bondmate when this is all over."

She knew him too well. There was no way he could stand by and watch Shadow be killed while he had a chance to do something about it.

"Leave him alone. I'll do what you want."

She nodded to the guard, who dropped his sword from Shadow's neck. Then she turned her attention back to the mages. "Do I have to remind you what you have to lose? All the children, all of your families. They go free as soon as this is done."

The mages peered around, their fearful gazes connecting with each other's and one by one landing on Delyth.

"It's all right," Delyth said, her voice firm. "You don't have any other choice. No one will fault you for your actions here tonight."

Ereni pulled her hunting knife from her belt sheaf. She walked past each mage and sliced through their bindings.

She saved Conall for last. He stared at her, his face cold. As she reached forward to slice his bindings, her fingers brushed his skin, and he recoiled.

She opened her mouth as if to speak, and her eyes filled with a glimpse of something he couldn't name. As quickly as the look came over her face, it vanished, replaced with a solemn stare. Her mouth slammed shut. Then she grasped his hands and tore away the rope from his wrists.

She stepped away, gone from his side before the rope hit the ground. He rubbed his wrists, his gaze returning to the behemoth of a wall before him.

"On my mark, place your hands flat on the Palisade," Ereni's voice boomed behind him.

He gulped, his heart beating madly.

He was really going to do this. All of Gael's warnings came rushing back. Would he still be the same man when this was over? It didn't matter. Shadow had saved his life. He would be a coward and a snake if he wasn't willing to return the favor.

He looked to the side. All the mages held out their hands, just short of touching the metallic gleam. He mimicked their stance, thrusting his hands forward. What would it feel like? He didn't have long to speculate.

"Now."

His skin made contact, and his face lit up with awe, goosebumps sliding over his skin. He'd expected the surface to feel cool, but it was warm. As warm as a rock that sat soaking up the sun. Even more strangely was how it pulsed, echoing the beat of his heart. Like something alive.

Suddenly, the wonder vanished. Pain rose to fill the void. Pain so intense it stole his breath. He hadn't thought he'd ever feel worse than on the day he'd fallen, his body bruised all over and pierced through with an arrow. But this—this was so much worse.

His every nerve ending was alive with fire. His bones rattled beneath his skin. He wanted to scream but couldn't. His jaw clamped shut. He closed his eyes and moaned instead, praying for the wall to fall before it killed him where he stood.

He opened his eyes to a changed world. He was floating. All around him, in every direction, the Palisade's metallic gleam filled his vision.

The pain was gone. So was the ridge, Mage Keep, and all the people who stood watch over him.

"Shadow?"

Panic flooded his chest when his bondmate did not reply. Wherever he was, he was alone.

No. Not alone.

From afar, he spotted something. Someone adrift in the magic like him. He squinted, unsure of who he was seeing, as they floated on the Palisade's undulating surface. If only he could get closer—

He gasped. The idea had barely formed in his mind before he found himself beside the far-off form.

His heart thumped wildly. How was that possible? He pushed the thought aside and took a closer look at the figure beside him.

It was Amora. She floated freely, eyes closed, her face calm and slack, as if asleep. He grabbed her shoulder and shook. "Amora. Wake up."

Her lashes fluttered open. She eyed her surroundings before turning to him. "Conall? Where are the others?"

He shook his head. "I don't know." Then he looked around. Off in the distance, he could just make out another figure floating.

This was it. This was his purpose in this strange void. He had to bring them together.

"Hold on." He grasped Amora's hand. Then he wished they were both beside the floating figure.

It worked! He grabbed the man and jumped again. This time, he found a woman. They jumped once more, with all the mage's hands linked. They roused the final man, and finally, they were all together.

"What do we do now?" asked the man he'd collected on the second jump. He looked older than Amora, his wrinkled skin deeply lined, his bushy white eyebrows raised in question.

Amora thrust out her hand. "We summon."

The words had barely escaped her lips before a ball of water formed on her outstretched palm. The other mages followed suit. The old man held out a ball of fire. The second woman materialized a ball of dirt, and the final man a ball of swirling vapor.

A flurry of sensations filled Conall as he floated beside the mages. His skin tingled from within and prickled on the surface, moisture and cold surrounding him. But despite the strangeness filling the void, nothing changed.

Then he felt it. The surface he floated on began to weaken. His gaze roved around as the shiny substance blurred.

As the void responded to the magic, its shimmering gleam dimming, the pulsating gyrations growing erratic and wild, a new feeling crawled across his skin he couldn't explain. The unmistakable sensation of being watched.

He jolted around erratically, searching for the source of his discomfort. There was nothing but the endless metallic sea. No matter how much he looked, he couldn't shake the squirming itch.

Was something there with them, watching?

A flash of the real world intruded into their shared vision. He saw himself and the mages from behind, all still holding tight to the Palisade. The onlookers gathered around, watching, their eyes stretched wide with horror.

Then the scene disappeared, gone before he could delve any further.

His stomach contorted. Why did their faces look like that? What was so terrifying?

"Conall. Come back." Shadow's voice reached him within the crumbling void, his usual calm tone now frantic. *"You have to come back now."*

His bondmate's terror set his nerves on edge. He could feel it, too. Something was wrong. He had to do something.

The Palisade needed to fall, now.

He stared at the mages. The balls had tripled in size. The void drew on their power, sucking at the elements held in their outstretched palms. They kept summoning, their faces the picture of deep concentration.

He stretched out his own hands, turning them over, staring at his palms curiously. Ereni had said he could summon. Maybe he could tip the scales. But how?

He recalled the way he'd jumped through the void. It had been so simple, action following thought. Could this be just as simple?

There was only one way to find out. He stared at the mages, watching the balls growing slowly. So slowly. He pictured each of those elements rising from his own hands. Then his mouth fell open as power took shape before his eyes.

On his right palm, an orb of fire warmed his flesh. The gently swirling wind tickled his fingertips. His left palm held a cool orb of water, and the earth's heavy weight floated above his left fingertips.

The sensations that started as the mages summoned intensified. His body thrummed with power.

All around him, the void responded. The gleaming fabric of the Palisade grew fuzzier. Weaker. He remembered Shadow's plea. He needed to do more.

He glanced at his hands, and a thought crossed his mind. He had to bring the mages together. Maybe he needed to bring the elements together, too?

He moved his arms close to each other until his palms were cupped together side by side. The power responded, the elements swirling quicker.

He gasped, as the balls conjured by the others responded in kind, creeping closer to each other as they expanded. His body shuddered, his teeth chattering. Yes, this was right. But it still wasn't enough.

He hesitated. The itch was still there, slithering across his skin. The phantom watched with great interest. Though he still couldn't see it, as the Palisade weakened, he could sense a presence there with them. Its sickening glee. It wanted this. For the Palisade to fall.

Indecision battled the certainty from just moments before. The magic on his hands swirled slower, the balls shrinking.

He took a deep breath and slammed his hands together. The elements collided. He was buffeted by a power so intense he lost all sense of time and place. Something inside of him screamed. It was a mistake! He was being destroyed.

Then he blinked. He was back on the ridge. He had just enough time to note the gorgeous scenery, visible again, before he collapsed.

He came to sometime later. It couldn't have been long; the ridge was still swathed in moonlight. People shuffled around uneasily, wearing shocked expressions and staring in his direction.

His mind was fuzzy, and the pain had returned with a vengeance, weighing down his limbs and making it hard to breathe. He sprawled out on the ridge, and someone pressed on his chest. He groaned, staring up into the handsome, dark face of a young man he vaguely recognized.

"He's waking." The man removed his dirt-covered hand from his chest. "I think he'll be all right, eventually." He stood and walked away, joining Ereni's side.

That's right. He was one of the young mages that helped carry the boxes and weapons earlier. Most of them still crowded around Ereni, but a few had broken off to tend to him and the mages he'd joined in the void.

He turned his head sideways, hoping to see the mages awakening as well. The sight he was met with was much grimmer than he'd hoped for. His stomach lurched.

Closest to him lay the oldest man. He was clearly dead, his body emaciated and shrunken. His expression was far from the calm concentration Conall remembered seeing last. Instead, his features were locked in agony.

The man's death stare brought tears to his eyes. He couldn't even remember his name.

Helpful, kind Amora lay with the others he'd barely known but who had helped him break free from that strange, undulating dream world. None of them had made it.

Tears welled in his eyes, the hope he'd held in his heart disappearing just as surely as the magic wall had. If only he'd realized what needed to be done sooner, had he not hesitated, maybe he could have saved them.

A commotion broke out somewhere behind him. The next instant, a warm weight settled by his side. Shadow.

"I heard you calling for me." His head tilted sideways, the fuzzy feeling wrapping around him again. *"Thank you, brother."*

"I'm here for you always, little brother." Shadow looked down at him, his muzzle still wrapped in rope, golden eyes filled with relief. *"You've been through a lot. Rest."*

His eyelids were already drooping. Sleep rose up to claim him.

When he woke next, daylight filled the sky. Two burly men in white robes lifted him atop a long wooden stretcher. Shadow sat beside him, his bonds removed, watching the men as they worked together to place him on the rough boards.

"Shadow, what's happening? Where are they taking me?"

"Good. You're awake." Shadow's tail wagged. *"I think they mean to bring you down this hillside. You're in no condition to do it on your own right now. Just relax and let them do the work for you."*

Conall tried to lift his arm and swallowed hard when it barely rose off the stretcher. He had the strength of a newborn lamb. He resigned himself to being carried.

A face appeared, hovering over his own as soon as the men had him situated on the stretcher. Delyth, the Sade Prim, peered down at him, her piercing blue eyes soft as they connected with his. "Thank you for what you did back there. I know it must have been an incredible trial."

The men stood, one at the foot and one at the head of his stretcher. He rose in the air with a groan. They began walking, jostling his body painfully with each step. They took ten steps before they both froze, their gazes locked on something far off on the horizon.

He lifted his head as much as he could bear. It caused pain to shoot down his spine but afforded him a view of what the men were watching.

His blood pounded through his veins. Down on the beach, where the campfire still burned, men the size of ants ran around screaming. Something was attacking them.

"Hurry," Delyth ordered. "We don't have long now."

"What?" he croaked out, his own voice sounding strange in his ears.

"They'll be everywhere within a few hours. Our only choice is to flee." Delyth kept pace with the men as they tramped down the ridge, back to the keep. "Most of the others have left already, heading for the mountain passes. I'm taking you with me. I'll need your help in Doln."

"Doln? I can't go to Doln." He shook his head, the motion sending a wave of dizziness through his body. "I have to find my sister. That's all that matters to me now."

"Do you know where she is? Do you have even an inkling?"

His stomach wobbled at the reminder. "No."

"What if I told you I knew a woman who could help you find her? The Winter Witch of the North."

He scoffed. "I'd tell you I don't believe in legends and myths."

"She's real. As real as you or I. She'll help you find your sister."

He shook his head again, groaning with pain as he tried to pull himself to standing and rise on his own two feet. "I don't believe you. I'm done with you mages. Shadow and I will find Lark on our own." The stretcher wobbled. The men struggled to keep it steady while he attempted to climb free.

"Lie back, Conall of Greenvale. You're as stubborn as a mule. Just like your father."

The words sent shock flooding through his chest. He fell back, lying still on the stretcher. "You knew my father?"

"Knew him? I know him still."

No, that couldn't be right.

He frowned. "That's impossible. He's been dead for more than a decade."

"I'm afraid you're mistaken." She stared down at him, and he spied the truth written on her face. "Come with us, help me reach the Winter Witch, and I'll tell you where to find him."

Could it be true? Was his father alive? The thought sent a surge of feeling through him. Anger and elation warred within him as he imagined seeing him again. He had to know. He owed it to himself and Lark to find out the truth. And if he could learn his sister's fate at the same time? It seemed he had no choice but to follow Delyth to Doln to seek the Winter Witch.

"She wants us to go with her, through the mountains to the north. What do you think? Should we trust her?"

"Trust her... No. But she is right about one thing. We need to leave. Do you feel that?" Shadow stopped suddenly, letting out an ear-splitting howl.

"What was that for? What are you talking about, brother? I feel nothing but pain." Even as the thought faded, a shiver slithered up his spine. There it was again. That odd tickle in the back of his skull that told him he was being watched. Shadow could feel it, too?

"I have to warn them. All my brothers and sisters out there. Whatever that was on the beach—it's coming." Shadow lifted his muzzle and howled with all his might.

Chapter 26

They caught up to the wagons outside of Bogsmouth. Muse sat atop her perch on the wagon, awaiting their arrival. *"Hurry, we're still not safe here."*

Surprise and delight painted the faces of the show members as they spotted Aren, Lark, and Sunny tearing into the clearing.

"Lark, you're back." Tiora beamed. But the smile fell from her face as she noted her friends' panicked expressions.

"There's trouble," Lark said between gasping breaths, "headed our way." She clutched her stomach, doubling over. "We have to leave, now."

"Leave?" Mazen's brow arched. "We just got here. And this town is always generous with tips."

Dausius hopped down from the colorful wagon and approached them quickly. "What's the trouble?" He reached out a hand to rub her back and stuffed a waterskin in her hands with the other. "Calm down, have a drink, and tell us everything."

She straightened and set the waterskin to her lips, gulped a few quick swallows, then tossed the skin to Aren. He caught it and began drinking while she recounted their tale.

"When I got close to Mage Keep, all the forest animals started going crazy. Running away from something."

"Yes, we saw it, too," Dausius replied.

"That's when Muse found me." She paused, her stomach in knots. "And she spoke to me."

"Lark, have you been drinking?" Mazen asked with a laugh. Meital shoved an elbow in his side, looking annoyed at the interruption.

"Bonding magic." Aren chimed in, handing the skin back to Dausius.

Lark stared at Dausius. His body was still for once, but she could see the wheels turning in his mind. He had to believe her.

Mazen was the first to speak, his voice incredulous. "You have bonding magic *and* elemental? I didn't think that was possible..."

"If Lark says she heard Muse speaking, then I believe her," Tiora said to Mazen, hands on her hips.

"I do, too." Dausius' hands shot out. He grabbed her arms and stared down into her face. "What did she tell you?"

A weight lifted off her shoulders. He believed her!

Her words came out in a rush. "She said some evil had been unleashed and that it was spreading. If I kept heading to Mage Keep, I would be killed. She told me to run." She glanced at Muse, remembering her final warning. "She says we're still not safe here."

Dausius turned to stare at Muse; she shifted from foot to foot on her perch. Whisper was behaving the same way. Both of the birds seemed ill at ease, their heads and eyes jerking all over on high alert.

He whirled back to her, his brown eyes searching her own. "All right. We run." Dausius spun her where she stood, turning her toward the wagons. "Hop in." Then he scooped up Sunny and deposited her inside the plain wagon before hopping into the front of his own. "Follow me closely, girls," he called back as he mounted the driver's bench and grabbed the reins. "We'll head straight for the docks."

Aren jumped into the back of Daus' wagon as it started moving, nodded to Mazen and Meital, and headed over to calm the birds.

Tiora held the reins for their wagon, but she reached over and squeezed Lark's hand as Lark settled next to her on the bench. "I'm glad you're back."

Dausius set a punishing pace. The wagons rattled over the cobblestone streets of Bogsmouth. This town was one of the largest they'd been in, but not nearly as big as Flamesmoat. People dove out of the way of their speeding wagons, cursing and shaking their fists.

Bogsmouth was full of fishermen, perched on the edge of the Boglands that bordered the Kingdom of Dracwood to the south. The Boglands were rumored to be dangerous, filled with carnivorous beasts, but that didn't stop the people of this town from reaping the riches of their waters. The smell of fresh fish filled the air, and Lark spotted a marketplace to the right of their path that appeared to be thriving.

Laughter bubbled in the air. As they rushed around a corner, she spotted the source. A schoolhouse sat to their left. Dozens of children played a game of tag in the yard. Lark's stomach clenched, and she shared a look with Tiora. "Shouldn't we warn them?"

Tiora shook her head, placing a hand on Lark's. "Do you think they would believe you without any proof?" she asked gently.

Lark frowned, her heart shattering. She knew she was right, but it didn't stop the sick feeling stabbing her stomach. She exhaled, tearing her gaze from the schoolhouse.

Soon they approached the dock section of town. Unlike the crowded streets near the marketplace, this area was practically deserted. Dausius pulled his wagon to a stop beside a rickety wooden dock on the far edge. He didn't even wait for it to come to a full stop before he hopped down, heading straight for a fellow sitting in a worn wicker chair.

"Dal, how good to see you, my friend." He sauntered forward with his arms spread open in welcome, a wide grin plastered on his face.

The man rose from his chair, holding up a tanned arm to shade his eyes from the sun. He was fit and trim, dressed in mud splattered overalls, his feet bare, and he appeared to be about the same age as Daus. "Dausius?" His brown eyes squinted. "That you?"

"Yes, it's me. I have a proposition for you. How would you feel about ferrying my friends and I through the Boglands?" He pulled out a coin purse, jingling it noisily. "I'll pay double if we can leave immediately."

Dal quirked a brow. "Make it triple, and you've got a deal."

"Done," Dausius agreed readily. "We'll need at least two boats. Do you have another sailor who can join us?" He tossed the coin purse through the air.

Dal caught it, hefting the bag a few times before stuffing it into his pocket with a smile. "Sure do. Let me grab my boy, Fillan. You and your folks can load what you want to bring in the two biggest canoes down at the end of the dock." His gaze skimmed over the wagons as he walked away from the dock to fetch his boy. "Two ought to handle it, if you pack light. Unless you want to bring the horses?"

"No, they'll have to stay with the wagons, I'm afraid," Dausius announced.

Mazen's face fell. He'd always taken the lead in caring for their horses each night.

Dausius noticed. "Horses don't last long in the jungle, son," he said quietly. "I'm sorry."

Mazen looked sick, but he nodded, then grabbed a crate from the wagon and carried it down the dock.

"All right." Dausius turned to address them. "Let's get those boats loaded. Only bring what we need. Food, a few changes of clothes, props for the show."

"And the animals." Aren grabbed a box and set off down the docks.

"Yes, of course." Dausius climbed into the back of the colorful wagon, dumped out a large bag, and started throwing things around, stuffing clothes and various props inside while discarding others.

Lark counted herself lucky she'd already packed. She grabbed her bag and whistled for Sunny to follow then settled both in one of the boats at the end of the dock. She returned to help with the food, carefully treading on the dock's shifting boards.

With everyone working together, they filled the boats quickly. Lark was just settling down next to Tiora in the largest canoe when Dal came back with a young man who looked like a younger version of himself. He even wore matching overalls and bare feet, though his skin was not so darkly tanned.

The man strolled up to the canoe she was in. He hopped in with a smile. "I'm Fillan. Nice to meet you all." He glanced around the boat, an expectant look on his face.

Tiora jumped in, making introductions. "Hello. I'm Tiora, and this is Lark and Aren."

They all exchanged nods, then Fillan's face lit up as he spotted the birds and Sunny sitting behind them. "You're bringing your pets, too?" His smile widened. "This ought to be fun."

Lark stared beyond Fillan. Mazen stood alone next to the wagons, unhitching the horses.

Fillan glanced over curiously. "Aren't you folks going to sell those horses and wagons before you leave? My dad could get you a good price for them."

"No," Aren said. "We have to leave now."

"Mazen." Dausius rose to his feet on the second boat. "Get on board. We're leaving."

Mazen gave each horse a gentle pat, then sprinted down the dock and hopped into the smaller boat with Dausius, Meital, and Dal. Meital threw her arm around his shoulders as he sat, squeezing tightly. Then Dal and Fillan stood in unison, untying the ropes that kept the canoes tied to the dock.

Lark sighed as they pulled free from the dock. They'd made it.

Then the screaming started.

They'd just pulled free of the docks when the sound blew in on a cool breeze. "What in the world?" Fillan peered back toward Bogsmouth. "Wonder what's going on back there?"

Though they steadily moved through the water away from town, the screams only grew louder. All of them stared in horror at the shore, their eyes peeled for the cry's source. Lark's heart thumped madly, the smiling faces of the children they'd passed on their way to the docks fresh in her mind. What was happening back there?

Movement on the dock's far side captured her attention. Her breath caught as a young woman staggered into sight. Her face was crazed, and she screamed at the top of her lungs. Her arms flailed about wildly, clutching her body.

Something was on her. A blur of motion climbing across her chest.

"What is that?" Tiora's eyes widened with terror.

Lark shook her head. She'd never seen anything like it. The small creature was barely bigger than a squirrel, with brown and silver-striped fur, sharp fangs, and claws. The creature tore a path across the woman's chest, slashing and biting her hands as she desperately sought to dislodge it. As the poor woman opened her mouth to scream again, the creature struck, launching on her face and viciously tearing out her tongue.

Lark's stomach lurched as the woman's screams stopped and she dropped to the ground. The creature held fast, tearing at her face relentlessly.

"Bloody blazes, what is that thing?" Fillan stared at the shore, his brown eyes round. Then he gulped as more creatures came bounding into sight. "How many are there?"

Lark blinked twice, not trusting her eyes. There were so many. Dozens bolted toward the fallen woman, covering her body in a blanket of writhing fur. Others spotted the horses where they stood on the edge of the docks and raced toward them.

The creatures were on them in an instant. Though the horses bucked and brayed with all their might, it was no use. They were overwhelmed by the sheer number of creatures piled atop them, tearing and biting at their flesh.

"I don't believe it," Dal said from the boat beside them. "The scourge. I thought it was just a legend."

"Is that what this is, then?" Dausius asked. "I suppose it must be."

"You know what those creatures are?" Lark grabbed Tiora's hand, clutching it tightly.

Dausius nodded. "There's a legend in these parts about creatures who lived long ago. The people here call them the scourge, but they have many names... *ichneumon*... dragonkillers."

Meital gasped, her arm wrapped tightly around Mazen, who watched the horses being slaughtered with teary eyes. "Those things could kill dragons?"

Dausius pitched his voice loudly, moving his hands animatedly, like when he told stories at the show. "They were said to be fast as lightning, fearless, and full of an insatiable hunger. They'll eat anything that moves, but they delight in finding and devouring eggs. Especially dragon eggs. They could even take down a fully grown dragon, sliding down their throat, tearing them apart from the inside."

Suddenly, the boat she was in lurched backward. Lark tore her gaze from Dausius and spun in her seat to find Fillan shoving a long wooden pole into the bottom of the bog. Tears streamed down his face.

"What are you doing?" Lark asked, her voice shrill.

"We have to go back." Fillan pushed again on the pole. "We have to help them. My friends…"

Tiora stood and placed a hand on his arm. "Listen. It's already too late."

Lark listened, too. She was right. The screams had died down. The scourge had already torn through, decimating the large town in mere moments. Her stomach heaved. All those people. The children.

Fillan broke down, sobbing. Aren stood slowly, the boat wobbling as he removed the pole from Fillan's shaking fingers. "I'm so sorry," Aren said as the boy sank down into a seat, holding his head in his hands.

"Aren." Tiora's eyes bulged, her hands twitching. "I hope you know how to use that pole."

Lark leaned sideways, sweat dripping down her spine. Their canoe still drifted toward the docks. The dragonkillers had spotted them. At least a dozen raced along the rickety structure, their beady eyes watching as the boat glided ever closer in the calm water.

"I'm on it." Aren shoved the pole into the bog, grunting. They stuttered to a stop, then slowly reversed direction.

Lark shivered as the creatures raced to the end of the docks. The one in the lead ran at breakneck speed. Its gaze connected with her own, and she yelped. It was going to jump!

It splashed into the bog barely an arm's length away from where she sat, spraying her face with droplets and disappearing below the murky water. She scrambled back from the side of the canoe as it resurfaced.

Her gaze locked on it, and she trembled, fighting off the nauseous ache that invaded her body from its stare. She stared into its eyes and saw the moment panic set in. It began to struggle. Then she exhaled a shaky breath as it bobbed up and down. The ravenous beasts had at least one flaw. They couldn't swim.

The dragonkillers backed away, making no attempt to save their drowning brethren or to reach the canoe as it steadily picked up speed.

Lark sat still in the canoe as her heartbeat slowed, her mind roiling with conflicting emotions. She was relieved, and so intensely happy to have escaped the savagery that had befallen that town. She looked to Muse, her heart filled with gratitude. There was no question she'd saved her life. All of their lives.

Some part of her had been in disbelief as she watched the scene unfold, but now the gravity of the mayhem she'd witnessed sank in. Those things were a menace. They would tear through the Kingdom of Dracwood, laying waste to everything in their path.

A lump formed in the pit of her stomach. If they'd made it this far, did that mean the mages had already been destroyed? If the strongest among them had fallen, what chance did the rest of them have?

Her heart broke for her friends back in Greenvale. All the gentle souls she'd sang for on their trip across the country as the Wandering Bards. The thousands of people in Flamesmoat. They had no idea what was coming for them.

Chapter 27

Kayda stared wide-eyed in disbelief. She had to be dreaming. She was standing in front of a dragon—and he needed her help?

"Come on, don't be shy. We've shared our thoughts already. Meeting in the flesh should be a simple matter."

She gulped. The single candle flame flickered in her shaky hands as she took a step closer. Her bondmate was covered in black scales that blended into the darkness so well she couldn't accurately gauge the size of him. Based on his head alone, she imagined he must be incredibly massive, at least the size of a small house.

She had every right to be afraid standing before this beast, but she took another step, the fear she expected completely absent. Something within pulled her closer until she stood beside his enormous head.

"I'm Kayda." Her hand reached out as if it had a mind of its own and stroked a hard, smooth scale on his jaw. *"What's your name?"*

"Kayda. It's a little short for my liking, but I suppose it shall do. I am Druturion the Black. Pleased to meet you, Kayda." He leaned into her touch, the motion so forceful it nearly sent her tumbling backward.

The name struck a chord within her. *"Druturion the Black,"* she repeated.

"It is a bit of a mouthful for you humans, I'm told. If you prefer, you may call me Dru for short."

That was it. *"My ancestor Algernon rode a dragon he called Dru..."*

Druturion snorted, and his breath sent her skirts swirling round her legs. *"Yes, yes, we're one and the same. He's pleased to meet you as well."*

Kayda stepped back. Her heart skipped a beat. One and the same? *"You can't mean... but that would make you five centuries old, at the least."*

"Hard to believe, I know, but entirely possible with magic on your side. I'll explain it all when we have the time. But now, we have to get out of here."

She nodded, feeling his urgency through the bond. *"What do you need me to do?"*

"I'm a fire dragon. We don't just spit fire, we need to ingest flames in order to keep up our strength. Could you bring that flame of yours closer?"

Kayda strode forward and lifted the candle up next to one giant, crimson eye.

"No, that won't do. It needs to be larger. Do you have anything else we can use as kindling?"

She shook her head, regretting the loss of her pack. *"No, but I can make it bigger with magic."*

"Good, do it."

Kayda took a deep breath and concentrated on the flickering candle. Instantly, it grew larger, the flame quickly becoming the size of her head. She wobbled on her feet, cold seeping into her skin, and the exhaustion returning with a vengeance. She ignored it, holding the candle aloft. *"How is that?"*

"Good, that should work nicely. Drop it in." His massive jaws opened, revealing a set of huge, sharp teeth that glimmered like deadly icicles in his dark maw.

She gulped but followed his instructions, dropping the candle in his mouth and stepping back. A heartbeat later, his jaw snapped shut, bathing the room in darkness.

Her heart jolted in the black room. She cursed herself for not thinking to leave herself some light. The thought had hardly crossed her mind before Dru swallowed and dizziness washed over her.

The next thing she knew, she sprawled on the ground in the dark, her mind swimming and eyes fluttering open to a world of black.

"You didn't tell me you conjured the flame on that candle. Stupid girl. You could have killed yourself, summoning without a source."

She sat up, cradling her head in her hands. *"Blazes, you don't have to yell. My head is already killing me."*

"Well, at least you won't have to worry about finding a source very often now." He opened his jaw, and she glimpsed a light—a flame—radiating inside his throat. The room was lit enough for her to see again, though much of the enormous chamber remained swathed in shadow.

She rose to her feet, her body feeling strangely heavy. Dropping her hands from her head, she patted her chest, her eyes widening as she palmed the rounded flesh that had somehow grown larger. She took a step, and her legs wobbled. Was she taller, too?

"You're not going crazy. You look a few years older, I'm afraid. The price you pay for summoning without a source."

She gasped, her hands roving around her body. Bloody blazes, of all the times to be stuck without a mirror.

"It's not too bad." Dru's voice was heavy with amusement. *"You were very young to begin with. I'd say it's actually a bit of an improvement."*

"I'm glad you find this funny," she said, trying her best not to scream. Although he had a good point. How many times in the past had she lamented that no one would take her seriously because of her age? Still, she couldn't help feeling like a stranger in her own skin.

Dru stood, and she stepped back, craning her neck, gaping as his head brushed the ceiling.

"Ah, yes. I haven't felt this strong in ages. Quick now, climb beneath me. I'm going to put a hole in the ceiling. This place is much too crowded."

She lifted a foot to follow his instructions, but set it down in the same spot as a thought flickered in her mind. Too crowded. Crossing her arms, she stared up at him. *"Wait a moment. How many bonds have you had?"*

Dru stiffened. His head tilted as a single eye fixed on her. *"Including you? Five."*

"Five?" Kayda's stomach sank. Her grandfather had struggled with two voices in his head. Now she was bonded to a dragon who had four other voices distracting him. What could go wrong?

"It's no challenge for a dragon, I assure you. Now get beneath me before you're crushed by the ceiling."

Kayda rushed forward, ducking beneath his neck and sliding between two clawed feet until she was hunkered down below Dru's chest. Then he rammed his head into the chamber ceiling, and dirt and debris rained down around them. The ceiling trembled with the force of his strikes. She covered her face with her sleeves, holding her breath to avoid choking on the dust swirling in the air.

He struck a half dozen times before a hole appeared in the roof and sunlight flooded into the chamber. She blinked and shielded her eyes from the light. A few more strikes of Dru's massive head, and the hole looked wide enough for him to stick most of his body through.

"That ought to do it," he declared. *"Well, what are you waiting for? Hop on my back. Let's get out of here."*

Her heartbeat picked up speed. She was about to ride a dragon.

Kayda climbed out from beneath Dru, using the piles of dirt to boost herself high enough to grab his long black neck. For a girl who spent much of her childhood climbing trees, it was no challenge. In fact, it sent a strange thrill racing through her as she perched atop his back. Her turquoise dress bunched up around her thighs as she wrapped her arms and legs tightly around his neck.

In the sunlight, she could finally get a good look at her bondmate. What she saw made her eyes widen with wonder. His black scales were not fully black at all but shimmered with flecks of purple, green, and blue. He was indeed as large as a house, but his body wasn't bulky. His long limbs, enormous wings, and svelte torso seemed almost feline in strength and agility.

"Are you ready?" Dru's body tensed beneath her.

Kayda's heart thumped against her ribs. Her skin tingled with anticipation. Part of her still couldn't believe this was real. But the greater part was alive with joy. She was going to ride a dragon!

"Yes, I'm ready."

Dru hopped up from the hole in the ground. A single leap was all it took to send them bounding free of the earth. They landed in the old decaying cemetery bordering the Church of the Dragon.

Kayda smiled. She'd always doubted the church's teachings, but no longer. The certainty she always longed for had found her last night. There was no denying she would have a part to play in the future of her country.

The church door flew open with a bang, and a group of priors clambered out, their faces filled with wonder. Some were crying, others smiling and laughing. A few dropped to their knees, while others clumped together, clutching each other, jumping and hugging.

She ached to stay, if only for a moment, to bask in the joy on their faces, but Dru was already tensing again, preparing to take to the sky. Unfurling his black wings, he pumped furiously. He took two running steps forward, and on the third, they sprang free from the ground.

Tears flooded her eyes. How many times had she wished for this? Countless times spent watching birds in flight, her heart longing for just a small taste of that freedom. The wind flew through her hair, and the world grew smaller as they climbed. And her heart soared with them.

"Who were those men back there in the robes?" Dru pulled to the left, circling the city from above. *"I would've thought the first humans to see a dragon would be quaking with fear, not filled with delight?"*

Kayda stared down at the ground, wondering what Dru was searching for. *"Those were priors from the Church of the Dragon."*

He stopped dead in the air and hovered in place. Kayda jerked sideways, the sudden stop almost sending her rolling off his neck. A sound filled her mind as Dru rumbled beneath her.

Was he laughing? The thought of his many bonds returned to plague her. Was this the first sign of madness?

"Church of the Dragon," he repeated between bursts of laughter. *"You humans will pray to anything, won't you?"*

She bristled, frowning. *"They were right, you know. They said drag-ons would return one day, and here you are."*

The laughter quieted as he continued circling. *"All right, all right,"* he mumbled angrily.

Kayda held on tightly, her stomach churning.

"I'm sorry," Dru blurted out. *"Algernon tells me it's not polite to mock your religions. I'll be more tactful in the future."*

His apology calmed her racing nerves, if only a little. *"It's all right. Tell me, what are you searching for?"*

They still circled. The city was so small from above. The destruction of the battle in Kings Keep last night stood out in stark relief, but from the looks of things, the castle guard had fought off the worst of the onslaught. Her heart felt heavy, thinking of all the people who'd lost their lives last night.

"I don't see any sign of the scourge. Good, they haven't made it this far."

"The scourge?" Kayda could feel the tension in Dru as the name filled her thoughts. Her body tensed in response. What could scare a dragon?

"You'll see, soon enough. If I've awakened, then so have they. The Palisade has fallen." He pivoted, heading east. Soon, they left the city behind and raced above the forested hills of the Kingdom of Dracwood, toward Mage Keep.

"Tell me, Druturion. I have to know what we're facing."

"Vicious little beasts. A horde of them. I can feel them. Their murderous glee. Their hunger." Panic laced his voice, and his body trembled beneath her. *"They're responsible for the destruction of my brethren. We have to burn them all."*

Her fingers clenched around his neck. What could be so awful, so terrifying, it sent panic through a creature so strong? And how could humanity possibly survive when these mythical beasts had fallen?

They blasted through the air. Her thoughts swirled, dampening the elation that had flooded her as they first took to the sky. She didn't know what to expect, but some part of her, deep inside, quaked with fear. Would she be ready to face the scourge?

Her breath caught as Dru suddenly picked up speed, descending like an angry bolt of lightning tearing through the sky. *"They're here."*

She craned her neck sideways, spotting a town perched on the Bogland's edge. She knew this place—Bogsmouth. Her grandfather had brought her to visit once before. She'd marveled at the open air fish market and admired the small town charm and friendly people.

As they flew closer, she saw all was not well in the small fishing community. Every street swarmed with chaos. Tiny, brutal creatures were everywhere, attacking everything that moved. The scourge.

Dru swooped down on the dock's edge above a large crowd of the silver and brown-furred beasts. His jaw snapped open, and fire blasted through the sky.

Her heart leapt as the first of the creatures burst into flame.

Dru hovered, bathing the beasts with flame.

The scent of singed fur and roasting flesh rose through the air. The piercing screams of pain flooded her ears.

Kayda spotted mangled corpses on the ground; the back of her throat clogged with saliva as she fought the urge to be sick. The people of this town had all been massacred. They were too late. Her soul filled with an anger so intense it burned from within.

From the corner of her eye, she spotted movement heading her way on the rooftops. Cold rage surged within her. Burning with righteous vengeance, her hand shot out. She pulled on the flames that made their home within Druturion's chest, and they answered. Fire flowed from her palms, scorching the creatures that loped toward them. Their beady little eyes filled with fear as the fire licked their skin.

Yes, they would burn them all.

They raced through the city, laying waste to every beast they found. Finally, the crowds of creatures began to thin, but Dru did not relent, painting the town red with fire. Suddenly, he stopped and landed in a large square.

Kayda recognized the space as the same open air market she'd marveled at so long ago. The smiling townspeople she remembered crumpled dead on the ground, their corpses barely recognizable as people, the flesh torn clean from their bones and covered in ash.

Dru strode forward on the ground, approaching a group of burning scourge. Their dying shrieks filled the air.

What was he doing?

He dipped his head, heedless of the fire still burning the creatures, and scooped them up inside his massive jaw.

Kayda held on for the ride, bobbing up and down on his neck as he went back for more, the crunch of bones loud in her ears.

"Shouldn't we be moving on?" She coughed, eyeing the burning buildings warily.

Dru stiffened and shook his head. *"You try sleeping for hundreds of years and not being a little hungry after,"* he said, sounding a bit irritated. But he left the rest of the creatures to burn and lifted back into the sky.

Within moments, they flew above Mage Keep. She'd been here before, too. The mismatched buildings looked deserted from above. She could see no movement in the streets from either people or the scourge.

Though she could see nothing, it didn't stop a strange sensation from scrambling up her spine. The further they traveled, the more the feeling spread, worming through her veins. It was almost as if something watched her approach. Some specter peering over her shoulder, waiting.

They climbed higher in the air, and finally, she spotted movement. There, beyond the cliffside that had once held the Palisade wall, a group of mages and soldiers in full metal armor had built a large circle of magic and fought from behind it.

The sight brought a tear to her eye. Someone had stayed to fight. But it was obvious from above the mages were losing. The scourge had them surrounded, their protective bubble slowly diminishing. They struggled beneath the onslaught of thousands of the beasts that threw themselves at the group relentlessly.

Dru saw it, too. He swooped down and flew in a tight circle around the group. Fire flowed from his mouth, burning the scourge from above. A cheer erupted from the people below, and her heart filled with pride. She added her own flames to the sky, sending the creatures skidding back from the group. They'd earned the mages a momentary reprieve.

"Can you land beside them?" she asked. *"We have to help them."*

He slammed down a moment later. The mages faces were filled with astonishment as she dismounted, her boots crunching on ash and stomping out cinders. A man jolted forward and pulled the metal helm from his face. A man she recognized.

"Kayda?" Tarquin's jaw hung low as his gaze flicked over her body. "Is that you? On a dragon?"

"Tarquin. What did you do?"

The bastard had the audacity to smirk. "Oh, you don't like what I've done with the place? It'll make a great port town after a little pest control. Come to help, have you?"

Kayda breathed in deeply through her nose, itching to slap the smile off his face. "You fool. You bloody, blazing fool. How could you be so stupid? You've condemned the whole world to deal with this evil, so you could build a seaport?"

"Don't be so dramatic, sister. We'll have this all under control by day's end. Just watch."

"Under control?" She shook her head. "You've already lost, and you don't even know it."

A brown-haired mage pushed forward, rolling her shoulders back and blinking rapidly. "What do you mean, Princess?"

"We just came from Bogsmouth. The scourge destroyed the entire town. They've already spread."

The mage's face blanched, the blue of her irises shrinking as her pupils dilated. She turned to face Tarquin. "It's over. We have to retreat to Flamesmoat."

"Retreat to Flamesmoat? Don't be ridiculous, Ereni. We have these creatures on the run."

"Kayda, get back now," Dru said, his mouth opening and spewing forth flame as the scourge circled back with a vengeance.

"Listen to her, Tarquin." Kayda raced back to bound atop Dru's back. "Retreat while you still have a chance."

Dru took to the sky.

"C'mon, let's clear a path for them," she said.

He swooped down again, and they both got to work shooting flames at the ground. More and more scourge popped free from the ground, swarming toward the group. All the while, that strange tingle slid over her skin, like eyes on her back she couldn't shake. They circled once, twice, three times, until they had a clear path away from the field and toward the forest bordering the keep.

The mages departed, leaving Tarquin and the guardsmen behind on the field. She cursed inwardly. The idiot was going to get himself killed.

She should be grateful to be rid of him. He'd plotted to kill her grandfather. And he'd never treated her like anything more than a nuisance and amusement, but she found herself absurdly upset at the thought of him dying at the hands of these vicious creatures. No one deserved that kind of death. Not even him.

"Take us closer," she ordered, holding tight to Dru's neck. He complied and hovered in the air near the guardsmen.

"Tarquin, please. Listen to reason," she yelled down from atop her perch on the hovering dragon. "I can't protect you from all of these creatures, and the mages are retreating. You have to join them."

His laughter set her stomach on edge. "You don't have to protect me. We men can handle ourselves."

The guardsmen's answering whoops reverberated in the air.

She couldn't help it any longer. She screamed. The stupid idiot of a man! He would lead them all to their deaths.

The guardsmen backed away in the face of her rage but did not move to retreat.

Fine. If he was set on dying on this bloody field and she couldn't stop him, then she at least wasn't going to let him go out without a fight.

"Let's burn them all down, Druturion."

He flew forward, flames spewing from his mouth. *"With pleasure."*

They blazed across the sky in ever widening circles. Their magic rained down on the scourge, sending all who touched it to a fiery death. The crowds began to thin. They were forcing them back, making them think twice about rising from the ground to quench their unfathomable hunger. For a moment, she thought it might be enough to save her brother.

Fear grabbed her, seizing her mind. The ghostly presence she'd nearly forgotten surged around her like a crushing wave. Her heartbeat thrashed in her ears. Then her heart shattered as dozens of the vile creatures broke free from the earth beside Tarquin's group. *"Dru!"* she cried out, *"Please, we have to help them."*

He spun in a flash, but Kayda could see it was already too late. Their circling path had driven them too far, and the dozens swiftly turned to hundreds. Their massive numbers overwhelmed the small group of guardsmen. In the blink of an eye, they collapsed under a wave of gnashing teeth and writhing bodies.

The last man fell, and something inside of her—something primal—screamed its rage into the sky.

Magic pooled within her, like ice in her blood. The fire burned, raging on the tips of her fingers. As they raced to the mound of fallen men and squirming, raving beasts, she thrust out her hands and screamed. Fire rained down, pouring out of her hands like a wave of death. She gripped Dru with her legs, her teeth bared and nostrils flaring.

Together, they set the scourge on fire.

Chapter 28

They floated just beyond the docks, neither Dal nor Fillan making any effort to quicken their speed as grief for all the people they'd known and loved in Bogsmouth filled their faces.

Aren crouched down beside her in the canoe. "Are you all right?" Lark gazed at him, and he must have seen something in her eyes. "I know what you're thinking, but we can't go back there. Not now."

A shadow blocked the sun for a brief instant, casting their boat in darkness. Lark looked up, her heart hammering. That was no cloud.

A dragon!

He raced across the sky, then swooped down close to the shore. Fire rained down on the scourge from above. They writhed beneath the flames, shrieking in agony.

Her breath caught. Some of the creatures had made their way to the rooftops. They were going to spring on the dragon from above.

Wait. A chill crept up her spine.

A second set of flames blazed to life, stopping the beasts in their tracks. The dragon tilted, and Lark's heart filled with hope. Atop the dragon rode a young woman in a blue dress, her red hair streaming behind her like a flame flickering in the breeze. Fire flowed from her fingers, her face fierce and fearless.

Lark stared at that girl and made herself a promise. As surely as that brave girl fought, she would do the same. She might be running scared right now, but she vowed to return. She would scour the jungle for someone to teach her to control her powers. And one day, she would return to help free her country from this blight.

Her face brightened as the heat from the shore drifted across the water to warm her skin. She would see her homeland again.

"How did you know?" Dal's anguished voice reached her from the second boat. He scrubbed his face and rubbed the tears from his cheeks. "How Dausius?" He stared at him, and the pain she glimpsed in his eyes tore her apart.

"I once knew a girl. Just a slip of a thing. But she had a voice..." Dausius smiled sadly, gazing off into the distance. "I've never in my whole life heard her equal. We traveled together in a different show. I was only a lowly puppeteer, but she, she was the star. People from all over were filled with laughter and tears when they heard her. Her voice was so moving, so sweet."

Dausius swallowed, a frown spreading on his face. "Then one day, she grew ill. The leader of the show wanted to leave her, find a replacement. But she and I, we'd become very close. I refused to leave her to die alone." He sighed, flicking his hand dismissively. "So, they left us both. I stayed with her, held her hand. And I was there in her final moments as she took her last breath."

"That's a sad tale, but what does it have to do with anything?" Dal's brow furrowed. "I asked you how you knew those things were coming."

"I'm getting to that. You see, what I forgot to mention was this girl, she didn't just sing. She had many talents. And when a person with certain talents is close to death, they often see glimpses of things that have yet to pass."

Lark leaned forward, open-mouthed. She'd told him about the future?

"I told her, as she lay there dying, traveling the world with her was my greatest accomplishment. That nothing I did would ever meet the same measure." He closed his eyes, the sad smile painting his lips once more. "She was so weak by that point, barely holding on. But all of a sudden, she sat straight up in bed and gripped my hands with the strength of two men. She stared into my eyes. And the words she said to me, I'll never forget."

Everyone was leaning in now. Even poor Fillan had dried his tears and stared at Dausius expectantly.

Dausius' brown eyes rolled over their boat and landed directly on Lark. "'You have much more left to do,' she said. 'One day, you will meet a songbird. Three times, you will set her free. Listen to her, trust her, help her fly. Together, you will save the world.'"

Lark sat back, her hand flying to her chest. Everyone turned to stare at her. She shook her head in disbelief.

Dausius cleared his throat. All eyes flicked back to him as he continued. "So, when I finally heard another voice that moved me the same way hers did, I listened." He grinned, looking at the twins and Aren. "We set her free. And when that girl"—his voice choked up, tears in his eyes—"our songbird, told me to run, you're damn sure I listened."

Tears welled in her eyes. Could any of that be true? Was she destined to save the world?

She glanced back at the shore. The whole town was bathed in flames. The dragon and rider were nowhere to be seen. Flames and smoke filled the sky as tears streamed down her face. It all seemed so unlikely. Would she ever have power like this? The power to render a whole town to ash?

Aren reached over and held her hand. She smiled at him, at all of them. She didn't know if she would ever be ready to save the world. But at least she had a few friends she could rely on. Whatever the future flung at them, they would face it together.

Conall awakened with a start, his breath clouding up before his eyes. He shivered, his nose filled with the scent of smoke. He raised his arm, sighing as it lifted easily and without pain.

"Brother, you've slept half the day away. How are you feeling?" Shadow sat next to him, watching over him.

"Much better." He sat up and rubbed his eyes as he gazed at his surroundings. He was on the stretcher on a mountainside in a large clearing. A few dozen people milled around, mostly children. Some of the youngest played nearby, oblivious to the anxiety filling the older children and handful of adults. *"Where are we? Where are the mages?"*

"We headed north, then they set you down with these people and turned back. I'm not sure why."

Conall stretched, his body stiff but free from pain. He lifted his tongue and winced as he tried to swallow. He grabbed his waterskin, hefting it and finding it empty.

"There's a small lake nearby. I can show you," Shadow offered.

He nodded and followed Shadow through the trees. A few people stared at them but made no move to stop them.

The trees at this elevation were sparse, affording a clear view of the land below.

Conall gasped. It was all on fire. Smoke filled the air, and flames undulated unchecked like a wave of red as the forest burned. Living in a forested country, he was no stranger to the odd forest fire, but this—this was like nothing he'd ever witnessed.

The mages were always called on to contain fires when they erupted. With their mastery over the elements, they could contain even the largest of blazes easily. Dousing it with water or soil. Stilling the wind so the flames would not spread. Even pulling the flame straight from tree trunks and extinguishing them with a thought.

This had to be deliberate. Was this why the mages had disappeared? To build a wall of flame to slow the enemy? A pit formed in his stomach. How frightened they must be if they were willing to set their home ablaze.

What of the mages and guardsmen who'd chosen to stay behind? His chest still burned when he remembered Ereni's betrayal, but deep down, he still felt a connection to her. Would she survive the inferno and whatever evil had awakened?

His thoughts drifted to his sister, and the pit in his stomach grew larger. What if she was out there somewhere, on her way to Mage Keep? Would she get caught in the crossfire?

He closed his eyes briefly and said a silent prayer for Lark. She had to be safe. He opened his eyes, clenching his jaw tightly. He would find her.

The lake lay ahead. Shadow raced forward and dipped down to lap at the water.

Conall hurried to join him, submerging his waterskin into the clear, cold water and draining it quickly. As he knelt down for a refill, he froze.

His reflection. It was all wrong. He stared in disbelief and slowly lifted a hand to his face.

Bloody blazes!

"It happened while you touched that wall," Shadow said. *"You changed as quickly as snow melting in the sun. I'm sorry, little brother."*

The youthful face he'd worn yesterday was gone. The skin on his forehead and around his eyes was wrinkled. His brown hair was full of scattered gray strands. He raked his fingers through his hair and captured a single strand between his fingers. He lifted it up to the sun, inhaling sharply. It shone silver in the daylight.

He shuddered, remembering the emaciated bodies of the mages who'd helped him destroy the Palisade. In a way, he'd gotten off easy. If they'd taken longer in that strange, glimmering void, he could've shared the same fate.

Still, he couldn't help feeling cheated. His stomach ached. Would Lark even recognize him when he found her?

He dropped the hair and watched it float away on the breeze. He sighed.

A twig snapped. Conall turned as Delyth stepped out from behind a tree.

"Well, you're looking much improved. I hope you both are ready to begin our journey," she said.

Conall rose to his feet, frowning. "You mages are unbelievable. Are you really going to leave the people of Dracwood when they need you the most?" He shook his head. "Didn't you take an oath to protect the world from evil? Why are you running scared?"

"Come, I'd like to show you something." She beckoned him to follow.

She led the way down the mountain to a group of old mages, their once pristine white robes covered with dirt, grime, and ash. On the ground beside them, an oval shape sat, shrouded with a dark blanket. The blanket swayed, and a strange snarl reached his ears.

There was something alive inside. Shadow's fur bristled, and he growled.

"It likely won't survive the mountain's extreme cold this late in the year, but the men and women of Doln will listen more closely if they see the carcass with their own eyes." Delyth lifted the blanket, revealing a metal cage with a large rodent inside.

Conall leaned closer and watched the thing cower in the cage, blinking its beady eyes at the light. Something stirred in his chest, a whisper of the same sensation he'd felt while the Palisade fell, but not nearly so strong. "Is that it? That's what has you so scared?"

The creature chose that moment to throw itself at the bars in front of his face. He flinched, backing away. Its vicious teeth snapped, and sharp claws tore at the metal.

Shadow growled at the thing, flashing his teeth. The creature showed no fear, despite facing a wolf ten times its size. Conall had no doubt it would have no qualms attacking them, if the cage were not there to stop it.

"They're called *ichneumon*—the scourge. There are already thousands of them out there, terrorizing the countryside. They've been living underground beyond the Palisade for centuries, mostly sleeping. Eating whatever snakes and mice they can find. Eating their own when they have to." Deylth glared at the creature with obvious disdain. "They breed faster than rabbits. The fire will slow them, but only for a time. Within weeks, they'll have spread throughout Dracwood. When the Boglands ice over this winter, they'll move south. And when the mountain passes thaw in the spring, they'll invade Doln."

She dropped the blanket back on the snarling beast. "The whole world is going to be swarming with *ichneumon* soon. We need time to find a way to stop them. I've sent riders in all directions with orders to send all the folk from the countryside to Flamesmoat. The ancient moat that rings the city will be lit, protecting all within."

Conall's heart thumped. "How do you know the answers you seek will be in Doln?"

Delyth marched forward and stopped before him, staring up into his face. "When I was a young woman, I traveled to Doln. I met the Winter Witch. She helped me see my future, the same way she'll help you find your sister. It's because of that vision I know I must return." She drew in a deep breath, her eyebrows raising. "Do you want to know what I saw all those years ago?"

"What?"

"I saw a girl who made the earth quake. Another girl reborn in flames. And a boy who held all the elements in his hands."

Conall's eyes widened. He hadn't told her what he witnessed while the Palisade fell. He hadn't said a word about what he'd done. How could she know?

"I saw myself as an old woman returning to Doln. Returning to the witch with two companions. A middle-aged man and a wolf."

He swallowed, his reflection in the lake flashing in his mind.

"We're meant to go there." Delyth laid a wrinkled hand on his sleeve. "I have to believe we'll find something there to help us win this fight."

Conall looked behind her at the mountain looming large on the horizon. He was so tired of worrying about the future. Would he ever find his sister? Would he, one day, be reunited with the father he'd thought dead all these years? If Doln held answers, then he was ready to find them.

"All right." Conall smiled. "Let's go meet that witch."

"What have we done?" Kayda and Dru stood atop the ridge overlooking the Abandoned Lands to the east and Mage Keep and the forested hills of the Kingdom of Dracwood to the west.

Mage Keep and the forest surrounding it had already been decimated, reduced to ash and smoldering debris. Fire and charred earth surrounded them in all directions, spreading through the forest to the west, heading inland toward Flamesmoat. Smoke clogged the air, making it hard to breathe. It was like she was living inside a nightmare come to life.

She swallowed and winced, her throat painfully dry. It had taken them most of the day, but finally, the scourge stopped coming. As the sun dipped low in the sky, the last handfuls of the vicious things had retreated, returning to the earth.

"We did what we had to do." Dru raised his neck, his nostrils flaring. *"This is not the last we'll see of the scourge. I can feel them still. They'll regroup. They'll breed. Within a few weeks, a few months at most, they'll be back terrorizing the land."*

She frowned, and her chest tightened at the certainty behind his words. It was the second time he'd said that phrase—he could feel them. His words brought back a shadow of the presence she'd felt during the battle. Had bonding with Druturion let her sense those things, too?

"Dru, how do you know so much about these things?"

His body stiffened. *"I did what had to be done back then, the same as we did just now."*

She backed up and eyed him warily. She rubbed a hand across her face, suspecting she knew what he was about to say.

"It was the only way," he continued. *"Bonding certain species lets you share abilities. It had to be done, so we could survive that long underground."*

"You bonded one of those things?" Her eyes widened as a certain word stood out in her mind. *"Wait a moment. What do you mean, we?"*

"It is very rare to find a human who can bond any species they choose. For dragons, it's much more common. I know there were others who made the decision to bond one of the scourge. We knew one day the Palisade would fall, and they would return to ravage the world." His shoulders slumped, his red eyes staring off into the distance. *"They slaughtered my kind. Devoured every egg. Destroyed our hope for the future. We will not let that stand. I don't know where the others are, but I intend to find them."*

She sucked in a breath. Suddenly, everything made sense. His weird connection to the scourge. The crazed hunger he'd displayed in Bogsmouth. A new appreciation for her bondmate washed over her. He was so brave to do whatever it took to ensure he would live to win this fight.

And also, definitely a little bit crazy. She could barely even fathom it. How strange it must be to bond one of the creatures responsible for the destruction of his own species...

Still, she couldn't help being thankful for his sacrifice. If he hadn't been there, sleeping beneath the ground, waiting for this day to come, then the events of today would've played out much differently. If there were more dragons out there, waiting to be awakened, then they would find them. She owed it to her bondmate to help him, just as he'd helped her.

Her gaze landed back on a certain spot in the Abandoned Lands. Tarquin. All that time she'd spent hating him, wishing to stop his plotting, had all been for naught. Her mind raced, questioning everything. Every single decision she'd made that led to this moment. All the "what ifs" plagued her. She flexed her fingers, tears pooling in the corners of her eyes. If only she'd been able to figure out what he was up to sooner, they wouldn't be in this mess. Maybe she could've saved him.

Her heart twisted. He'd always been an arrogant jerk. But he was still *her* jerk. She'd wanted to stop him. She'd wanted him brought to justice for the role he'd played in her grandfather's attack. But she didn't want this. She didn't want to watch him die.

She leaned on Dru for support. Her whole body ached. Exhaustion weighed her down. But she couldn't rest. Not yet.

"What now?" she asked. *"Can the Palisade be restored?"*

"No. It took the life energy of hundreds of dragons and mages to conjure the Palisade. And it was never meant to last forever. Honestly, I'm surprised it lasted this long."

She bit her lip. There had to be some way to pen these things in now that they'd retreated beneath the earth. *"What of a normal wall? One made of stone and earth?"*

"The scourge would only dig under it, given enough time. The Palisade went down as deep as it stood tall."

She could see no other options. They had to find some way to stand and fight. *"Can you fly us back to Flamesmoat?"*

Dru tilted his head and stared at the towering inferno that was only just this morning a sea of unending green foliage. *"No, not now. The battle has me spent. I need to rest. In the morning, I could fly through the fire, but you'd never make it without air talent to clear the smoke. We can wait it out or go around."*

She shook her head, and her gaze landed on something else. A large boat anchored offshore. A Jorian shipping vessel.

It reminded her of something. She was supposed to uncover a second mystery today. Izora's hasty declaration that Prince Gideon was not her father.

But the Sade Prim wasn't here to explain. She couldn't be sure if she'd survived the fire and scourge. Even if she had, she could be anywhere by now. There was no point in searching her out if she hadn't a clue where to look. She could question Izora back in Flamesmoat, but it might take them weeks to fly around the smoke and ash.

There was one other place she might find answers. And maybe she could find some others to help win this fight while she was at it.

"Dru, I have another idea. I think it's about time I met the other side of my family. How about a little detour to Joria before we head back home? I have a feeling if the Princess of Dracwood and her new bondmate sail back with the Jorians' lost ship, they'll be willing to talk."

Dru stretched out his wings and crouched down close to the ground. *"I could use a sand bath right about now. Hop on."*

Kayda took a last look at the devastation surrounding her as she vaulted on top of Dru's back and wrapped her arms and legs tightly around his neck. She had to admit she was frightened. Who knew what she would discover when she went digging into her past? Who was her real father? Why make her a princess when she wasn't? And why did Prince Gideon, even now, believe he was the man who'd fathered her?

Despite the fear, she was ready. Ready to find the answers, no matter what they might be. And even if she discovered she wasn't a royal, maybe it wouldn't be so bad. For once in her life, she was free from all the responsibilities of royal life. She had to admit, despite all the death and destruction, she was enjoying the freedom.

She tossed back her head, her long auburn hair blowing in the breeze, and smiled. *"Let's fly."*

Epilogue

The forest burned all around her. Animals that hadn't the sense to flee were incinerated. Dense clouds of smoke clogged the air. Massive, ancient trees toppled over like saplings in a windstorm.

Ereni sucked in a breath of cool, moist air, her skin tingling as magic surrounded her. She and the young mages had a front row seat to the destruction from within their protective bubble of magic. Dozens of them worked together to do the impossible. To survive where all should be destroyed.

Wind mages cleaned the smoke. Earth mages flung dirt to deflect any fiery debris that came too close. The fire and water mages worked in concert to extinguish the flames before them so they could take step after careful step through the burning forest.

She grinned. It was a thing of beauty, to be sure. Just days ago, some of these mages hadn't even known how to summon. For so long, the Palisade Mages had made them wait to learn how to twist the elements to their will. For so long, they had to wait and pay. Pay with their very lives to maintain a dying wall of magic.

Those days were over. Now they could return to the old ways. Where young mages learned of their abilities when they needed them the most. She'd experienced this for herself years ago. How a mage could gain access to their abilities in a time of great stress and great need.

All the young mages around her had learned this, too. As soon as the scourge attacked, all of those who'd not yet manifested abilities quickly received them. And because they'd not been made to sacrifice their power to the Palisade, they were, by far, the strongest mages the world had known in many generations. Together, they would be enough to defeat the scourge. She had faith in them all.

At long last, they broke free of the wall of flame. Ereni turned back to survey the inferno they'd strolled through. The fire stretched from north to south, splitting the entire country in two. It was miraculous they'd survived. Her heart soared with pride. Just think of all they could accomplish.

She gazed at the group of mages beside her. They would never wear the white robes of the Palisade Mages, but they were all living proof that clothes and tradition were not what makes a mage. Every one of them, in their plain traveling clothes, glowed blue so strongly. All of them looked at her expectantly.

She smiled. "Baris, Oriana, head northwest. Edrik, Karina, you two go southwest. Stop in every town you pass. Tell all the people you find who haven't left already to head for Flamesmoat. The rest of us will travel straight west. We'll meet in Flamesmoat, light the moat, and make our stand."

The mages all nodded and separated quickly, leaving on their respective missions. Ereni led the way west, calmly walking at the head of the group until just before sunset.

They found themselves in a small town. It didn't surprise her to find it already deserted. They were still close to the forest fire. Most people in Dracwood knew to flee when they spotted a fire so large, even if only to wait in a neighboring town for the mages to come and extinguish the flames. Little did they know this time would not be like all the rest. This time, they had to let the forest burn.

"We'll rest here for the night," Ereni said. "Roan, you have first watch. Everyone else, spread out and check there's no one hunkered down waiting out the fire."

The mages scattered, all of them listening without complaint or question. Ereni rubbed a hand across her chest and paced down the main street until she found what she was looking for. Then she turned and entered a large building on the outskirts of town.

Perfect. She made her way into a huge, empty bathhouse. It appeared the town they were in had the good fortune of being built atop a natural hot spring. She seated herself on a stone bench in front of a shallow pool of steaming water and began freeing the laces on her sturdy brown boot.

The action brought back the memory of another night not long ago. Taking off the same boot with a set of eyes watching her every move. A bittersweet smile crossed her face.

For her whole life, she'd always tried to live without regret. To be true to herself. To follow her own heart, her own conscience. Until yesterday, she would've thought she'd done a good job of doing just that. Not any longer.

Ereni finished removing her boots. She folded her socks methodically and placed the little folded bundles atop her boots, which she set neatly beside each other.

She sighed. She couldn't stop picturing Conall's face. The way he'd stared at her with hate in his eyes when she'd threatened Shadow. How he flinched from her touch when she'd freed his hands. Her stomach churned as she lifted her tunic over her head and pulled down her trousers. She might wash the smoke and dirt free from her skin, but that look, that feeling, would not wash away so easily.

Blazes. If only she hadn't listened. If only there'd been another way.

She knew in her heart there wasn't. If he had known, there was no way he would have left with her mother while Ereni remained fighting. Not Conall. He would've stayed with her, no matter the cost to himself.

Ereni had chosen to trust her mother, the Sade Prim. When she'd said it was time, Ereni had listened. She'd done her part to set the plan into motion. And when she'd returned and her mother said Conall had to travel with her to Doln, she'd trusted her then, too. She'd done what she had to do to ensure that would happen. She only wished it didn't hurt so much.

If they'd only had more time to think, then maybe they could've thought of another plan without so much lying and subterfuge. She wouldn't have been forced to stand by the prince's side and act like she couldn't care less about Conall, while secretly her heart crumbled into a million pieces.

She sighed again, leaving her pile of neatly folded clothes behind and sinking into the hot spring's warm waters. She would regret the decision to lie to Conall for the rest of her life. But she'd needed to be the villain to save him. To save the world.

Her gaze trailed down her naked belly. At least there was one decision left she didn't regret. Her rare seer eyes had just picked up something new. Something wonderful. Radiating from her lower belly was the most beautiful purple glow.

She traced her fingers over her stomach and smiled.

Also By

Would you like to read more about Dracwood? Sign up for my newsletter for a free standalone prequel novella that tells the story of how the Palisade was built centuries ago.

You'll find the link on my website amberlwerner.com

And look for the next books in the Palisade Trilogy
Muses That Align Us — March 2023
Lines That Drew Us — May 2023

Acknowledgments

There's a lot of work that goes into making a book. I'd like to take a moment to thank some people who helped me get this story ready to publish.

My critique partners, Nicholas Redmon, Jesse Vail, A.K. Watkins, Monica Kieb, and S.M. Lovin. I've learned so much working with all of you, and had so much fun reading your incredible stories while you tore mine apart and helped me make it better.

My early readers Scott Werner, Karen Underkoffler, Thomas Werner Sr, Shane Lee, Josh Grinar and Dave Tosta. I don't know if I would have had the confidence to publish without a few people enjoying the story enough to read it all the way through in its early stages.

To my editor Claire Ashgrove, thank you for smoothing all the rough edges so my words could shine.

And thank you Nadia at Miblart for all your help bringing my cover art design to life.

About Author

Amber L. Werner loves to write about magic, monsters and mythical creatures. She lives in Norristown, PA with her husband and two children. The Palisade Trilogy is her debut series.

Follow her Facebook page Amber L. Werner
Or Instagram amberlwerner

Sign up for her newsletter and receive a free novella.
Find it here amberlwerner.com